The Murder (

It is Scotland in the 1870s. Old Tom Morris – the Grand Old Man of golf – and his even more gifted son, Young Tom Morris, dominate the game.

Their stronghold at St. Andrews is fast becoming the pre-eminent course and the Royal and Ancient Golf Club is set to govern the rules of play.

But this does not necessarily suit the purposes of the other two important courses – Prestwick and Musselburgh. Jealousies abound and there is much at stake, not least the future of the Open Championship.

One by one, members of the Morris family start to die what look like natural deaths.

Newly returned from the Ashanti Campaign, war hero Captain David McArdle of the Black Watch seems more than casually interested in these affairs.

Police Constable Murdoch of the St. Andrews police has his suspicions. A local doctor returned from the Indian Service, the Superintendent of a mental institution, various professional golfers with reputations to protect and an expert in potato rot are all added to the mix.

Taken from the recently-discovered writings of Fife's Chief Constable, James Fleming Bremner, released one hundred years after his death, this remarkable memoir puts the history of St. Andrews, the Fife Police and the game of golf in a whole new light and uncovers a bizarre series of murders – if murders they were!

McArdle – champion or villain? War hero or phoney? Bremner leads us through the tangled skein of society, politics and golf in Victorian Scotland.

"Whether your interest is golf, St. Andrews, social and military history or just a well-crafted mystery, the first volume in the McArdle series is a cracking good yarn!"

Amazon review

i

THE MURDER OF YOUNG TOM MORRIS
By BRUCE DURIE ISBN 1-4716377-5-1

GATH
ASKELON
PUBLISHING

Published by Gath-Askelon Publishing®,
Edinburgh, Scotland

Available from Lulu and Amazon

mcardle@brucedurie.co.uk
http://www.brucedurie.co.uk/McArdle

ABOUT THE AUTHOR

Bruce Durie was born in Fife, where golf is compulsory. He has been a science journalist, a senior academic at various universities, Director of the Edinburgh Science Festival, a regular contributor to New Scientist and other periodicals, broadcaster, radio panel games host, maker of medical videos and Professor of Genealogical Studies.

His book *Medicine* was short-listed for the first COPUS Prize and his parody of Sherlock Holmes, *The Mystery of the Pneumonic Numismatist* was performed nationwide and in Chicago by Simon Williams and William Simons. He produced and performed his one-man play *MacPherson's Rant* at the 1992 Edinburgh Fringe and despairs of anybody ever buying the screenplay.

He is best known for his BBC Radio Scotland genealogy series *Digging Up Your Roots* and his genealogy/history books, including *Scottish Genealogy* from The History Press.

He lives in Edinburgh, and feels grateful that it is close enough to Fife without actually having to live there.

http://www.brucedurie.co.uk/McArdle

ALSO BY BRUCE DURIE

From *Mercat Press/Birlinn*
The Pinkerton Casebook
Dick Donovan: The Glasgow Detective

From *Gath-Askelon Publishing*
The High History of the Holy Quail – A Fantasia
Volume the First in the End of All Magick saga

The Dick Donovan series
The Man-Hunter –
Stories from the Notebook of a Detective
Caught at Last! –
Leaves from the Notebook of a Detective
Tracked and Taken:
Detective Sketches
Romances from a Detective's Case-Book –
Dick Donovan in The Strand Magazine

From *The History Press*

A Century of Glasgow	**Glasgow Past and Present**
Kirkcaldy and East Fife	**A Century of Dunfermline**
The Story of Stirling	**Dunfermline in Old Photographs**
Scottish Genealogy	**Documents for Genealogy & Local History**
Not a Guide to…Glasgow	**Not a Guide to…Edinburgh**

THE MURDER OF
YOUNG TOM MORRIS

BRUCE DURIE

CONTENTS

FIGURES

INTRODUCTION

Had it not been for the fortuitous occurrence of Fife Constabulary handing over its records to the County Archives, and their release from time to time under the 100 year Rule, it is unlikely that these extraordinary memoirs would ever have come to light.

They concern a personal record of the police force in the 1870s in North East Fife, and specifically in the ancient Toun of St. Andrews, written by James Fleming Bremner towards the end of his life. It is a matter of record that Captain Bremner was Superintendent and then Chief Constable of Fife from 1863 until his death in November 1903 just short of 77 years old. His long service saw many innovations which laid the basis of modern policing.

As for the part played in his life and professional efforts by the enigmatic David McArdle, this memoir tells it all, or at least the beginnings of it. Should further instalments come to light, perhaps I shall be allowed leave to re-present them to a later century.

Meanwhile, I should record those who played a significant part in bringing this confection to the boil:

Peter Stubbs, the man with a photographic memory for photographers; the staff of the Fife Archives; Thomas H Smyth, the knowledgeable Archivist of the Black Watch Museum, Balhousie Castle, Perth; Emma Jane McAdam, Assistant Curator at the Golf Heritage Department of the Royal and Ancient Golf Club; Prof. Sue Black OBE, tireless champion and world-class giggler; Captain James Bremner (albeit posthumously by 100 years); Jill Martin, ministering angel; numerous helpful people at various golf courses who managed to contain their laughter at my attempts to play as if Queen Victoria were still alive; and, as ever, Carolyn, who helped with the re-conception, never missed a chance for a visit to Fife and knew a thing or two along the way.

And a special mention is due to the lovely American lady encountered while she was looking for her military grandfather.

"He was in the Black Watch and died in the World War," she said.

Which World War did he die in, I asked – First or Second?

"I don't know. He fought in both!"

Bruce Durie, Fife, 2003

PREFACE

Rarely, it comes to us to meet remarkable men in remarkable circumstances. One such was Captain David Frew McArdle of the 42nd Highland Regiment of Foot, more popularly known as the Black Watch. I feel it incumbent on me to record, independently of any official records which may be drawn up for reasons of necessity, administrative order or statute, the circumstances under which I came to encounter Captain McArdle, and his part in a series of related deaths in St. Andrews in 1875. I leave it to the longer text which follows, to expound the habits and nature of this officer. The public at large will already know from newspapers and certain sensationalised fictions, some of the details of his life and fortunes.

During the years I had the honour, privilege and – at times – pleasure to be Superintendent, a rank later and more commonly called Chief Constable, of the Fife Police, I was in the singular position to observe the formidable personage of McArdle and – I think I may claim without forsaking modesty or foreswearing probity – taking some small part in shaping his career.

Indeed the very word "career", applied to the choices one makes in one's employment or engagements, is a most inappropriate one for the generality of persons, redolent as it is of the headlong dash or the bounding lope, while, as most of us are aware, progression through one's station in life is mostly a steady plod occasioned by circumstance, enabled by accident, and enlightened – if one is fortunate – by acquaintances.

In these writings I have taken it upon myself – who perhaps can justifiably term himself McArdle's inventor, or at the very least a modest Pygmalion to his towering Galatea – to relate the circumstances by which he came to return St. Andrews after years of military service abroad, and the particulars surrounding the most opprobrious and too soon demise of that fine man and finer golfer, Mr. Thomas Morris Jnr. Later memoirs may, should Providence provide, treat of McArdle's better known exploits anent the attempted abduction of Her Majesty and the violation of her royal person by the Huns; the seminal role played by the good Captain in the matter of Greatorex, the foul murderer of that much-missed peace officer Mr. McCall of Glasgow; the circumstances in which the noted designer and architect Mr. Charles Rennie Mackintosh happened to choose the Arts over a position in the Glasgow Constabulary like his father; how young Dr. Doyle came to write detective fiction; the pursuit and apprehension of the fraudulent Dr. Leishman of Dunfermline; and – furth of Scotland – the unacknowledged part McArdle played in the Eastern Question which earned him the high regard of the Russian Tsar and of the French, and the lifelong enmity of Bismarck and Germany.

ix

There may also be occasion at some time to relate the place McArdle holds in the pantheon of heroes over the ocean in America. His courage and ingenuity in saving the life of a President of that far but familial land; his engagement with Allan Pinkerton during the latter days of that great detective and exiled Scot; and not least the little-recognised part McArdle played in bringing the hallowed and ancient practice of golf (some call it a game!) to the New World.

But all this in time, should eyesight and bodily vigour not desert me, nor yet the amber comforts of the Wine of Scotland which sits at my elbow and serves as both muse and palliative. My son, Frederick, who has become a fine if somewhat fussy physician, tells me my liver will kill me before the year's end, in an act of revenge for the torment I have given it over the years. The other Leeches around me concur and I shall do my best not to disappoint them all, as there is no more disagreeable specimen than a medical man proved wrong over a patient who outlives a diagnosis.

I cannot foresee, nor do I imagine, whether these jottings will be read and, if they are, whether they will be enfolded and catalogued with the official record of my tenure at Fife Police; nor whether, should any further historian choose to explore their veracity, they will be found wanting in detail or precision[1]. The most I can claim for them is that they represent, as best as I might render them, my recollections of the sundry events and happenstances surrounding Captain McArdle's more momentous involvement with myself and the police force of the Kingdom of Fife.

I pretend no merit as to Literature, nor yet to history. My guide is Mnemosyne and perhaps Hubris. At worst, I am scratching a long itch. At best, I may bring long-overdue recognisance to worthy personages. But if these amateur scribblings enlighten, inform, beguile or – vainglorious hope – entertain, then "this auld grey heid had lain easy"[2].

This day 1st January, 1903, at Sandilands, Cupar in the Kingdom of Fife

My hand,

James Fleming Bremner

Chief Constable of Fife

---

1 Bremner is occasionally wrong or remiss in small particulars (such as referring to McArdle as his 'Galatea', who was female) and I have indicated these in footnotes. I have also added further comment where it shines an interesting sidelight on the history of the period, or where some explanation is perhaps necessary for better understanding by the 21st Century reader.

2 A case in point – this is a slight misrendition of a line from the third verse of a polemic against the Union of 1707, attributed to Robert Burns, *Such a Parcel of Rogues in a Nation*. The line goes: 'My auld grey head had lain in clay/Wi' Bruce and Loyal Wallace'.

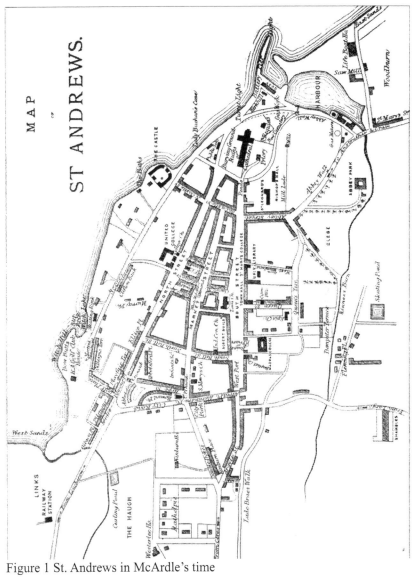

Figure 1 St. Andrews in McArdle's time

CHAPTER ONE

The first hole at the Old Course in St. Andrews is known as The Burn Hole, and is a well-known tester of a golfer's mettle, perhaps even more so in 1875 than today. It takes its name from the Swilcan or Swilken Burn, the small stream that runs down the left of the fairway towards the green, turns straight across the front of it and then curves back up the fairway and to the right, making an inverted U-shape with its open end towards the tee.

On this fine Wednesday afternoon, the last of June in that year, the bright sunshine did not make its 370 yards look any shorter. A deceptive hole, it led many a golfer into a powerful drive straight forwards, to avoid as much as possible of the burn. Their idea was to afford themselves an easy second shot, but invariably most drives ended up short, and the second in the water, making a par four impossible. A dispiriting way to start a game of golf, many a player thought.

Others, perhaps distracted by contemplation of the stream before them, sliced it to the right and ended up out of bounds or facing a long and tricky second along the burn anyway, or having to cross its meander three times.

The wiser golfer – or the better advised – played a wee bit to the left and just beyond Granny Clark's Wynd which crosses the fairway about 150 yards out, then aimed for the back of the green, hoping for a roll back and two putts.

I could tell that these were the very thoughts going through the mind of the man standing at the first, bulger in hand and his gutty ball ready on a small pile of sand at his feet. He looked back at his caddie, a young lad of 12 or so, who was carrying the other half-dozen clubs under his left arm. I had just approached the First tee with my own caddie and was waiting patiently for the earlier golfer to take the honour.

"Come on then, young Archie," the man said. "What's the shot? I haven't played this thing for a score or more years, and it was different then."

"Wee bit to the left, Captain McArdle, and dinnae melt it."

"Just what I was thinking," the man evidently called McArdle replied. As he was preparing himself to address the ball, I emboldened myself to call out to him.

"Ho there! Forgive me, but the Starter says you're playing alone and new to the course. Perhaps you would not mind a partner and a bit of company on the round? I fancy I know a trick or two on this devil of a course."

I had an ulterior motive, too, in that a caddied pair could play though any lone golfers we met.

1

"If you can show me the bits to avoid, I'll be in your debt," McArdle said, extending his hand towards me.

"Oh, I'll do better than that," I averred, taking McArdle's hand and shaking it vigorously. "I'll probably land in every bunker, slap of water and bit of rough there is, so you can see exactly where they are! Bremner, Sir."

"McArdle. Glad of your company, especially if you're going to make me look good. I was just saying to Archie here, I haven't played these links since I was a lad not much more than his age, back in Daw Anderson and Allan Robertson's days."

"Ah, well. You'll notice the new first green then. Ever since Old Tom Morris put it in back in '70 and separated the seventeenth, we play the course right going out and left on the return. Did anybody bother to tell you that?"

"Archie here mentioned it. I heard that you played it clockwise one week and the other way the next. Is that not the way any more?"

"After the first Open Championship here a couple of years back we've sort of kept to the widdershins," I informed him. "All the other greens still have two holes, though. White flags for the front nine and red flags on the way back."

"So why don't you take the honour and show me how it's done, eh?"

McArdle lifted his ball and I replaced it with my own on the sand pile. I was using an old cleekie driver I was fond of at the time, and gave the ball a ferocious thwack. Unfortunately, I hooked it left and what was intended to be a good lie on the fairway was in the margin of the rough and looking straight along one arm of the burn as it headed north-west towards the green. It ran the risk of finding water whatever shot I played next. So I sighed. "Oh, I don't know why I play this blasted game."

Taking his stance with a grin, McArdle decided on the brave approach and belted the ball straight ahead. It flew a good two hundred yards, caught a small hummock beyond The Wynd, which diverted it slightly to the right, and pottered to a stop right where the Swilcan runs due north along the front of the green.

"Well done, Captain McArdle," Archie cheered, as aware as any caddie that the size of his tip would depend not so much on his advice as to how he made his 'man' feel about the day's game.

As we walked together down the fairway, our caddies cradling the clubs, I kept the conversation going. "So you weren't here for the Open in '73, then?"

"I would have, but the Army had other ideas. Somehow they felt I would be more use in Africa," McArdle replied.

I addressed the ball for my second shot and caught just enough grass to slow it down. I remember sighing as it skidded towards the burn and breathing a sigh of relief as it stopped just short. "So, Army, are you? Which regiment?" I asked as we headed for McArdle's lie.

"Royal Highland Regiment, 42nd Foot," he replied, indicating to Archie that he would use an iron club.

"A Black Watch man, eh? Here, is that one of the new Forgans?" I asked, nodding at the club.

"Collected it this morning. I had a look in at Forgan's place in Market Street and took a liking to this. They call it a lofting cleek, kind of a metal baffy. It's a sort of coming-home present to myself." McArdle used it to good effect, lifting the ball over the burn to land not far short of the pin.

"You'll be getting more clubs like that, then," I said in admiration, mentally adding it to the long list of ideas and implements that might, one day, improve my own game. Every golfer knows that imperfections in his game can reasonably be ascribed to the fault of his implements, the course, inclement weather, a badly-cooked breakfast, an unsympathetic caddy and many another independent variable.

"Oh, perhaps. I like the old ones, though." He indicated the other six clubs, all wooden and five of them long-nosed. "These are the set Tom Morris gave me when I was a boy. They're all old, except the bulger. He made that for me especially, when I went away to sea. I can't think what use he thought I'd have of it on the 'vasty deep', can you?"

I laughed at the image this conjured of a young man blasting balls far out over the ocean from off the Poop or Quarter-deck or whatever part of a ship from which one might do such a thing .

"So you're a local laddie, then?"

"Born and raised here."

"And you know the Morris family."

"My father knew Tom Morris. He would let me hang around the shop and caddie for him now and then. He taught me the game, really."

"Then you'll know Young Tom as well."

"He was very wee when I left. In 1850 that was."

There was something about that date which didn't ring correct with me, but I let it pass for the time being. "Before they built the Clubhouse," I said, indicating the building behind us. "It went up in 1854. You'll not have been in it?"

"I have not. I well remember the old Union Parlour in Golf Place. I'd certainly like to see the new clubhouse, but I'm not in the Royal and Ancient, or the Union, so a visit will have to wait until I can join one or the other. Which do you advise as the better club to belong to?"

"Oh, it hardly matters, as I fancy the two will merge before very much longer. But I'm sure something can be arranged. Especially as I'm a member of both of these fine clubs."[3]

"Are you now? You're obviously a man to know."

"Oh, you've no idea! Mind you, the fees are crippling. My wife – who complains of very little and grudges me less – is a termagant on that matter. But didn't you see your friend Mr. Morris when you collected your caddie?"

"He wasn't in. I went to his shop to see if he was around, but they said he was in Edinburgh visiting a customer. I'll try to see him tomorrow. I'm glad in a way because I want to surprise him. As I say, I haven't seen him in twenty-five years. In the meantime, I'm a Stranger."

I realised what had been puzzling me from McArdle's narration. "But tell me, how is it that you went to sea if you were in the Army?"

McArdle waited until I had baffed my third shot high and nodded in appreciation as it thudded near the flag and came to a sudden halt. "I went to sea first. But one day in '56 we were docked at Dover and I found myself talking to some Black Watch sojers in a tavern. Next thing I knew, I was in front of a recruiting officer and taking the shilling!"

I laughed. "Terrible persuasive, those Highlander sergeants."

"So is their whisky! But it was a fine life, wearing the Red Hackle. Never regretted it for a moment."

McArdle putted first, missed by an inch and I indicated that he should just tap it in before sinking my own short putt and halving the hole with McArdle. Both caddies went to great pains to point out how well their respective men had played the hole.

"And now you're back home. Mustered out?" I asked as we handed our putters to the caddies.

"No, I'm still in, at least in theory. I was wounded last year and got a home posting. So I'm on full pay but light duties for a year while the Army works out what's to be done with me. I'm back at Perth and this time it's me doing the recruiting. Or looking after it, anyway. It's still a big Highland sergeant called Geddes that does all the work."

"Probably the same one as you encountered in Dover."

---

[3] Bremner is obviously showing off to the reader, here. He would have known that this inevitable event occurred in 1877. The imposing sandstone Clubhouse, one of the most instantly recognisable buildings in the world, was initially a smaller H-shaped building with high windows. Members of the R&A and the Union Club shared the premises until amalgamation. Over the next 70 years, further development extended the Clubhouse to its present format.

"It wouldn't surprise me," McArdle laughed as he was handed his bulger by Archie for the second hole, known as Dyke for good reason.

"Take the honour, McArdle," I offered, "and if you'll take my advice as well, play to the left of Cheape's."

"I can't see the hole. I'd forgotten that."

"Indeed! But maybe you'll remember the gorse and the other bunkers on the right."

McArdle played a creditable shot just short of Cheape's bunker and I'm pleased to say that my drive passed his by a good twenty yards. Both had a sight of the pin and our second shots reached the green and avoided the chain of small sand traps leading to it. Mine had landed squarely to the left while McArdle's ball had rolled away down the diagonal towards the sixteenth hole, which shared the green with the second. I putted out for a birdie, but McArdle finished with a handy four.

By the time we had finished the third hole and Ginger Beer, we were even again, and I had extracted from McArdle that he had been born in St. Andrews in 1835 or so, schooled at The Madras College and had thought perhaps to become an apprentice clubmaker and greenkeeper, like his benefactor Old Tom Morris. Circumstances, chiefly the death of his hard-drinking father, had led to his leaving St. Andrews on one of the coasters which berthed at the harbour. There was no mention of a mother. Brought up in the warren of warehouses and cramped fisher-folk's homes which clustered around the quayside beside the gasworks and the Cathedral's eastern wall, the boats and yawls had been part of McArdle's boyhood landscape. Vessels like these had brought his grandparents from Shetland fifty years before, imported with other islander families to revive the St. Andrews fishing fleet devastated in a storm with many men lost. In 1850 they had taken the young David McArdle away to Edinburgh, and thence to Africa, America and elsewhere.

But he had no great love of the open main, he said, and even less for the brutality and greed of the merchant service. At the first opportunity, he had joined the infantry, as he had explained to me. It was indeed his good fortune to find the Black Watch, ever the local Regiment for Fife, Angus and Perthshire, despite its often being called the 'Royal Highlanders'. But within half a year he found himself at sea again, this time aboard one of the six ships bound for Calcutta to help put down the Mutiny. Private McArdle arrived on the sub-continent in November 1857.

I dare say it was not until we had turned and were on the sixteenth hole, known as Corner of the Dyke, where McArdle had landed in the Principal's Nose bunker 180 yards out, that he seemingly realised he had given me almost his whole life history, yet knew all but nothing of his interlocutor in return. It was a situation he clearly resolved to remedy. He later told me that he had initially found me pleasant enough, and every bit his match on the golf course, but had to admit that I had a patient and insistent way of ferreting out detail without giving much away in return. Perhaps I was a lawyer or a schoolmaster, McArdle had thought, so he had reckoned to stand me a whisky or two and loosen my tongue a bit.

We halved the long seventeenth and started the eighteenth all-square, each of us a stroke under par. The Swilcan Burn was less of a hazard, being just in front of us, and the best shot, as I told McArdle (but he remembered anyway) was to aim straight for the clock at the Clubhouse, landing just before Granny Clark's Wynd once more. He also recalled, on his second shot, that the buildings surrounding the green make the yardage look deceptively short. He aimed left and long and landed with a lengthy but uncomplicated putt to finish.

Not so myself, whose second shot had found the other natural hazard on the hole – the Valley of Sin, which guards the green's frontage. I had no choice but to loft my third ball, which was therefore short, and I took two putts on the enormous green. McArdle, also taking two putts, was down in four, taking the hole and the match.

As the caddy complimented us effusively – and was rewarded for his efforts with an additional (and highly unofficial) sixpence – McArdle suggested that, as the winner, it was his privilege to stand me a drink. It now being almost seven of the evening and a mist coming in that would shortly turn to a summer shower, we agreed upon the tavern opposite his hotel in Abbotsford Crescent. He would forego the pleasures of the new Union Clubhouse until he was dressed for the occasion, he said.

"Archie, take my clubs up to Rusack's Hotel and have the desk get them cleaned and ready for tomorrow, would you?" McArdle asked his caddy. "Say I'll be back in a moment to change my shoes and I'll be taking dinner later on, maybe in an hour or so."

Young Archie paused for a moment as if in two minds as whether to comply. At the time, I put it down to him wondering whether yet another sixpence might in it, but he scuttled off up Golf Place. While I took my clubs back into the clubhouse, McArdle resolved to meet me outside his hotel. In fact, he was waiting for me at the corner of North Street – where I saw him quietly give a shilling to a College student begging for food, as they often did – and we made ready to head for a nearby tavern. But I stopped McArdle short, grasped his arm and indicated along the road.

"Ah. Now you get to meet one of St. Andrews' finest," I informed him.

Walking towards us down North Street at the regulation two miles-per-hour was a large, imposing figure in a police cape and a tall helmet. "All quiet, Constable?" I asked. At the mention of the word 'Constable', I noticed that the student who had been squatting on the corner quietly quickly gathered up his belongings and took his leave.

"So far, Sir," the Constable replied, saluting me and giving McArdle the well-practised once-over that says: *You probably haven't done anything yet, but I'll be keeping my eye on you just the same.*

"You two are well acquainted, then," McArdle said, surmising that I was perhaps a magistrate or some other local worthy.

McArdle has the good grace to look astonished. "I've met the Chief Constable once or twice afore, aye," Murdoch replied.

"Well, well. Chief Constable, eh Bremner? No wonder you were so good at getting me to hold forth back there on the links," he laughed.

"I've been having eighteen holes with Captain McArdle, Constable. A local man come home again. And Black Watch, like yourself."

"McArdle?" the policeman mused. "Black Watch, is it?"

"That's right. And you would be..."

"Murdoch, Sir, and I had the privilege of serving in the 42nd, as Mr. Bremner says."

"So you did," McArdle exclaimed delightedly, shaking his hand. "Pipey Murdoch! I remember you from India. You were one of the old sweats when I first joined up"

"Well this is remarkable!" I exclaimed. "You two served together?"

The large policeman stood straight to attention and threw his burly chest out even further, staring straight ahead and announcing in a voice that was learned early on the parade ground, "Aye Sir. Although I first got my knees brown at the Crimea with Campbell. Then in India during the wee bit of bother, as you'll recall, Captain." I'd not heard the Indian Mutiny called a 'wee bit of bother' before.

McArdle grinned. "We were never in the same Company, so we didn't really get to know each other. Anyway, us raw recruits gave the older men a wide berth so as not to annoy them! Especially the pipers. I'm right in remembering you were a piper, Murdoch?"

Murdoch murmured an assent.

"And you'd have been at Lucknow, I imagine?"

"Aye, Sir. I was there when Lieutenant Farquharson got his Victoria Cross." He puffed out his chest further still, standing proud in the reflected glory of famous campaign and a famous officer.

McArdle clapped Murdoch on the shoulder. "At ease, man. You'll strain something. But you're a Dundee man, as I recall. Whatever brought you to The Kingdom?"

"Ach, well, I got married – a lassie local to here – and she never took to city life. Her folks were getting on and... well, I was in the Polis by then and asked if I could join the Fife establishment. Mr. Bremner was kind enough to have me."

As Murdoch relaxed ever so slightly in telling his tale, I interjected, "So the Black Watch got a V.C., eh?"

"Oh they've got a few, Sir," Murdoch affirmed. "That was 9th March 1858, and the Regiment's very first Victoria. I was there for the next three, as well." He gave McArdle a sidelong glance, the import of which I missed at the time.

"Is that right, now?" I interjected. "Murdoch, you're a lad o' pairts, right enough."

"As you say Sir. We marched to Rhoadamow in April. That bastard – forgive the Gaelic, Mr. Bremner – Nurpert Singh was holed up in Fort Ruhya. 'Rebel chief' he called himself. Just a bandit, in my view. We were four companies plus the 4th Punjaub rifles. Plucky lads, all of 'em. The brigands had men firing from the parapets and even in the trees. We lost Brigadier Hope, Lieutenant Douglas and Mr. Bramleyhere, a sergeant and six privates. Above thirty-five of us were wounded, if I remember aright, before the rebels slunk away at night. We acquitted ourselves well, if I can make so bold."

"More V.C.s?" I asked, amused but also interested in the Constable's association with his regiment's laurels.

"In India, Sir, aye. Quarter-Master Sergeant Johnny Simpson, Lance-Corporal Eck Thompson, and Private Jimmy Davis. Wee Jimmy was a friend of mine. Our lieutenant had been killed at the gate of the fort and Jimmy volunteered to carry his body back to the regiment under heavy fire. Later he said he'd often had an officer on his back, but he didnae mind this time, as he couldnae think o' a better shield against bullets. Great sense o' humour, Wee Jimmy. Edinburgh man, lives there still. About ages with yourself, Mr. McArdle. Mind you, his real name was Kelly, though he kept it quiet."

"Well, he would," McArdle agreed. "But what happened to you, Murdoch?"

"I was invalided out at Bareilly the next month and after we came home I took up the Polis, like my father afore me."

"And do you still play the pipes?"

"When I can. The wife disnae like the noise much."

McArdle turned to me. "You know, Mr. Bremner, when I joined up in '56, the exploits of Murdoch and his comrades in Crimea were well known. I was glad I'd been inspired me to muster with the 42nd and no other regiment, even though the 73rd were recruiting strong. Murdoch, did you get to see Sir Hugh Rose – the Commander-in-chief in India, Bremner – when he gave the Regiment its new colours? And its old name, eh?"

My Constable nearly broke his back straightening up again. "Richt enough, Sir. We always knew we were the Black Watch, but it was nice to get the old name back, as you might say."

"New Year's day 1861 it was. Imagine listening to a two hour speech with a Hogmanay hangover!"

"Indeed, Mr. McArdle. But you'll pardon my presumption – we didnae get the auld name back official-like until the July of that year. Her Majesty was graciously pleased to let The Royal Highland Regiment also be called by its first name, The Black Watch, once again. Am I right? I missed it, I'm sad to say. I came out just before that in the March, when three companies were detached to Futteghur and the headquarters moved to Agra. You must have got my old commander back as your Colonel – Major-General Sir Duncan Cameron, him as led us up the slopes of Alma."

McArdle laughed. "So we did. He's still in harness, as Governor of the College at Sandhurst. This is some man you've got here, Mr. Bremner. Piper, hero and military historian to boot. Is he as good on the beat?"

"None better. Runs a quiet parish, does our Murdoch. But to hear some of his war stories – as I often have, I might tell you – and it's a wonder he didn't get half a dozen V.C.s himself. I take it the Black Watch won a few more, then?"

Murdoch started counting off on his fingers. "Gardner, Davis, Simpson, Spence, Thompson, Farquharson, Cook, Millar. That's eight in India by my tally. And a brace at Ashanti, of course. That would be right, Mr. McArdle?"

McArdle chose that moment to examine some mud on his shoes and seemed to be ignoring the policeman. Murdoch's moustache twitched slightly and he glanced sideways at McArdle before addressing Bremner again. "Beggin' yir pardon again, Sir, but if I'm not mistaken this'll be the same McArdle that got the V.C. himself, same time as McGaw."

I spun to face McArdle and I dare say my mouth and eyes were wide in genuine surprise.

"McArdle! You? The V.C.? Good grief man, would you credit that!"

McArdle flushed slightly and threw Murdoch a sideways glare. The Constable merely smiled and continued to stand at attention. "Well, it's not as difficult as it sounds," my erstwhile golfing partner demurred. "You just have to be injured badly enough for everybody to feel sorry for you, but not enough to die. And so much the better if it happens when there's something dangerous going on."

Murdoch chipped in again. "Aye. That, and lead your men through the bush to safety throughout the day, even though you were badly wounded early on. First Ashanti Expedition, I believe. Battle of Amoaful, January last year, was it not? I read about it in the paper, Sir, if you can believe the paper."

McArdle ignored the obvious slight. "Lance-Sergeant McGaw's was the better deserved. But how right you are, Constable. I was a Sergeant at the time, which is a bit of good luck, really."

"And how's that, McArdle?" I asked, truly fascinated by this unexpected revelation.

"Ah, well, an enlisted man who scores Queen Victoria's cross gets an extra £10 a year to his pension. Keeps me in *usquebaugh*." He looked towards the tavern across the road. "And I'll stand both of you a small one out of my good luck, if you'll allow me. Murdoch, do you take of the strong drink."

"Never on duty, Sir!" the big galoot replied, conscious of his superior. But McArdle cut the Gordian knot for him.

"Well, doubtless Mr. Bremner's on duty too, so he can hardly discipline you without arresting himself into the bargain. What do you say, Bremner?"

"Och, it's a cold, wet night coming for all it's July tomorrow, and Murdoch could probably do with a medicinal one. For his chest."

McArdle poked Murdoch's inflated, barrel-like rib cage with his fist. "I don't think his chest needs any more encouragement. Let's say it's for his feet, shall we?"

"Let's say that very thing," I agreed. "And I'll buy them, just so there's no misunderstanding. Murdoch here can hardly refuse a direct order from his Chief, now can he?"

Murdoch clearly had no intention of doing so, and followed us into the tavern. Any reluctance he might have felt was compounded by embarrassment when the tavern-keeper, seeing the constable enter, gave out with a cheery "Evening, Murdoch! The usual, is it?"

I turned to look at my subordinate somewhat sharply, expecting an explanation. "I usually just poke my head in the door about this time, Sir. Just to see there's no bother, like. And I sometimes have glass of lemonade. For the thirst." He said it loud enough for the tavern keeper to hear and realise his gaffe. McArdle laughed and said, "Never mind, Murdoch, you'll have a wee whisky with us now, won't you? Just this once. Much better for you than lemonade. Three quarter-gills, cold, if you please."

As the whiskies arrived, Murdoch did not lose the opportunity to give the tavern keeper a fierce *I'll talk to you later* stare. Then he raised his nip glass in salute, to which I and McArdle responded in kind.

After we had each downed our whiskies and replaced the glasses on the bar, I had a question to ask of our guest. "But listen, McArdle. If you were a Sergeant not a year and a half ago, how is it you're a Captain now?"

"I was wondering that myself, Sir, if it's not too bold." Murdoch added.

"Ah, well. More luck, if that's the word for it. I was field-commissioned to Sub-Lieutenant, but really only because my Colonel knew that an officer would get a cushier berth on the troop ship home. After I convalesced, I got talked into helping the War Office with a spot of trouble and woke up one morning to find myself gazetted Lieutenant. And when I came back to Perth to organise the recruiting and some other bits and pieces, they realised they were a Captain short of the establishment and picked me. So I'm not an officer really. More a jumped-up Queen's Man."

"Rather unusual, isn't it, to be commissioned like that? If you don't mind me saying," I inquired.

Murdoch butted in. "Not so very, Sir. I knew three Sergeant-Majors myself that were promoted out of the ranks – Wilson and Lawson were made Ensigns in 1854 and the next year Granger was made up to Lieutenant in the Land Transport Corps, then to a Captaincy. Lawson became a Captain as well, but he died at Mooradabad – whether of the wounds or the fever, I couldn't say."

"It was a bit of both, I'm afraid. And exhaustion from the forced march. The Regiment always lost more men from disease than from steel or bullets. Murdoch will remember John Wilson – enlisted man who became a Brevet-Major," McArdle added, "and a good friend of mine until he retired two years back. So I'm really not as queer a fish as you might think."

"And what are you doing now, Captain McArdle, if I might ask." The whisky had clearly emboldened Murdoch.

"Well, it's quite boring, really. We got back to Portsmouth in the Spring of last year and some of us had to go up to Windsor for a chat with Her Majesty…"

"And get your medal, Sir," Murdoch intervened.

"Aye, that too. But when many of the lads were preparing for Malta, I was given a wee job in the War Office. Then I was sent to back to Perth to help with recruiting, and a few other matters. So here I am. That's it."

"Keeps you busy, I suppose," I mused, and called up another three whiskies, which the tavern keeper indicated were on the house.

"Not really. In fact, I'm thinking maybe it's time to find something else to do. I've come back to see if maybe there's a place for me in the town I left more than half a lifetime ago. Farming maybe. Horses, I fancy, although a wise man once told me never to keep an animal that eats while you sleep. They cost too much. Or perhaps I'll get to make golf clubs after all. I'll go and

11

see Tom Morris tomorrow, and maybe I'll ask him. He'll know of a good position for a local man, or one who once was."

"I'll ask around too, McArdle," I offered. "Perhaps somebody has a suitable opening. Have you a trade as well as your soldiering?"

"Not a bit of one. And don't bother suggesting the sea again. I've seen quite enough of boats and foreign shores. Something quiet and landward for Davie McArdle from now on."

We had a final toast to the sentiment.

As we three left the hostelry, I said my goodbyes. Murdoch walked ostentatiously away from the tavern and around a corner while McArdle headed back towards Abbotsford Crescent. I crossed the road and sheltered in a doorway as I gathered my thoughts, from where I saw Murdoch peer back around the corner, checking that the coast was clear before nipping back into the howff. The rascal! I looked across the street and saw McArdle also watching Murdoch from the other corner. He smiled and shook his head.

In the event, it was a blessing that I had chosen to remain and see what transpired next. McArdle had stopped in the doorway of his hotel, looking at the sky and perhaps wondering what promise it held for the next day's weather. It was as much to his surprise as it was to mine when a rough looking man bustled past him, clutching a leather box. McArdle suddenly cried out. The ruffian looked back over one shoulder, saw McArdle, and took to his heels, sprinting away up North Street. I heard McArdle shout: "Hiy! That's mine!" The thief accelerated, clasping the box even closer to his shallow chest, bending low in his flight.

It was then that I had the first evidence that McArdle thought along a different vector from most of humanity. The normal reaction of anyone who suspected a fleeing figure to be carrying something of theirs, would be to give chase and shout 'Stop! Thief!' Or some such. Not McArdle. He looked to both sides of him, saw a golfer trudging home carrying four clubs, reached over to abstract the putter from the crook of the man's arm, and swung it back behind himself. The said golfer, deprived surprisingly of what was undoubtedly, at that moment, his favourite club, made to remonstrate with the one who had relieved him of it, but even he stopped when he saw what happened next. McArdle bent forward and flung his arm around, releasing the putter with a spinning motion. It gyrated away from him, perfectly level with the pavement, whirling as it went, and caught the retreating miscreant at knee height, entangling itself in his legs. The man fell sprawling to the ground, the leather box tumbling from his grasp and falling open in the road. Winded, he raised himself on all fours, unsure what mysterious power had deprived him of movement. By the time he stood upright, somewhat groggily, he was doubtless further surprised when McArdle hit him at full tilt, driving him into a wall and causing him to expel all his breath. Even from my vantage point some thirty yards distant, I fancied I heard a rib crack.

My duty was clear. I looked back into the pub we had so recently left and saw Murdoch raising a glass that contained the fluid which did not resemble his 'usual' lemonade. "Constable Murdoch," I shouted from the door, causing that worthy to drop the glass, stand bolt upright, spin around and put his hat on, all in one fluid movement which the most talented ballerina could not have emulated with a month's practice. "Come with me! Now!"

"Sir," Murdoch replied instantly, and was out of the door quicker than 'knife'. I have no doubt he was fearful of his position, but I grasped his sleeve and pointed up the street to where McArdle was standing over the now-fallen ruffian, holding him by his collar.

"Do your duty, Murdoch. I shall follow."

Murdoch set off at a velocity commendable for a person of his bulk and habits, and reached the altercation. I followed a few seconds behind. McArdle saw Murdoch approach and said, "Sorry, Constable. I appear to have dented one of your citizens". He also collected the putter from where it had fallen and returned it to its astonished owner with effusive thanks and apologies. The still-amazed golfer, standing open-mouthed, must have thought his club lost forever. But he clearly took comfort from the sight of Murdoch's uniform and continued on his way, shaking his head and muttering.

Murdoch was now in full possession of the felon, McArdle having released him into the constable's tender care. Holding the fellow with one huge fist to the collar, Murdoch used the other to take out a large red kerchief from a capacious pocket, then he removed his hat, placed it under his arm and mopped his brow.

"This is no 'citizen', Captain McArdle. This miserable specimen is Twa Ba' Wullie!"

If McArdle was as intrigued by the appellation as I was, he gave no sign of it. But Murdoch clarified the confusion immediately, addressing himself to me.

"William Joyce, Sir. Once a caddie, but dismissed by Mr. Morris for his practice of finding his man's lost golf ball while managing to stamp the other player's ball into the ground. Many a wager Wullie's won for his man by carrying an extra ball in his boot heel and burying the opponent's!"

"Ah yes, I recall hearing the name," I said. "A shameful thing to be dismissed as a caddie. And now he's adding thievery to his misdemeanours, is he?"

"It seems so, Mr. Bremner. Not to mention evading the pursuit of an official of the law."

McArdle took issue with his last statement. "But Murdoch wasn't pursuing him. I was."

I knew what the constable was getting at, and nodded towards the whistle slung on a chain across his breast. "Do your duty!" I instructed.

Murdoch obligingly put the whistle to his lips and blew three shrill blasts. "There you are McArdle!" I exclaimed. "A hue and cry was raised by Constable Murdoch, as everyone in this vicinity will later attest."

McArdle looked around. "So will more policemen come? It seems unnecessary."

"No need, as you say," Murdoch announced, bodily hefting the criminal to his feet. "I've got him."

"You had him anyway," McArdle observed, frowning.

I felt I had to explain.

"What Murdoch and I realise, McArdle, is that while attempted theft is an offence punishable most probably by a fine, evading an official hue and cry will not endear Mr. Joyce to the Sheriff-Depute, and he'll likely find himself at Her Majesty's pleasure rather than mine. Let him be Perth Prison's problem for a while rather than the Toun gaol's."

At times like these I regretted the passing of the old Tolbooth with its thief-hole and jougs.[4]

"Ah! I see," McArdle nodded. But still, you'll have more constables here in a moment, won't you?"

"Unlikely, Sir," Murdoch said. "There's only one other policemen in St. Andrews and I happen to know he's visiting his sister in Crail the day."

McArdle looked stunned for an instant, then laughed. "I see very little escapes you two. St. Andrews is a safer Toun under your guard than it was when I left it."

"We aim to serve," I affirmed. "And I commend you on your quick thinking with that flying putter. Hardly a proper use for a short club at such a distance, but remarkable aim nonetheless."

---

[4] Bremner could not have known the old Tolbooth, which as in most Scottish Burghs served as police office and gaol, as it was demolished in 1862, to be replaced by the Scottish Baronial-style Town Hall nearby in Market Street. The site of the Tolbooth and Mercat Cross is now occupied by a particularly hideous memorial fountain erected in 1880 to the long-forgotten Victorian novelist George Whyte-Melville (1821-1878), often confused with his more famous father John Whyte-Melville (1797-1883), the longest-surviving Captain of the Royal and Ancient and one of its stalwarts for sixty years. 'Jougs' were a kind of collar by which a miscreant could be chained to a wall.

"Sheer necessity, Mr. Bremner. My leg doesn't run so fast since the wound. So I didn't have much choice."

"Commendable all the same. You're an interesting man, McArdle. Wouldn't you say, Murdoch?"

"Aye, Sir. Interesting." I could see that Murdoch wasn't wholly sure about McArdle – Black Watch and Victoria Cross or not. And the last thing any policeman wants in his bailiwick is anyone or anything 'interesting', which always leads to trouble. A peaceful parish and no surprises, that was Murdoch's dream, and I could not, in honesty, disagree with him.

"But what of this valise, McArdle?" I enquired, keen to resolve the matter. "I take it you immediately recognised it as yours. I can see why. It is rather distinctive. Spanish, is it, perhaps?"

"Marykin[5] leather, Mr. Bremner, with carved wooden locks. Not valuable, but we've been together for a while. I'll doubt there's another like it in Fife, if not the whole of Scotland."

"Begging your pardon, Sir," Murdoch interjected. "But how did this creature get into your room?" He shook the miserable Wullie for emphasis.

"Begging *your* pardon, Constable. The real question is – how did he know he *could* get into my room?"

Murdoch looked puzzled and I confess I was confounded for a moment. Then light dawned. "Ah! Murdoch, I see what he means. Who would know Mr. McArdle wasn't in his room and might not be for a while?"

Murdoch was quick on the uptake. "Anybody who saw us together in the street would think twice. Did you tell the hotel staff you were going out?"

"There was nobody at the desk when I left," McArdle said.

"Then nobody could have tipped Joyce off, but it does explain how he could slip upstairs. What do you say, Wullie?" Murdoch shook his captive again for emphasis.

"I'm sayin' nuthin'," he muttered.

"You'll say something later!" Murdoch threatened.

"But who would know where you're staying and when you'd be going?" I asked.

McArdle pursed his lips and said, "I do have an idea."

"On, come now! This blackguard could have entered the room any time you and I were playing. In fact, it would be less risky to do it then. Two or three hours he would have had."

"That's the point, Mr. Bremner," McArdle added. "He could have, but he didn't. Which suggests he didn't know about me until we'd finished. And he

---

[5] Moroccan - *Ed*

15

didn't know me by sight, or else he'd never have pushed past me in the street. He'd have gone the other way towards City Road or up a close. So somebody else tipped him off about a stranger staying in the hotel but not until after we'd finished our game. He just scooted upstairs and waited until he heard a door close and someone walk down the stairs. Isn't that right, Wullie?"

At the sound of his name, Twa Ba' Wullie cringed away from McArdle and whimpered, "Dinnae let him hit me again!"

Murdoch shook him once more and said "Shut it! I'll deal wi' you later."

McArdle had by now picked up what had spilled out from the box. I saw a medal case, a scroll, some letters in a bundle, a bound notebook or journal of some sort and a few trinkets, plus a small soft leather purse. (And lest anyone think that I am pretending to some prodigious feat of memory after all these years, I should make it clear that Murdoch later asked McArdle for a list of its contents, a record which I later saw and agreed with, as a witness to the attempted theft.)

"Anyway, for the moment, I'm happy to get my possessions back," McArdle stated, collecting up the items. "And I'll be having a wee word with the hotel to suggest they keep a better eye open for skulkers like this one. In truth, the box itself is more valuable than the contents, in sentimental terms anyway. I would hate to have lost it. We can pursue the matter further in the morning. And a few other matters foreby."

"Do I take it you have another idea about this, McArdle?"

"I do, Mr. Bremner. And if Murdoch would accompany me tomorrow morning, I venture we'll find an accomplice or two in this matter. Then I can make my statement. Will you come, Murdoch?"

The constable stood to attention and saluted. "I pass this way about 9:15 on my usual beat, Sir. Will that suit?"

"It will indeed, Murdoch. But now if you don't mind, gentlemen, I've had a very good game of golf – thanks to Mr. Bremner – a nice wee drink and a bit of unexpected excitement. So it's a bath, dinner and bed for me. Until tomorrow then, Murdoch."

Murdoch clicked his heels by way of salute – something he'd never done for me. All the same, I could see he was not altogether sure of the man.

"And you, Mr. Bremner – you've made my homecoming very… eventful."

"I hope it doesn't put you off the old place, McArdle. Not everyone gets robbed and not everyone is a criminal."

"It's a good thing some do and some are, otherwise you two would be looking for other engagements elsewhere. Eh?"

I laughed and we parted, Murdoch propelling Joyce towards the gaol so fast his feet could hardly keep up, and myself thinking that doubtless I would meet McArdle again.

I rode home to Cupar that evening somewhat bemused as to McArdle's assertion about accomplices to the theft. But I was happy to leave that to Murdoch. Twelve years as Chief Constable of Fife and a few before that as Superintendent in Kirkcaldy had taught me to let my men do their job without me tripping their heels.

I resolved to inform Provost Milton about our new arrival to St. Andrews, but all in good time. Meanwhile I would content myself by telling my wife Isabella. She would be fascinated by the news of the dashing V.C. who had frustrated a criminal before my very eyes, as would my daughters, especially Mary. Oh yes, wee Mary would be very interested indeed.

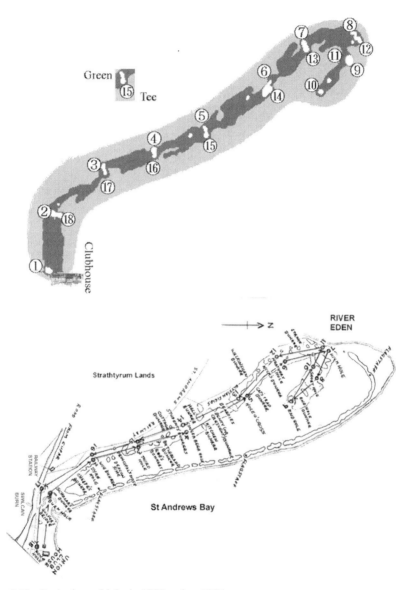

Figure 2 The St. Andrews Links in 1857 and ca 1886
Historians of golf may be interested in these two drawings of the St. Andrews Links, known as the Old Course after 1895 when the New Course was designed by Tom Morris Snr. Note the change of playing direction, from clockwise to 'widdershins', as Bremner put it.

CHAPTER TWO

W hat I know of the next day's remarkable events comes wholly second-hand from what Murdoch put in his official reports and what McArdle himself later told me. Therefore the actual exchanges between the persons concerned are, it must be said, a fancy of my own although I have every reason to believe them to be close to the real occurrences and not to take too many liberties with veracity. Knowing the speech of those involved, I feel justified in putting words into their mouths I did not myself hear. The reader will perhaps excuse this conceit on my part and regard it as not so much a lapse from the normal practice of accurate recording to be expected of a senior police officer, as a way of enlivening what might otherwise run rather dry as a narrative.

In any event, I believe Murdoch was as good as his word in presenting himself at Rusack's Hotel at 9:15 precisely the next morning, to be told that their guest had breakfasted and gone to take an early stroll, resolving to return in time to meet Murdoch. The constable being expected, and having a few moments on his hands, he took it upon himself to inform Herr Rusack of the previous evening's occurrences and further to suggest that if he wanted to keep his customers, he might pay more attention to the comings and goings of non-residents like William Joyce.

I have no doubt that Murdoch also left a strong impression that while there was no actual proof of collusion with the criminal element in this case, he, Murdoch, would be keeping a weather eye on the establishment for some time to come. As an alien and a newcomer to St. Andrews, he was under particular scrutiny.[6] The hotelier was doubtless relieved when McArdle appeared a few minutes later and took the Constable away.

In the street, Murdoch told McArdle that he had been unable to get Joyce to confess to having an accomplice and that in fact the prisoner had said very little. Murdoch made it clear that he simply didn't believe that Joyce was acting other than alone and on an impulse. McArdle replied that he felt they

---

[6] Readers may be confused by this reference and by the placing of Rusack's Hotel in Abbotsford Crescent. Johann Wilhelm Christof Rusack (1848-1916) was a German of French Huguenot extraction who came to Britain in 1871 after the Franco-Prussian war and was naturalized in 1885. Along with his first establishment, he also took over the Star Hotel in Market Street, the Temperance Hotel, Kinloch House and a farm. In 1887 he opened the famous Marine Hotel hard by the Links, where it stands to this day.

might resolve the matter either way if they headed down to the golf course and spoke to the caddie master.

"You surely don't suspect him of any wrong doing? Come now, McArdle!"

"We'll see," McArdle said, "but first, we might clear up part of the mystery right away. Look over there." He indicated a young man walking along the other side of the street, carrying a strap of books.

"What, a College scholar? Why?"

By way of reply, McArdle took Murdoch across the street and intercepted the young man. "Excuse me," he said, "but I believe you were the young man on the corner over there last evening. I give you a shilling."

The youth, seeing Murdoch's uniform and being accused in his presence of begging, was struck dumb and could not reply, opening and closing his mouth in turns. McArdle realise the boy's distress. "Oh, it's all right. You're not in any trouble."

"Oh isn't he?" Murdoch said, good policeman that he was, giving the scholar a very old-fashioned look.

"No he isn't, Constable. Not from me at any rate. Not if he can answer a couple of questions. For instance, you noticed me have an altercation with a man in the road, am I right?"

The youth nodded, looking from one to the other of his interrogators. "Good. And did you happen to notice that same fellow hanging around there just before that?"

The boy recovered his wits sufficiently to speak. "Er, no Sir. That is, he wasn't hanging about. But I saw him going up Abbotsford Crescent just before you did yourself."

"And what made you remark him?"

"He spat into my hat, Sir. Not a nice thing to do. You yourself stopped, found you had no small change and said you'd give me something later. Which you did, God bless you."

"There you are, Murdoch! Joyce was just ahead of me and knew where was staying. We have this young gentleman to thank for confirming my suspicions and we should commend him on his reliability as a witness."

"Reliability!" Murdoch spluttered. "A student beggar?"

"Come now, Murdoch. A lot of the students have to resort to soliciting money to make ends meet. It was always the way. What do you study, son?"

"I hope to enter the ministry, Sir. Providing I get my M.A. first."

"You see, Constable? A divinity student. More power to him."

"More shame you mean! Wanting to be a Meenister of the Kirk and you begging for coppers? Tchah!"

The boy found the courage to speak again. "Well Sir, Christ himself was a poor man and relied on the kindness and charity of others. I see no shame in following our Lord's example!"

Murdoch spluttered but McArdle laughed. "Well said, Mr..."

"Garlands, Sir. Michael Garlands."

"Well, Mr. Garlands. Here's another sixpence for your good cause. Can your parents not afford to keep you at the College then?"

"They're just farming folk from Ceres, Sir. My mother gives me a sack of meal when she can and when my father comes to market here he'll maybe bring me some potatoes and bacon or a few herring. But it's never quite enough. Then there's lodgings to pay for, clothes, books. It's not their fault, with six other bairns to feed and clothe."

"Mr. Garland, I have no doubt that they are proud of you and that you will make them even prouder yet. But why are you still at the College on the first of July?"

"I do some extra tuition for small fees. School children and next year's bejants," he explained, referring in that quaint and particular term to the scholars who would enter their first term in the following Autumn. "It may give me enough to last me until I can earn something at the berry-picking and the potato harvest later in the year."

"Better get along then, and stick in at your books, mind!"

Relieved and grateful, the youth tipped his hat and sped off. I confess I now wonder if this was the same Garlands who later became lauded for his missionary work amongst the poor and was eventually appointed Moderator of the General Assembly of the Church of Scotland. Of course, I may have misremembered the name. But if it were indeed so, perhaps that short exchange was in some way character-forming. Murdoch, however, did not regard it so. "Bluddy college scholars! They're just a blamed nuisance with their begging and their loud ways. Poverty is it? Never stops the limmers getting ale-headed on Lammas days, I've noticed!"

It was, we should remember, an expensive business being a scholar. It would cost a young man some £15 a year to live and study. If that seems a trifling sum now, it behoves us to recall that in 1875 a working family had barely twenty shillings a week to live on and that a four-pound loaf of bread or a stone of potatoes cost sixpence. There being no Hall for the scholars to live in, local landlords had them at their mercy, often charging as much as five shillings a week for mean diggings. Studying was considered so expensive that St. Andrews had scarcely 130 students at the time and the Colleges were considering closure altogether.

21

But to the matter in hand! McArdle was resolved to see the caddie-master, although Murdoch had not fully grasped the reason or the need for this. Nor had I, I freely confess. But the surprise was McArdle's when he entered the clubhouse asking to see the caddie-master and was met by none other than Old Tom Morris himself! McArdle had not known, and could not have known, that Old Tom had added this responsibility to that of Green Keeper. When McArdle had left St. Andrews in 1850, the Keeper was Auld Daw Anderson, he who so improved the fifth green by cutting the two holes we have today. In 1856 two worthies were appointed his successors, Alex Herd and Watty Anderson, sharing the duties and the annual fee of £6. But it was Tom Morris who raised the profession of Green Keeper to its rightful standard when appointed in 1863, receiving the princely sum of £50 annually. Of the three great professionals who graced the Links in 1875, Wilson and Forgan preferred making clubs to managing caddies, so Morris took over Superintendent duty as well.

McArdle's surprise at seeing Old Tom was no greater than that of his old friend seeing McArdle again. It took him but a moment to recognise in the 40-year-old man the resemblance to the 15-year-old boy he had last seen. Murdoch knew that Tom Morris was Caddie master, but it had not occurred to him to say that to McArdle, assuming that as old friends, McArdle would be apprised of this intelligence. But he was not. The two men fell upon each other on first sight, the one not more surprised than the other, shook hands and exchanged their news as Murdoch walked about examining the pictures and notices on the walls, wondering why he was even there, I imagine.

But soon, the natural politeness of Messrs Morris and McArdle tore them away from their reminiscences, resolving both to continue them later, and they included Murdoch again in the conversation.

"Tom, we had a wee spot of bother last night at my hotel."

"Aye. Mr. McArdle's room was robbed," Murdoch added.

"No! Surely not! Did you lose much?"

"Oh, we caught the offender, but Mr. McArdle here is convinced he was tipped off that the room might be empty."

"Is that so? Old Tom asked. "Not by me, you don't think!"

McArdle laughed. "Well if so, you were a very convincing actor when you pretended to see me for the first time just now! But I do have to ask you about your caddies. You see, the gentleman concerned was a certain William Joyce."

"Twa Ba' Wullie? But he hasn't worked this course for a while. It was me that caught him at his shenanigans and I saw him off sharply, I can tell you. Can't have caddies that aren't as straight as a die. It's one thing for Members to get up to nonsense but never one of Tom Morris's caddies! I have rules about such behaviour, and more foreby."

The Constable was studying a notice on the wall. "Aye. I noticed your new rules, Mr. Morris. Do you think you'll make them stick?" Murdoch was referring to a printed notice on the wall of which I have kept a copy and make bold to include at the end of this chapter for the purposes of completeness. Call it Exhibit A in Evidence, if you like.

"Och, it's the only way. You can't have just anybody caddying for the gentlemen. We have high standards to keep up, Murdoch. Mind you, the last time we tried it, in '70, there was a strike!"

At this, Murdoch would have pursed his lips, I imagine, having not a high regard for the denizens of the Course. Murdoch is not a golfer and like many a policeman, he prefers it when the citizenry is firmly indoors where it can't cause any bother, rather than out in the open air carrying dangerous instruments and projecting hard balls at high velocities.

"The fact remains, Tom, this Joyce didn't follow me – he was ahead of me, in fact. But he knew where I was staying and the only other persons who had that knowledge were my playing partner Mr. Bremner..."

"The Heid Polis?" Old Tom exclaimed. "Well look no further for your miscreant, Davie!"

Murdoch was not amused. "Aye, very humorous, Mr. Morris."

"Yes, well, I had rather excluded him from the picture myself. But my caddie yesterday was a lad called Archie."

At this, Morris's eyes narrowed and he nodded. "Ah, now. You might have something there. Caddy second-class is Archie, and more to the point, his surname is Joyce!"

"What? A son to Wullie Joyce?" Murdoch asked.

"No, a nephew. His dead brother's boy, I believe. The whole family's a bad lot, but the boy's never caused any trouble so I had no reason to let him go. Couldn't punish him for the sins of his uncle, could I? And he's probably the only breadwinner in the whole family." Tom Morris consulted a ledger below his desk. "He's not engaged to any gentleman right now, so we'll find him hanging about." Tom Morris strode outside and re-entered not minutes later dragging the said Archie by his ear. "Is this the one, Davie?"

"Aye, that's Archie. Remember me, son?"

The boy took one look at McArdle and burst into tears. The whole sad story tumbled from his lips. It transpired that he had, in fact, been coerced by his uncle to tip him off when a stranger was in town who looked like he might be worth a shilling or two, and where the man was staying. They stuck to out-oftowners because a local house was rarely if ever unoccupied, what with wives and servants about. Normally, Twa Ba' Wullie would indeed have had a couple of hours at least to obtain entry to the man's rooms and rifle them. In this case, Archie had not discovered McArdle's residence until the end of the game, when he was asked to take the clubs there.

"You also knew I intended to change my shoes and then go out for an hour or so. So your uncle Wullie barely had time to get to the hotel before me, hide up the stairs, see what room I was in then wait for me to leave, surmising I'd be out at dinner or in a tavern for a good while. Is that it?"

"I don't know, Sir," the boy Archie bawled. "I haven't seen him since yester e'en."

"That's because he's having Toun porage wi' me," Murdoch glared. "And you might fancy a bowl of that yourself, eh?" The boy howled even louder at the thought of gaol and at the fierce look he was getting from the thoroughly furious Morris.

"And how did you get the hotel staff away from the desk, Archie?"

"When I telt them you wanted your clubs washed, they took them to the back scullery."

"Leaving the coast clear for Wullie, eh? Well, that was my fault. I did ask Archie to do that."

"Ye wee villain! Leave him tae me, Mr. McArdle!" Murdoch said, lunging for the boy.

"Just a minute, Murdoch. And Tom, you can let the boy go. I don't think he'll be running away. Archie, take off your shirt, will you?"

"Wh-what?" the boy asked, doubly amazed at his seeming reprieve and the unusual request from the man he had conspired to rob.

"I want to see your back, boy. Show the Constable your back."

Archie lifted his shirt over his head and revealed a narrow torso covered by a welter of bruises and recently-healed scars. "And would I be right in thinking your Uncle Wullie did that to you? You can put your shirt down now."

The boy complied and blubbed his confession, doubtless grateful to have it off his chest. William Joyce, it seemed, had beaten the boy into agreeing to inform for him in the manner described, and had administered even more whippings when a tip-off did not materialise or produced nothing of worth. And when a robbery did come right, Joyce would drink most of the proceeds, return home drunk and dispense more violence solely on that account. Further, he took all of the boy's caddying wages, leaving Archie to scavenge for food or surreptitiously spend what tips he got and could conceal from Joyce. His Uncle knew that a Second-Class caddie got a shilling a round and sixpence if

24

another round was played immediately, and questioned the boy closely each evening as to his takings. Clearly, Archie had a miserable life. It transpired that they had been working this dodge for over a month and that there had been perhaps ten such robberies from local hotels.

"Didn't you know of this, Murdoch?" McArdle asked.

Murdoch's professional pride was probably piqued at this. "We've had no such reports, Sir," he would have said, for indeed we had not.

"I don't wonder," Tom Morris put in. "Most hoteliers wouldn't want it getting about that their places of business are insecure. They probably make good any loss and tell the guests they'll inform the police later, which they never do. One or two might even be in on the business!"

"We'll be seeing about that!" Murdoch stated and proceeded to take down in writing as much detail as Archie could give him on the places and dates of likely thefts. When Murdoch later registered the matter we made the appropriate enquiries and found a good half-dozen actual thefts unreported and in two cases clear collusion between Joyce and the hotelier in question. Not, I am pleased to report, at Rusack's hotel, but suffice to say that the practice stopped forthwith and every hotel owner in St. Andrews was put on strict notice that failure to report any crime instantly was grounds for another visit from the Fife Constabulary and some rather close questioning. Joyce himself confessed when faced with Archie's testimony. I supposed it was either to his credit that he hadn't wanted to involve the boy in his prosecution, or was perhaps a calculated act, figuring that he would be able to turn the same trick when released, if Archie was still in place. Either way, he did not get the chance to involve Archie again.

McArdle now turned his attention again to the boy, who had calmed down and was sitting miserably in a corner. "Right, Archie. Tell me, do you go to school?"

"It's required of them, Davie, and Sunday School, too!" Morris informed McArdle.

"Aye, but does he do it? I sure he'd rather earn a shilling than read a book."

The boy wiped his nose with a sleeve and looked up at McArdle. "I went to the Flagpole, but that's stopped now."

McArdle looked at Tom Morris for enlightenment. "General Moncrieffe – one of our Members – has long had the caddies' education at heart. He started an outdoor "reading room" for caddies around the flagpole outside, and arranged to have them to be fed coffee to keep then alert and warm. The ladies of the town taught reading and figures. But it didn't last."

"Why's that, Tom?"

"Well, not to put too fine a point on it, there's only so much coffee the young body can take without wanting to relieve itself, and the ladies felt the flagpole was getting used for, what shall we say, ignoble purposes. It offended their sensitivities more than somewhat. So they gave it up. But the General's now got the Greens Committee to work with the School Board and there's evening classes at the Fisher School."

"You don't say! I learnt my first letters and numbers there before I went to The Madras," McArdle said, and thought for a moment or two. Suffice it to say that McArdle extracted a promise from Archie that, if Morris let him stay on as a caddy and Murdoch wouldn't press the matter of his conspiracy in theft, he would attend the classes at the Fisher School opposite the old Cathedral ruins.

Murdoch now had plenty of work to do, what with Joyce to interview further and reports to make out based on Archic's confession, so he left McArdle and Morris to themselves, the two old friends wanting to catch up.

Morris invited McArdle to his house and shop and got Kirky, his personal caddie of long standing, and no mean golfer and club maker himself, to stand in for him. It must have been as they walked together towards Old Tom's premises, close by the fairway, that they were met by his wife, Agnes Morris, running towards them, obviously in a state of distress. "Tom! Oh, Tom!" she was repeating over and over as she reached them and collapsed in her husband's arms.

"Whatever's the matter, lass?"

"Tom, it's Auntie Janet. I think she's dying!" And Agnes collapsed on her husband, weeping.

RULES

REGARDING

PAY AND DISCIPLINE OF CADDIES,

ADOPTED BY

THE ROYAL AND ANCIENT GOLF CLUB OF ST. ANDREWS,

At a Special General Meeting of the Club, held on 3rd February, 1875.

I.—All Caddies shall be Enrolled,—none being admitted under 13 years of age.

II.—Members of the Club shall employ only Enrolled Caddies.

III.—A List of Enrolled Caddies shall be placed in the Club Hall, and also in the Clubmakers' Shops.

IV.—Caddies shall be divided into Two Classes, according to skill or age, and their services shall be rated as follows:—

First Class Caddies.—Eighteenpence for First Round, and One Shilling for each following Round, or part of Round.

Second Class Caddies.—One Shilling for First Round, and Sixpence for each following Round, or part of Round.

V.—No Caddy, unless previously engaged, can refuse to carry for a Member, under penalty of suspension for a stated time.

VI.—Names of suspended or disqualified Caddies shall be posted.

VII.—Complaints regarding Caddies shall be made through the Keeper of the Green to the Green Committee, who shall award an adequate penalty.

VIII.—The penalty shall be awarded by not less than two of the Green Committee.

IX.—The Keeper of the Green shall have charge of the Caddies, and Members shall apply to him when in want of a Caddy.

X.—Members are particularly urged to report all cases of misconduct on the part of the Caddies, whether during their time of service or otherwise,—such as incivility, bad language, abusing the Green, or any other form of misdemeanour,—which may merit censure or penalty.

XI.—Tom Morris shall be Keeper of the Green, and Superintendent of the Caddies.

Figure 3 The Rules of Caddies 1875

27

CHAPTER THREE

N either myself nor Constable Murdoch was witness to most of what happened subsequent to Captain McArdle and Mr. Thomas Morris receiving the news that Mr. Morris's aunt was dying. However, I do have to hand McArdle's own record of the events to draw on. He was careful to note his observations and the actual words spoken by him and others. I have rendered these into the third person for reasons of narrative consistency and I can only ask the reader to take my word for it that I have not added or elided anything of substance, nor have I embellished, except where an event occurred, seemingly insignificant at the time but which, with the benefit of hindsight, turned out to have been important or had some moment in the light of later events.

It is a matter of record that Miss Janet Morris died at 1 A.M. on the second day of July 1875, aged 92, at Kincaple, a hamlet some three miles west of St. Andrews. She was unwed, having worked as a domestic servant and had remained resolutely independent all her life. Some, lacking perhaps in Christian charity, may say that a lady of her age had had a reasonable run for her money and was fortunate to have lasted so long, but as events were to prove, she could well have gone on to an even longer life and possibly might have reached her Century.

Tom Morris's wife, Agnes, was fond of her aunt-by-marriage, and was understandably distressed when the news came of the elder's debility and likely final hours. However, it should be remembered that Agnes, being sixty years of age at the time, and some five or six years older than her husband, was thus not in the first flush of youth herself. She was in no condition to rush to the bedside of an aged relative, however dear to her. Tom Morris himself was so stunned by the news that he had to retire to his house in Pilmour Links and compose himself while McArdle organised a trap to take them out to Kincaple. And so it was that he accompanied his old friend to the cottage of his aunt.

They arrived there not long before noon on the first of July, to find various friends and relatives in attendance and Tom naturally went immediately to his aunt's bedside. He was distraught to find her coughing blood and barely able to breathe. There were enough females around busily making tea, bringing towels and emptying blood-spattered enamel basins, so McArdle led Tom into the other room where they might sit and await what was, obviously, the soon demise of old Janet. Whisky was provided and tea brought, as the women tried to offer what comfort they could. But an observant person might have noticed McArdle wrinkle his nose and furrow his brow while in the bedroom of Janet, although he said nothing at the time.

As the evening wore on, Tom found comfort in talking about Janet and about his own life. It is a feature, I have found, of bereavement, that it turns the thoughts of the bereft to their own mortalities and those of their loved ones, living or already passed away, and they take comfort in talking, as if to connect again the deceased and the long-passed with the surviving and the generations to come. McArdle engaged Tom in conversation of this kind and gently encouraged him to talk about his family. In truth, McArdle was happy to receive the news of the Morris family and also conscious that he was affording his old friend an opportunity to give voice to things he had perhaps not discussed for a long time.

Tom spoke first of his eldest son, known universally as Young Tom, who was now widely considered to be the finest golfer in the land.

"Young Tom will be sorry he didn't see his Nanny Janet before she went. They were specially fond of each other."

"Is he away playing just now?"

"Aye, he is. A tournament in Edinburgh. And he'll win, I'm sure. He's twice the golfer I ever was, Davie. And he'll be a fine clubmaker too, with a bit more practice. But he's ower keen on the playing at the minute. Mind you, so was I, when I was younger. He's already won the Open Championship four times, and him not yet twenty-five. He'll win it again, mark my words, never mind if they change the rules."

"What do you mean, 'change the rules'?"

"Och, it's the Edinburgh lot. The Honourable Company of Edinburgh Golfers. 'Honourable' indeed! Do you know, Young Tom was playing as a Professional when he was thirteen! When he was just sixteen he came fourth in the Open and the next year he won it! That was 1868, and the runner up was furious, I can tell you!"

"Who was the runner-up?"

"Why, it was me, of course!"

McArdle laughed. "You've won it yourself a few times."

"Aye, I have that. We held very first championship at Prestwick in 1860 and I nearly won, but Willie Park took it. Mind you, I took the title in 1861, 1862 and again in 1864, when I was back at St. Andrews. Then I had a couple of busy years, but I won the Belt again in 1867. That'll be the last time, though, with Young Tom and the other youngsters that are coming up. Better clubs, better balls, better courses – it all makes a difference."

"So when did Young Tom win? In 1868, you said?"

"And again in '69 and '70. Three times in a row, so he got the Championship Belt outright! Not only that, he won by twelve strokes. A last round of 47 on that 12-holer at Prestwick. I doubt anybody will ever do that again. It didn't please the Edinburgh lot, I can tell you, nor the Prestwick men, even though Young Tom was raised there. But we were back in Fife by then so he was considered an outsider, and so was I. In fact, the Championship was suspended for year. The excuse was that the sponsor died, but really they wanted to work out a way to stop one of us winning it. The three clubs got together – the Royal and Ancient, Prestwick, Edinburgh – and subscribed to a new trophy, since Tom had the belt outright. Beautiful big silver claret jug it is, to be played for at Prestwick, St. Andrews and Musselburgh by turns. Didnae work, though."

"He won it again?"

"He said to me, 'Pa, that's a fine-looking jug, and it would fair set off my mantelpiece. And if it doesn't, it'll look just as good on yours'. He'd fair set his heart on it."

"Did he get it?"

"Oh aye. He took the 1872 and I was runner up. I tell you, the betting was strong that day. There was many had a shilling or two on me to win my fifth, and many more had their luckpenny on Young Tom to equal my four. He took it from me, but not by much."

"And which way did the two of you bet?"

"Aye, that would be telling! But we both did well enough out of the day's wagers. And we managed to irritate the Edinburgh men again, which is never a bad idea. But after that I said to him, 'Tom, time to knuckle down and get settled. There's more money in the clubmaking and the balls than in the playing.' And I said he should find himself a nice girl, too, give him a reason to stay at home more."

"Did he?"

"He married Margaret Drennan last year, and she's expecting, in a couple of months as it happens. They have a pleasant enough house in Playfair Place."

"You're very proud of Young Tom, aren't you? I hardly remember him, of course. He was just a wee boy when I left in 1850."

The elder Morris looked thoughtful for long moment. "Davie, that's not the same Tom. Did you not know? Our first wee lad, he died when he was but four. And 1850 it was, the same year you left St. Andrews."

31

"I'm sorry Tom. I really didn't realise." They were silent for a moment, but McArdle judged that Old Tom wanted to talk. "Then you left St. Andrews for Prestwick?"

"Aye, we did, the next year. It was a bad time for me, that. Agnes was devastated, just devastated. And at the same time, I had fallen out with Robertson again."

"Allan Robertson that you were apprenticed to? But you and he were great friends, and unbeatable golfing partners."

"We were that. But the new gutta-percha ball had come along in '44 or '45, just about the time I got married. I was all for it – it flew straighter than the old featherie if you dented it a wee bit, it lasted longer and it stayed spherical so you could putt it. But Allan just saw it as a threat to his featherie ball business and wouldn't countenance it. He even tried to buy them all up and burn them – can you believe it? He took my enthusiasm for the newer pill as a kind of desertion and he genuinely thought he could tell his former apprentice what to do. That was why I started up my own business. But by '50 he had realised the gutty was where the future lay, and he tried to grab the whole trade for himself. So I reckoned some time and distance away from St. Andrews was best for all. I was offered the Greenkeeper's job in Prestwick in '51 and I took it."

"But Young Tom…"

"Ah, he was born in April that year, almost a year to the day since wee Tom had died. Agnes said he was an extra gift from God and we should call him Tom as well. He's always been special to Agnes. And to all the other women in the family. That's why Auld Janet doted on him so much. It was like we'd been given a second chance at our son. Then the next year Elizabeth comes along, then James in '56 and John – Jack we call him – in '59. All born in Ayrshire, but by God I made sure to get them all christened in St. Andrews as soon as Agnes was strong enough to travel."

"A daughter and three sons? Your cup is fairly full, I'd say."

"Aye, and they're fine bairns, all. Bairns! Elizabeth was married not four months back."

"So when did you come back to St. Andrews – 1863?"

"Aye, it was about then. I missed Fife. I accepted the position as Keeper of the Greens and later they made me Honorary Professional."

"What about Old Daw Anderson, though?"

"Daw retired in '56. Watty Alexander and Eck Herd did the job with a bunch of rabbits to help," Morris explained, meaning by the term 'rabbits' the temporary workers who swept rabbit droppings and other debris from the greens. "But Daw set up a ginger beer stall on the ninth. And if you asked nicely, he might sell you something a wee bittie stronger, 'to warm the inner man', as he always said. Did you not see the stall yesterday?"

"No, but it was evening by then."

"Ah," Morris continued. "Anyway, I started up the club and ball making business again in what was the old sweetie shop – do you remember it? Then I moved to the new place hard by the Links. Like I say, it was a busy couple of years. No wonder I didn't win the Open until 1867, which again annoyed the Prestwick men. They thought I was nothing but a turncoat and a traitor!"

McArdle was amused by this. "There's still a fair bit of jealousy in the golf, then?"

"Ocht, you've no idea! The Ayrshire men think they're the greatest because the Championship was always held there until two years back, as I said. The Musselburgh men, they didn't mind my first two wins as I was working at Prestwick, but they dearly wanted Willie Park to take it in '64 – which he didn't, I'm pleased to say, though he did in '66 – and the Ayrshire men wanted their own man to get it in '67. The Edinburgh Golfers – well, they just think they're the bee's knees and the oldest and all that. They hate St. Andrews being called 'Royal and Ancient' just because Old King Willie got a game there and they think that since they had the first rules, they should make all the rules. But we don't let them get away with that."

"So Young Tom won it in '72, eh?"

"Aye, then Tom Kidd from here, and last year Mungo Park, Willie's wee brother. He was twenty years at sea and came back a better golfer. Imagine that. This year it's at Prestwick again and I fancy Young Tom might see off the Parks one more time. That would be braw!"

The two spoke of other events, people and places they had known and as it grew dark towards 10 o'clock, McArdle spoke of his times on the oceans and at war in India and Africa, and of his thoughts for the future. If his intention was to keep Old Tom Morris's mind away from thoughts of his dying auntie, he was successful in this. The rest of the family and acquaintances were glad enough of it, as they had their private grief to cope with. The women banked the fire when necessary and kept up a steady supply of cold meats, potted head and sandwiches. Tea, whisky and bottled drinks were replenished betimes. Either Janet kept a happy cupboard and pantry or others gave of their own provender, bringing it as needed. Both of these were probably true. It is my observation over many years that when attending the dying, everyone is glad to have something to do and sharing victuals is a wordless way to join in the moment and the sentiment.

About half-past the midnight hour, a female relative came and put a hand on Old Tom's shoulder. He nodded and rose to go through to the bedroom. McArdle stayed put in the parlour, feeling that Janet's very last was a time for her nearest, not for long-gone strangers. He nursed a whisky and water until, just after one in the morning, Tom returned and said, "She's away, Davie."

McArdle stood. "There will still be things to do, Tom. You don't need me in the way."

"The women will wash and dress her. My part's to register this and see to the undertakers."

"Should a doctor not be called to certify her death?"

Morris said nothing for a few moments. "You know, I've seen people cough blood like that before. Maybe she had the consumption. It's a terrible disease. Or maybe she didn't."

"It's possible, Tom. Or maybe she had some other lung trouble. The house does smell a bit musty."

"Either way, the last thing anybody needs is a scare of the tuberculosis. I think the least said the better, Davie. No-one will find it strange that an old lady of 90-odd died in her bed. I'll explain it to the doctor in the morning. I'm certain he'll agree. Then he'll maybe come and check a few folks' lungs quietly, just to make sure."

And indeed, that must have been the way of it. In fact, Tom waited until Saturday the third to visit John Sorley, the Registrar in St. Andrews, probably taking the rest of the Friday to compose his thoughts, comfort his wife and deal with his regular business – including a particularly troublesome and demanding client, apparently – as well as making various arrangements for Janet's interment. I have to hand the extract from the register of Deaths and it merely states 'Old age and general debility. Not certified.' With 'Thomas Morris, Nephew' given as the Informant. Doubtless Old Tom and Registrar Sorley felt that this was a likely explanation for Janet's demise and that no medical man could add to it.

As we shall see, McArdle had thoughts otherwise, but at the time he took no more part in the matter other than to take Old Tom back to Pilmour Links, return the trap to its owner, a neighbour of Tom's, and get what sleep he could for the remainder of the night, but not until making notes upon the evening. It had been McArdle's habit for years, it seems, to keep a journal of his activities and thoughts. For this, we were later to be most grateful.

The Friday McArdle spent on the golf course again, as had been his plan. He looked in on the Morris household to see if there was any more he could do, but it was clear that there was not and the family was engaged enough with its own affairs. At Tom Morris's workshop, he found his old friend in earnest discussion with a small, dwarfish-looking man who appeared to be arguing over the exact shape of a putter head. McArdle signalled to Morris that he would return at another time and left him to his commercial discussions.

He also took the time to see Murdoch and make a statement concerning William Joyce and the contents of the valise at the centre of the attempted robbery. There was, in addition, a telegraph message from myself, instructing Murdoch to ask McArdle whether he might be free to visit my house in Cupar on the Sunday. My news about the war hero had been received with much bright-eyed interest by my wife and family. Mary, as I had predicted, was instantly englamoured by the thought of a handsome officer and transmitted her enthusiasm to her younger sister, Keith. Isabella implored me to invite McArdle to visit us, and my boys, James, Frederick and Herbert, spend the intervening days marching around the house with wooden swords and paper hats on their heads, re-taking Alma, Sebastopol, Lucknow and probably Camelot and Agincourt as well, with commendable gusto but no care for historical order or accuracy.

As it happened, McArdle had intended to travel back to his barracks on the Sunday and found it not inconvenient to break his train journey at Cupar, planning later to catch the last train to Perth from there. He arrived at our house, Sandilands, in time for lunch.

It is fair to say that the call McArdle paid us was an unalloyed success. Isabella was a gracious hostess and made a great fuss of our guest. She and Janet Miller, our domestic at the time, had prepared a fine collation that we were able to eat out of doors, the weather being clement. Mary took pains to proffer McArdle platefuls of sandwiches, pastries, cakes and tea until he was fit to burst, but she did it with all the dainty grace of a Princess that a nine-year old can effect. After we had eaten, young Mary pleasured us with a piece from her piano lessons and little Keith gave a recitation, something from her *St. Nicholas* paper, I imagine. The boys patiently waited their turn, then bombarded McArdle with requests for war stories. Isabella was unsure of this idea, but McArdle winked at her – capturing her heart and her confidence in an instant and making it clear that he would not dwell too much on the gorier side of soldiering.

When McArdle consented to give us a story, Isabella gathered everyone in the parlour, with the boys sat around his feet and the girls primly on the ottoman, but no less enthralled. James made it his business to memorise every word and, as it later became apparent, wrote it practically verbatim from memory that evening. Frederick and Herbert joined in with questions. And little Lewis, being

35

barely 16 months old, ignored us all except to draw attention to his own needs from time to time. I will give the screed James wrote without the various interjections, questions and gasps of wonderment, which were many, supplemented by what recollection I have of the occurrence.

McArdle said:

"Do you know the tale of the Crimean Reveille? No? Well, I'll tell you. I was in a regiment called the Black Watch. Actually, it's really called the Forty-second Regiment of Foot, or the Royal Highland Regiment, and has been officially for some fourteen years now. But Black Watch is a good name, too. Now, I didn't join up until 1856, but just before I did, the regiment was fighting in a place called Crimea, in the south of Russia, as part of Sir Colin Campbell's Highland Brigade. The morning of November fifteenth was freezing and a mist was swirling as dawn broke over the entrenchments. Only one man was awake – a piper of the Black Watch. Through the harr and the murky dawn light, he saw a huge army advancing towards them, ready for a surprise attack. Russians! Armed to the teeth! And all bent on massacre and a quick victory! So what did the plucky piper do? He did the thing he knew best how to do – he grabbed his bagpipes and started to play. He played all the tunes he could think of. Other pipers heard him, and took up the same tunes. Soon, all along the Brigade lines, other pipers joined in. Now, it's a well-known fact that no Scottish soldier can lie in bed when the pipes are playing. So every one of the troops was out and up in a flash. Of course, they saw the Russian attack troops and, far from it being a surprise, the Russians found themselves facing a fully-awake Highland Brigade, stirred by the skirl of the pipes. They were routed! And to this very day, on the fifteenth of every month, the regiment parades at six-thirty in the morning and the pipes and drums play the Long Reveille. The same tunes that piper played in Crimea. Do you know what the tunes were? I do, and I'll tell you. It's important they're played in the correct order. So I want you boys to remember them. And maybe your sister Mary, who's so good at the piano, can get the music and play them for you. Here they are: The Soldier's Return; Granny Duncan; Sae Wull We Yet; Miss Girdle; Chisholm Castle; and Hey Johnnie Cope.

McArdle finished his story in an absolute hush, broken only when Herbert piped up, "But you didn't tell us about when you got your medal!" It will surprise no-one that the boy became a lawyer.

"Another time, Jamie, another time," he said and tousled the boy's hair.

The other children joined in the clamour for a further story, but McArdle was let off the hook by reminding everyone that he had to catch his train to Perth or he'd be posted as a deserter, coupled with a promise to come back and tell more tales. Isabella bustled all her little chicks off to bed, but not before the girls had curtsied prettily and the boys shaken McArdle's hand, then marched in good order out of the room.

"Thank you, McArdle, for not going to town on the blood and shot," I said, clapping him on the back. "The boys do love all that, but I don't think it's necessary to glorify it."

"In truth, there wasn't much honour and glory in the Crimea campaign, from what I've heard of it. A war of incompetence. Twenty thousand good men died and three parts or more of them from disease, not Russian steel. In our Regiment alone there was only one officer and fewer than forty men lost in the campaign itself, but a good two hundred succumbed to disease and another hundred and forty had to be sent home with wounds and poor health. I'm glad I missed it."

"The piper story's true, though, isn't it?"

"Oh, it's more than true. It's legend! And I think you'll find, if you inquire closely, that the piper concerned was a man called Murdoch. It didn't strike me when we met the other day, but I've had time to reflect on it since then."

I was stunned. "You don't mean our Murdoch!"

"I don't know. And if you ask him, I doubt you'll get a straight answer. I've found that the old soldiers are usually happy to tell you a cock-and-bull tale about battles they weren't in and the bravery of others and the stupidity of their officers. But when it comes to their own exploits, they're strangely reticent."

"Well, I'm sure he'll tell you, if you question him on it."

"Oh, I don't think Constable Murdoch's all that taken with me," McArdle confided. "I'm sure he regards me as a jumped-up Private and no better than I should be. Plus, I'm an officer and pipers never respect an officer!"

I found I had to laugh at his self-effacing candour. "Never mind. The children liked your story, anyway."

"There was a part I didn't tell them, though."

"What was that?"

"Seemingly, there was a piquet officer who was supposed to be on watch. But the regimental officers had had a rather good dinner the night before and he'd fallen asleep at his post, drunk as a lord. What's more, the piper in question had only got up to relieve himself after a night's beer took its toll. So the whole occurrence was a lamentable piece of dereliction of duty saved by a stroke of luck. The regiment doesn't take much pride in that aspect of it."

"Doubtless. But yourself, McArdle. Back to your recruiting, is it?"

"I'm afraid so, Mr. Bremner. I wouldn't say this in Perth, but my mind isn't really on it. Especially after coming back to St. Andrews. Despite all the turmoil of the past few days, I do feel drawn to the place. Another year'll do me, as there's a particular duty I have to see to next Spring. Then I should find another direction."

"Ah, yes. You said you might try your hand at farming."

"I might, if I could get the tack of a small piece of land."

"It's good growing country around these parts, as you'll know. Especially over here in the Howe of Fife. Look, if you like, there's a famous potato man coming to Cupar to give a talk next week. Some Professor or other. I'll get you invited, and you'll meet some of the local growers, get your face known. Agreed?" I went back into the house, found a handbill about the lecture and gave it to McArdle. "Professor Braid, that's the man. Edinburgh fellow, I believe. Quite famous from some mixture he's concocted which keeps away the rot. Will you come?"

"Duties permitting, Mr. Bremner. But I don't see the Huns or the Turks invading Perth within the next few days so I imagine I'll get the leave."

"Splendid! And you can stay the night with us here at Sandilands. Isabella will insist. Now, where's all your tackle?"

"Oh, I left my bag and my clubs at Cupar station. I really should go and catch that train. It's the last one today."

And taking his leave, he started walking.

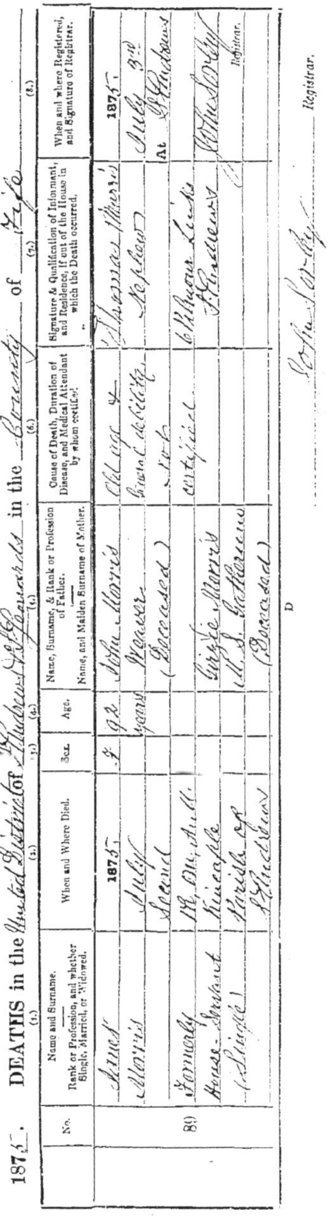

Page 30.

DEATHS in the _District of_ _____ in the _____ of _____

Janet Morris Formerly House-Servant (Single)
1875 July second 1h 0 min A.M. Kincaple Parish
of St. Andrews
F   92 years
[Father] John Morris Weaver (Deceased)
[Mother] Grizel Morris M.S. [Maiden Surname]
Gatherum (Deceased)
Old age and general debility Not Certified
Thomas Morris nephew
6 Pilmour Links St. Andrews
1875 July 3rd at St. Andrews John Sorley
Registrar

Figure 4 Extract from the Deaths Register entry – Janet Morris

39

CHAPTER FOUR

It occurs to me that I have not yet given a description of David McArdle. The reader will perhaps excuse this lamentable lapse, and understand that, as someone with many years' intimate knowledge of the man and his manners, I have no difficulty in conjuring his image to my mind's eye. But others will require a way to picture him, so I offer this word depiction of McArdle as he was a quarter century and more ago, when first we met.

As a good police officer, I should state the clear facts first. McArdle was tall, standing a good five feet and ten inches, and well-muscled, especially about the upper body. He was moustachioed but beardless and his hair was perhaps marginally longer than might be expected in a military man. He stood with a slight stoop – which I later came to understand was due to his protecting the injury of an old wound to his abdomen – and walked with a barely noticeable limp to one leg, courtesy of his war service. His complexion was initially browned from his years at sea and otherwise abroad and, even when he later lost this swarthy aspect in the pale sun of Scotland, his visage retained a weather-beaten and ruddy cast not unusual in fishermen and farmers of this area. In fine, he would not have stood out particularly in a crowd, other than being half a head taller than most.

Also, McArdle tended to speak quietly. This had the paradoxical effect of causing others to pay more attention to his words. He once told me that almost twenty years of service in the army had taught him that if you want a man to obey you at once and without question, it is necessary to shout. But if your aim is to get a man to understand and attend to you, it is best keep the voice low and reasonable.

McArdle did not overall give the impression of a military gentleman but looked more like a son of the land. Therefore he did not seem out of place when he visited Cupar for Professor Baird's lecture the next Friday. He had entered the hall in the company of another man whom I recognised but could not immediately place. Seeing me, he came over to where I was standing, in conversation with a Cupar landowner of my acquaintance named Doig.

"Ah McArdle. Glad you could make it. No Ashanti incursions on Perth then?" I enquired, in reference to his parting jest the Sunday before.

"If so, they are doing it quietly. So I have a weekend leave. I trust you won't mind that I brought along an old friend, Dr. William McIntosh. William, this is Captain Bremner, Chief Constable of the Kingdom of Fife."

McIntosh shyly extended me his hand. "Of course I know Mr. Bremner. In fact, he is friendly with my father, John McIntosh."

I recalled instantly the man, whom I had not seen for some years. He had been a fresh-faced boy when last I beheld him but now had a full beard and an earnest expression on a pallid countenance that spoke of too many days indoors and too many nights working. "Ah yes! William. But Dr. McIntosh now is it? A medical man?"

"William is Superintendent of the Murthly Mental Hospital at Perth," McArdle.

"So either you're here in charge of this dangerous lunatic, or else you figure to find new inmates amongst the farmers of Fife. Which is it William?"

McIntosh blushed and grinned, saying nothing. I remembered him well enough as a coy young man, given to scholarly pursuits. His father was a prominent businessman, most outgoing and ebullient, if somewhat robust in attitude. His mother Eliza, had borne five daughters besides William as the only son. Perhaps the upbringing in a house full of females had contributed to William McIntosh's self-effacing demeanour.

McArdle explained that the two had been boyhood friends, meeting at The Madras College, and spending hours and days together combing the St. Andrews sands for sea creatures and plants. This was despite a good two years' difference in their ages. Later, McIntosh had attended college at St. Andrews at the age of 15 and after this had read for a medical degree in Edinburgh.

"We continued to write to each other," McArdle further elucidated. "In fact, in all my years away, William and his sister Roberta were my only regular correspondents. They would send me letters about the local wildlife and all sorts of new worms and crabs and periwinkles that William had discovered. And Roberta did the most beautiful drawings. For my part, I fear I sent back the most boring stuff about military matters."

"Not at all, Davie," McIntosh said, finding his voice again at last. "Your descriptions of faraway places were most illuminating and a welcome diversion from an otherwise dreary existence. Many a wet evening my sister and I would get out your letters and read of Tortuga or China or the Far Indies."

"But what's your interest here, William?" I asked, genuinely puzzled. "Not potatoes, surely."

Perhaps, I mused, the medical profession had found some new cure for dropsy or ague in tattie leaves, and I would not have been surprised. It seems that hardly a week passes without some learned doctor or other proclaiming that this leaf or that root has the most beneficial effect on one bodily organ or another. At the time, or possibly later, there was an American called Kellogg who was promoting the healthful digestive benefits of flakes made from boiled wheat or toasted corn, and their role in reducing the desire for the Sin of Onan.[7] Interestingly, these nutritive evangelists also, to a man, inveigh against tobacco and alcohol, which suggests to me that they lead most mournful lives. It is no wonder they spend their energies contemplating the lower bowel and the consequences of self-pollution. But enough of such matters.

"Well, yes, in a way," McIntosh replied quietly. I have a deep interest in all plants. In fact, when I worked as assistant physician at Murray's Hospital in Perth, the physician superintendent Dr. Lauder Lindsay – a keen botanist himself – allowed me to set-up a Natural History museum and to give regular lectures for the patients. We found it to be most conducive to their recovery. Now I'm in charge at Murthly, I have a similar facility and also a small laboratory. We grow potatoes and other vegetables in a kailyard garden, and I hope to learn something from Professor Braid which I can take back and have the inmates try out. There was a dreadful blight last year."

"Can lunatics grow potatoes?" This was from Doig, the man I had been speaking with before McArdle and McIntosh arrived.

"Well, you seem to manage!" I chided him. "Gentlemen my apologies. Mr. John Doig, who farms here in the Howe of Fife. Root crops and cereals, isn't it?"

"Aye. Tatties, barley and porage. It's what Scotland grows best. And I gather Mr. McArdle here is the one you've told me about. Fancies his hand at the growing. Caught a thief too, I believe. With a putter, no less!"

"What's this, Davie?" McIntosh asked, surprised. "Getting involved in police business, are you?"

McArdle laughed. "No, not really. There was a particularly ham-fisted attempt on my hotel room, but the felon had the bad luck or poor judgment to bump into me at the doorway."

"Really?"

"And with the Chief Constable and one of his men right at hand, which was poor judgement."

"Well, I wouldn't expect much excitement here tonight, McArdle," Doig exclaimed. "In fact, when one of these science fellows speaks, I'm usually sleep by half-time. Better than valerian, the professors!"

---

[7] In fact, Dr. John Kellogg and his brother William, whose family originated in Fife, are credited with the invention of corn flakes around 1884, which again suggests that Bremner's memory was occasionally faulty. These cereals were initially promoted as a nutritious way of reducing the desire to masturbate and calming unnatural lusts.

"Oh, I think you'll find Professor Baird most interesting," McIntosh said, suddenly animated. "There is no better man for fungus in Scotland. I read that he has a new treatment for various blights. This will, I'm sure, be a fascinating evening." And as if embarrassed by such a long and impassioned utterance, Dr. McIntosh looked down sheepishly and fell silent again.

I spotted the President of the local farmers' organisation, our hosts for the evening, enter with a stranger, and I made the obvious deduction. "Ah, this must be our esteemed lecturer now." I noticed McArdle's back stiffen as he turned to see the man. "Do you perhaps know him, McArdle?"

"No, but I have encountered him before. Last Saturday at Tom Morris's shop. He's having clubs made, I believe."

"Aren't we all!" Doig interjected. "And it takes a blamed long time, I'll tell ye! If him or Young Tom got down to their commissions instead of gadding about playing competitions all the time, we'd all get our clubs that much faster! And if Old Tom's not away playing gowf elsewhere, he's off designing courses for people. Do you know, he charges one Pound a day? A Pound a day! I wonder anybody can afford him!"

"Anyway, we're about start," I interrupted, before Doig's rant intensified. "Come, gentlemen. Let's see what this Braid has to say for himself."

I later realised that Professor Braid was the same personage who McArdle had referred to as 'dwarfish' when he had seen him in Morris's shop the day after the old aunt's decease. In truth, he was a strange-looking bird – small, thin, with unusually long arms and short legs, a balding head wreathed by unruly tufts of hair and largish ears. Overall, he had something of the aspect of a chimpanzee. The President made a fulsome introduction during which much was made of Baird's having categorised or catalogued vast numbers of mushrooms and the like in Turkey and around the Caspian, and that he had received, for his pains, some medal or other from the Mufti or the Caliph or some other local potentate. This eulogy over, during which the eminent Professor had affected to study the ceiling, he then got to his feet and began his oration. He strode about the stage like a small, dumpy crane, droning on in the most monotonous voice about this potato and that blight and the other fungus. The details were largely lost on me, being neither a farmer nor a naturalist. Doig was, as he himself had predicted, fast asleep and snoring gently within 15 minutes. McArdle appeared mildly interested. But Dr. McIntosh was taking copious notes, clearly fascinated, and hanging on every word. The import of it seemed to be that Braid had a solution of chemicals which, if applied to potatoes early the season, would abort any rot or blight.

For my part, I was really not sure why I was there, other than that an excuse to get away from a house full of children made a welcome change. And there would be a glass of wine or Madeira at the close. But, ever mindful of my police duties, I would generally take the opportunity at such gatherings to enquire gently of my various friends and acquaintances about the goings-on in Fife, whether my Constables and other officers were quick at their duties or rarely seen, and similar matters.

Finally, though, Braid had finished. There was sporadic and polite applause, sufficiently loud to arouse Doig, who immediately joined in most heartily, as if he had just seen a marvellous variety show. The President called for questions. First to his feet was an old farmer who simply wanted to know whether the Professor preferred one seed-potato to another. The answer was that he, Braid, was unconcerned with potatoes *per se*, but in their diseases, although he had heard it said that so-and-so a variety was generally felt to be hardier and more prodigious than such-and-such and offered this intelligence for what it was worth. A second inquisitor required to know whether the Professor felt that certain rots were particular as to climate, which question evinced a rather lengthy reply concerning rainfall, spring temperatures, earthing-up and other matters doubtless of deep moment to the growers present. A third was curious as to whether Swedish turnips were bigger in Fife or in Angus, of which the Professor admitted to knowing little and left the obvious impression that he cared even less.

But then Dr. McIntosh raised his hand, somewhat hesitantly. I confess I had imagined the diffident doctor would not have put himself forward in such a manner. He had always given the impression, even as a young man, that he would not say so much as 'Boo!' to a goose. Quite what the boy McIntosh had found in common with the boy McArdle, I could only but imagine. But on his feet, and on his subject, William was a different man. At the President's nod, McIntosh arose, glanced once his notes, grasped his coat lapel and addressed Braid.

"Professor, your chemical solution is most intriguing. If I understand you correctly, this is an admixture of three parts of anhydrous copper sulphate to four parts of hydrated lime?"

"That is correct, Sir. You have understood me well."

"And would I be correct in surmising that this compound, as well as stemming both early and late blight in potatoes, would be equally effective against the various mildews which attack soft fruits such as berries?"

"You would, Sir. I am aware that this area and the land north towards the Carse of Gowrie are also renowned for summer fruits, and I would commend the use of my formula on these growths also."

This caused a murmur of approbation in the hall, as if an additional item of magic had been revealed. I expected McIntosh to take his seat at that point, but he continued.

"And would I be further correct in assuming that it is equally effective against black rot and powdery mildew on grapes?"

Braid inhaled sharply. I could not see where this interrogation was headed, but McArdle was watching his friend intently. I smelt blood.

"Sir, I have little knowledge of nor interest in viticulture," Braid stated, clearly upset and irritated for a reason I could not fathom. "You may well be correct, I could not possibly say. Now if there are no further..."

But McIntosh would not let this particular bone go. "What puzzles me, Professor, is that this mixture, which you claim as your own invention, is all but identical to the Bordeaux Formula widely used by the wine-growers of France, primarily to deter theft of their grapes. But it is also said that it has anti-fungal properties. I believe it is currently under investigation by Professor Millardet of the University of Bordeaux, for this very purpose."

"As I said, Sir, I am no great expert on grapes or wines."

"Nor I. In fact, as a lifelong abstainer, I abhor such beverages. But the same cannot be said of Professor Millardet. His reputation is substantial. You are acquainted with the learned gentleman?"

"I could not say. One meets so many people. Really, I ..."

"Yet you cite him extensively in your most recent book, albeit in up a different context. You claim to have visited him and discussed his radical proposals to transplant French vines onto American vine root stocks which are aphid-resistant, in order to defeat the pernicious *Phylloxera*, an idea of which you were quite dismissive. I understood this visit to have taken place immediately after the cessation of hostilities in the recent Franco-Prussian war."

Of course, I missed the import of McIntosh's questions. What I had thought was a simple clarification of some point of chemistry was, it soon became apparent, much more serious than that. As I later came to understand, Dr. McIntosh had, in fact, accused Braid of scientific plagiarism, the most heinous crime in the calendar of academic misdemeanours. But the learned Professor did not miss the point of Macintosh's charge. He looked shocked initially and his eyes blazed, but he recovered his composure, took a breath and gripped the lectern.

"I fear, Sir, I do not know your name."

"Dr. William McIntosh. Of Perth."

"Ah. I was unaware that the fair city of Perth had a university, let alone a department of chemistry or mycology," Baird sneered.

"I am but a medical doctor, but I retain an amateur's interest in your field."

"Well, Dr. McIntosh. Let me assure you that M. Millardet was by no means the first to propose nor to the first to administer this so-called 'Bordeaux mixture'. If you were conversant with the published literature in the area, you would know that my own speculations and solutions predate those of any French chemist. In fact, I bid fair to say that it was clues and suggestions I left after visiting France which subsequently led others to confirm my work and publish it as their own, making, I might say, a pretty penny in selling their nostrums to the gullible French growers."

He clearly thought this tirade had seen off the impudent questioner and made of to take his seat. But McIntosh continued.

"Indeed, Professor, I am quite familiar with your earlier work. And if I recall correctly, your first publications concerning this formula were in 1874, last year. This was after your return from France. Also, I seem to remember that as recently as 1869, you dismissed the very idea of copper-based anti-fungals as being, and I quote, 'a fancy'. Yet you appear to have changed these ideas markedly since your visit to Bordeaux. Or do I, as an amateur, have these specifics wrong, too?"

Braid was now shaking with anger. A look crossed his face which I can only describe as pure, uncut hatred. By way of reply, he disengaged his glower from McIntosh and turned to address the President, who by now had gathered there was something amiss.

"Sir," the Professor said through clenched teeth. "I have come today to Fife at no little inconvenience to myself, to give what I feel to have been valuable information to those might benefit from it. I did not expect to be interrogated and insulted by laypersons. I believe I have fulfilled my commission to your Society and must now take my leave. I bid you and your members a very good evening!"

And with that, Braid stalked from the lectern and strode down the centre aisle, pausing only to give McIntosh one last, venom-filled glance as he passed.

"Oh, dearie me," Dr. McIntosh muttered, once again seated and back to his diffident persona. "I suspect I have insulted your guest and embarrassed your society. How can I apologise?"

It was Doig who saved the day. "Embarrassed?" Havers! We haven't had such excitement in Cupar since the Scanlon brothers were hanged in '52. Needs livening up, this place. And that Edinburgh fellow wanted taking down a peg. I just didn't reckon to him. Too full of himself by half. Now, come and have a glass of wine with us. You'll be the toast of the evening, I assure you!"

We repaired to another room where fortified wine was indeed on offer. Dr.

McIntosh kept to flavoured carbonated water as a lifelong adherent of the temperance persuasion, and that doubtless as a reaction to his father.'s tendencies to the contrary While a genuinely good and stable man, John McIntosh could occasionally be a brute when in drink. However, William's passion had subsided and he visibly recoiled when the President of the society came over to us, and evidently expected a reproof of some sort. In fact, the opposite occurred.

"Dr. McIntosh! Let me shake your hand, Sir!"

McIntosh did so, somewhat taken aback. "You are not angry? I did rather disrupt your meeting."

"Not a bit of it. I have had the so-called 'pleasure' of yon Braid's company all afternoon, and I can honestly say I have rarely met a more pompous, self-important old blellum. Needed taking down, he did, and you tripped him nicely. My hand again, Sir!" And with that, he was off to see some other Committee member. Fife farmers may be bluff and gruff, but you generally know exactly what they think about you, I have found.

So, the evening had been more interesting than anticipated. Doig also shook Dr. McIntosh by his right hand, and said that if McArdle was indeed minded to try his hand at tattie farming then he would help in any way he could, with seed crop, supplies and such men as he could spare until McArdle got organised. Then we left.

McArdle and I walked McIntosh to the station where he would take the train back to Perth. Hello "So, you obviously consider Braid to be a fraud?" I enquired.

McIntosh thought for a moment. "No, he really does have a reputation as the greatest expert on exotic fungi in Scotland. He has collected specimens from all over the world and keeps a special hothouse to grow them, I gather. But in this one case, I think he has been less than honest about the origins of this formula. The French have been working on this for some time although I do not think Professor Millardet has yet published a definitive work on the subject."

"But why does it matter? Isn't it just some salts and lime in a bucket of water."

"To you and me, yes. But to a grower of potatoes or berries, it could be the difference between yield and disaster in the growing season. And where there is potential catastrophe in agriculture, there is potential profit. I expect to see 'Braid's mixture' for sale to farmers very soon. Depend on it."

"I see."

We both quizzed McIntosh more on Braid's marvellous mixture (if it was indeed Braid's!) and learned that it had been used initially to deter anyone who attempted to steal the grapes. When eaten, it would cause gastritis, diarrhoea, bloody stools and eventually anaemia. That it also killed rot was an unexpected bonus. I made a mental note to remember the symptoms of this poisoning for future reference, should such facts ever be needed. Then, after giving our goodbyes to McIntosh, the two of us continued on to Sandilands. On the way, we discussed Braid further. "You said you'd seen him in Pilmour Links last week?" I asked McArdle.

"Aye, and he seemed to be giving old Tom Morris a to-do all about some club head. Now that I've heard the man, it's clear he is – what did your President say, - 'pompous and self-important' was it? He certainly gave that impression. Old Tom can hold his own, but he was getting quite an ear-full from Braid."

"I realise I've seen him before too, you know, "I mused. "At a golf match in Musselburgh perhaps two years ago. He's one of the Edinburgh Golfers. He and his partner got beat by Old Tom and Young Tom playing together. And he wasn't pleased, I might tell you. Why he should be giving good money to the Morris family, instead of some Edinburgh clubmaker, is a mystery."

"Perhaps he felt the advantage was in the clubs, so he should get a set for himself. Or maybe he felt his best revenge was to commission clubs and have an excuse to give Old Tom a hard time about it." McArdle laughed.

I joined in. "It may be so, McArdle. It may be just so. But how does your friend McIntosh know so much about chemicals and plants and such?"

"Oh, William's not just a doctor. In fact, that's the least of his interests. I went to visit him earlier this week at the Murthly Hospital. He does have a laboratory there. He grows salmon eggs and all other kinds of fish and animals, just to study them. Then his sister Roberta – did I say she was a talented artist? – she drew and coloured them in marvellous detail. William even thinks crabs have brains, although his explanation is lost on me. What does a crab have to think about? I asked him and I am not sure I even understood one tenth of his answer. In truth, I think he'd be happiest at a university, peering into his microscope tube all day, rather than pacifying lunatics like..."

He left the rest of the sentence unfinished, but as we had reached Sandilands by then, I did not press him to continue.

Isabella had a warm supper waiting for us, and an even warmer welcome. She showed McArdle to his room, saw that he had towels, water and a razor, and went to set the dishes. When McArdle came down again, he and I shared a small whisky, then were called to table. The first course was a large bowl of hot, thick soup. As McArdle picked up his spoon, he smiled. Isabella noticed this and, her eyes twinkling, took him gently to task for it.

"Why, Captain McArdle! My soups have caused various reactions in my guests, but rarely humour. Or are you just fond of soup?"

"My apologies, Mrs. Bremner. I was recalling that once I was given dinner by a regiment of Austrian Hussars. The soup arrived in a tureen quite like yours, and the first thing they all did was to plunge their hands into it. I was surprised, I can tell you. It turned out that the Colonel was some distant relation of Beethoven. It seems that when the great composer was young he would go to play at grand houses – as he did for money, because he had hard times early on in his life – and he would usually walk the journey. Then, at the house, he would ask for a bowl of soup before playing. But rather than eat it, he would steep his hands in it, explaining that he found this the best way to get them warm and supple ready for the piano. The Colonel always did likewise and so, of course, did his officers."

"I can hardly believe that," Isabella exclaimed.

McArdle tasted his broth. "Apparently, Beethoven also said that 'only the pure at heart can make a good soup'. I compliment you on both attributes, Mrs. Bremner.

Isabella and I laughed heartily at this. "Well, I hope you won't be dripping soup on my piano later on, Captain."

"Have no fear of that, Mrs. Bremner. I am completely untalented at music, except that I can pick out a few tunes on the concertina or the jaws harp from my sailing days. Your piano is in no danger from me, I assure you. But perhaps you will grace us with a piece yourself later?"

As we bent to our soup and the beef which followed it, I gave Isabella a recounting of the evening.

"It seems excitement follows you about, Captain McArdle," she commented. "First, beating my husband at that unfathomable game, then the experience with your thief, on top of which your old friend's sad bereavement, and now we have an altercation at a Farming Society lecture of all places. I wonder you can walk in the street without elephants falling on you!"

"I assure you, most of my life's been rather sedate."

"What, even at sea and in war?"

"Especially then. A sea voyage is possibly the most dreary way yet devised for man to spend his time. And somebody once said that soldiering was 'long periods of boredom interspersed with brief bursts of panic' or something like that."

"Not in a battle, surely!"

"Battles are the smallest part of a soldier's service. Mostly it's marching somewhere, usually to turn around and march back begin. Or it's occupying some fort or other, waiting for something unspecified to happen, which it rarely does. Or cleaning a thing, purely in order to get it dirty once more. I sometimes think that if all the armies in the world could just arrange beforehand to fight their wars in a certain place at a certain time, we could get most of our soldiering done in two weeks each year and spend the rest of the time doing something useful."

"Like growing potatoes?" I ventured.

"At least it has a purpose, and it's steady."

"Are you still taken with the farming idea, then?"

"I plan to see a small place in Kettle next month. If I like it, I may take the tack on it. It will be just big enough for me to work, maybe with one boy to help and a couple of horses. I'll keep a pig and a cow, some chickens and perhaps a sheep or two."

"And what about a farmer's wife?" Isabella enquired. I have noticed that there is nothing which quite upsets the sensibilities of the ladies so much as the sight of a marriageable man unwed, and they expend vast energies in conniving to rectify the omission.

"There are no candidates for the position of Mrs. McArdle just now."

"Well, you could do worse than a Kettle girl. They are healthy and hard-working. Or I can introduce you to..."

"Now, now, Isabella!" I interposed. "The man's back in Scotland not a month and already you're wanting him tied down and married off! Anyway, he's still in the Queen's service."

"That is so," McArdle agreed. "It's no life for young lady to be billeted in a garrison, and a Captain's pay does not stretch to outside quarters. So maybe I'll just bide my time."

"If you wait ten years or so, our Mary will be full-grown. She's fair set her cap for you, you know!" she added, with that twinkle I had come to associate with mild mischief.

McArdle laughed it off. "You have lovely children. I hope one day I'll be so blessed. But I doubt it somehow. I'm already 40 years old."

"Come now, Isabella," I chided my wife. "Let the man enjoy his meat instead of spoiling his appetite with your scheming about his private concerns!"

She was not to be put off, however.

"I gather your old friend Dr. McIntosh is also a bachelor."

"That is true, Mrs. Bremner," McArdle averred. "A confirmed bachelor, I'm sure, although he enjoys a full family life of a different sort. I was telling your husband that William and his sister Roberta wrote to me throughout my soldering. Roberta was a brilliant watercolourist and illustrated William's natural history works. Sadly, she died a few years back."[8]

"Oh, I didn't know that," I said, somewhat taken aback. I had rather lost touch with the family since the father's demise.

"She was married – a man called Albert Gunther, another naturalist. They had a son, Robert, and William is very fond of the boy although he sees him seldom[9]. But his other sister, Agnes, is really William's closest companion. She has looked after him ever since he went to work at Murthly – in 1863, I believe. William sees no need of a wife, I'm sure, just as he sees no need of alcohol or tobacco."

"Well, I have a need great of both and I trust you'll join me in them after our meal, McArdle," I suggested, to his assenting smile.

After supper, Isabella played the piano for us as requested, and McArdle and I took a pipe together. He spoke again about young Archie the caddie and it became clear that the boy's experiences mirrored McArdle's own. His father had died when he was young and he caddied to make money to help his mother. An only child, he was not obliged to work to pay for younger children, so he had a full-time education at The Madras College under the admirable Mr. Crichton, where he and his friend William tutored younger boys in their letters and numbers, as was the Reverend Dr. Andrew Bell's Madras system. They even helped to look after the pig which Dr. Woodford, the Classics master, kept in the small yard behind Madras House East, until Provost Playfair forced the school to have it removed on the grounds of possible contagion. McArdle also came under the influence of the Languages master, the Swiss Samuel Messieux, famous for driving a featherie golf ball 361 yards at St. Andrews' Elysian Fields in 1836, further than any man before or since. McArdle, it transpired, had shown a reasonable facility with languages, leaving school with more than adequate German and French and had picked up other languages on his travels, including certain Indian dialects.

The Morris family had indeed taken the young McArdle under their wing to some extent, and seen that he got good caddie money. It appeared that his forebears being Shetland fishing folk had led to his choosing a career at sea,

---

[8] In 1869, to be precise.

[9] This boy was to become the noted zoologist and antiquary Dr. Robert William Theodore Gunther (1869-1940), first curator of the Oxford Museum for Science. From the early 1900s, McIntosh became very close to his nephew and they collaborated on various scientific projects

initially. But whether his mother had died by then, or died later, he said nothing of it. He had told me before, that he had no relations in St. Andrews.

Of his maritime career he said little, but I gained the impression he had visited many lands. In the Black Watch he had fought in India, seen other service at home and abroad and finally, in 1873, had sailed for the Gold Coast to take part in the Ashanti campaign against 'King Coffee' as the head savage was nick-named. It was during the capture of Kumasi, the Ashanti capital, that McArdle had won his Victoria Cross but, as was usual for him, he made light of this sterling achievement as if he were in some way embarrassed by it.

As for his present duties, it seems that the War Office in London felt that changes were afoot in the British Army once again. The Black Watch came out of this period remarkably well. In 1881, it re-merged with the old 2nd Battalion, which, as I remembered, had been given the separate status of the 73rd (Highland) Regiment of Foot in 1786. The 73rd had had a distinguished record since that time, although in 1809 it had lost its 'Highland' appellation and served in Australia (where it was engaged more in civil engineering than soldiering), in Argentina, in South Africa fighting the Kaffirs and in India. In 1869 another name change rendered it the 73rd (Perthshire) Regiment. On the merger with the 42nd, which was really more of a takeover, the 73rd lost most of its great traditions, adopting those of the Black Watch. It was rumoured at the time that there were just too few Scots enlisting in the army and, having to look to England for recruits, things had got to a situation where there were more Englishmen in the regiment than Scotsmen. It was also said that some officers of the 73rd were sympathetic towards the Irish Freedom movement. It seems that what McArdle had earlier referred to as 'helping the War Office with a spot of trouble' was in some way connected with this and with the Detective Branch of the Metropolitan Police in London. I knew there were moves afoot to form a Special Irish Branch to deal with the Fenian terror campaigns and naturally the Police would look to the Army to help root out sympathisers within its own ranks.

Now, it seemed, in anticipation of the merger of battalions and the need to boost the number of Scots in the 42nd and other regiments, McArdle was responsible for recruiting throughout Scotland. Then we spoke of this and that while taking a final pipe, and so to bed.

On the Saturday, he returned to Perth (although indirectly, as I knew he wanted a game at Ladybank on the way, a six-holer which Old Tom Morris was designing[10] and which incorporated his revolutionary proposal that tees

---

[10] Bremner's memory must again be unreliable. Morris did not design this course until 1879. Bremner may have meant Lundin Links.

and greens be separated). But he did not leave before again entertaining the children with tales of far-flung places, although he shied away from battle stories, realising Isabella's preferences on the matter. The boys hung on his every word and Mary mooned at his feet.

McArdle departed after lunch, and as we waved goodbye, Isabella took my arm and said, "You know, James, there is a lot of sadness in that man. A good, young wife is what he needs, right enough."

"Oh, wheesht, woman! You ladies always think a man's greatest lack is a wife and that a marriage will solve all his ills. Whereas, it is usually the start of a whole new set of them."

"Oh, indeed, James Bremner? And how old were you when we married? Nearly 40 yourself. And look at you now. Do you think you would ever have made Chief Constable without me to see to you?" And she gave me that wifely look which sees right through your eyes and into the mind behind them. Women! Cunning Vixens, all.

Figure 5 A Black Watch soldier of the period
The uniform is similar to that which McArdle would have worn, but possibly slightly later.

CHAPTER FIVE

I did not see David McArdle again for two months, almost to the day. It was Saturday, September eleventh. I can be specific about it, because it was the day on which Mrs. Margaret Morris, wife of Young Tom, died.

I was playing the St. Andrews Links and had teed off early, largely to avoid Sir John Low of Chatto. While I liked the man when he was on his own two feet, his regular habit of going about the golf course on the back of a pony irritated me. Not only did it slow up the play of others – with all his mounting and dismounting – but the animal itself was a hazard. It left what can only be termed 'loose impediments' all over the course, which had occasioned a few new rules to be written to take into account these noisome hazards. And it simply got in the way, as animals do. While the gentle beast appeared to suffer the occasional thwhack from a ball with a certain stoic equanimity, the shot was ruined and so therefore was many a player's temper. But such was the affection and reverence felt for Sir John, who had been Captain in the 1860s, that this eccentricity was tolerated, and even emulated by others who fancied the game but not the walk. Rarely on the course before noon, Sir John could be avoided completely by the knowing golfer who rose early and started by ten o'clock, especially if he took an official caddie with him, which afforded the privilege of playing through lone golfers as I have previously explained.

An early start was no difficulty for me as I had spent the previous evening as the guest of General Moncrieffe after a golf club dinner and we were playing together that morning. By eleven of the clock we were a good few holes into the game. I happened to know we would see McArdle because, as we collected our caddie from James Morris, Old Tom's second son, he had informed us that they were expecting the Black Watch captain later that morning for a game and to visit the Morrises afterwards as their guest. He said it was his father's intention to persuade McArdle to enter for the Open Championship in October, as he had been playing a great deal since returned to Scotland and was now, in Morris's words, 'the equal of many a professional and the better of some'.

James Morris also said, with a wink, that his father and brother were 'keeping oot o' the way' because Young Tom's wife, Margaret, was due to give birth any day and 'the place is fu' o' wummin'. They were playing their annual one hundred pound challenge match against Willie Park and his brother Mungo at North Berwick, confident to be back in time for the happy event on the Sunday or Monday. Opinions varied on this; apparently Dr. Moir, the family's physician, held for a Monday birth but the various wise women, crones and biddies who always gather at a confinement like gulls at a trawler, had all decided it was to be a Lord's Day baby.

As we played round, I told Moncrieffe about David McArdle and vouchsafed that he, the General, would find a meeting interesting. Thus it was that McArdle, playing alone, encountered us on a green shared between one of their outbound holes and our inbound. Introductions were made, an invitation to lunch issued and hands shaken on it. I was amused to see that McArdle's caddie was Archie, the boy so recently implicated in the attempted theft and I had no doubt that he had been asked for specifically. I later mentioned to Moncrieffe that Archie was one of those young caddies now enrolled in the General's evening school system. Moncrieffe and I watched as McArdle hit a shot with his Forgan club a good 150 yards! I complimented him on the shot and McArdle, graciously, put it down to Morris's new bramble-patterned ball. My partner and I continued, finishing just as Sir John Low was to be seen trotting his steed to the first tee, and we bid him a cordial good day, doubly pleased to see him so well for his age and not to be sharing the fairways with his nag. Moncrieffe and I then dallied in the clubhouse for half an hour or so awaiting McArdle, taking coffee and speaking of sundry municipal matters and the likely merger of the Union with the Royal and Ancient.

It was possibly twelve-thirty or one in the afternoon, and we were expecting to see McArdle arrive, with an appetite ready for a luncheon. Instead, when he entered, with the caddie Archie close behind him, his was face dark and troubled. He espied us in the club room, and came over.

"What is it, McArdle?" I inquired. "Some difficulty?".

"I regret I shan't be joining you Mr. Bremner, General. James Morris has just told me that Margaret had the bairn, but stillborn. And she herself has a bleeding that will not stanch. A doctor is with her. I offered to telegraph North Berwick to get the Morrises back as quickly as possible. I thought I would write it here and have it run to the office, to save time."

"A good thought, McArdle," I agreed and signalled to a club steward, who brought a telegraph form and pencil upon my command, and I told Archie to stand ready to take it speedily for transmission. It may seem strange to us now, who are so used to telephonic communication, that we had perforce to use such an unwieldy method of contacting North Berwick, but we must bear in mind that this was 1875, the very year in which the son of my old friend

Bell[11] was busy inventing his telephone device. It would be some time before we had the benefit of it in Fife.

The telegraph form hastily finished and Archie quickly dispatched, McArdle accepted a whisky from me. After downing it, McArdle had said he would return immediately to Perth as he had no wish to intrude on the family and as there was nothing more that he could do in St. Andrews, he took his leave of us, telling Moncrieffe that he hoped they would meet again in better circumstances and the General returned the compliment. I also excused myself from my partner, all thoughts of luncheon now forgotten, and made for Morris's shop to see if there was any way in which I could be of assistance.

On the way I noticed a party of four starting to play. I recognised two instantly. One was an ex-Captain of the Honourable Company of Edinburgh Golfers called Wharton-Todd[12], and the other was Professor Braid, whose lecture at Cupar we had attended in the July. I nodded to Wharton-Todd, as I knew him well enough from competitions. Braid did not know me and in any case was surveying the fairways. I heard him say something disparaging about 'this St. Andrews conceit of separating the tees from the holes' and watched him set up his ball on a sand pile placed ostentatiously two club lengths from the final hole before playing it. He sklaffed the shot and it skittered about 60 yards and into the rough. The reader may forgive me the secret smile I allowed myself.

At Morris's shop, I inquired of Kirky how Margaret was, and told him to pass on my condolences at the baby's death and my wishes for the mother's speedy recovery, adding that I had seen the Telegraph despatched and was sure that Young Tom would be back as quickly as the trains and the Burntisland ferry would allow. This was, readers will realise, some years before that miracle of the Engineering Age, the Forth Bridge, was erected. The journey across the estuary was either by ferry or by one of the coastal steamers which plied from North Berwick to Leith, Elie, St. Andrews and other coastal towns.

---

[11] What are we to make of this throw-away remark? Alexander Graham Bell was born in Edinburgh, Scotland on 3 March 1847, son of the noted speech educator Alexander Melville Bell. He was educated at Edinburgh High School and thereafter receiving special training in his father's system for treating speech impediments. He moved to London in 1867, then went to Canada with his father in 1870 and to the United States two years later, introducing his father's system of deaf-mute instruction and becoming Professor of Vocal Physiology at Boston University. By 1876 he had invented and was producing his telephone system. It is conceivable that Bremner, who married Isabella in Edinburgh in 1863, could have known Bell's father, who was five years Bremner's senior, and could well have been acquainted with the son.

[12] Bremner has the date slightly confused. In fact., John Wharton-Todd was not Captain until 1876-7.

At around this time, North Berwick was starting to acquire its reputation as 'the Biarritz of the North'. Unlike many places, it had an operational telegraph office, which had moved from its original home in the foyer of the Dalrymple Arms Hotel in Quality Street to the Post Office at 37 High Street. The Royal Burgh was now a town of some one thousand souls and the express railway engines and plush carriages of the North British Railway were bringing the well-to-do from not only Edinburgh, but as far away as London. I calculated that the Morrises could travel on one of these fast trains to Waverley with a change thence to Granton and so by ferry to Burntisland, from where a further train journey would alight them in St. Andrews. This journey would take him at best six hours. (It is not often realised, I must add in passing, that Robert Napier's 'Leviathan', built in 1849 for the North British Railway's Granton to Burntisland service, was the world's first train ferry.) However, if they could find a coastal passage direct from North Berwick to Elie, a distance of only ten miles or so, the two Toms might arrive in a couple of hours or less.

In a somewhat sombre mood, I made my way to Murdoch's house and station, hoping to tell him what had occurred, or leave a message. He was in, just sitting down to his dinner. His wife Jessie, a fine woman if easily flustered, nearly dropped the plate when she saw me. Murdoch put on his braces and made to don his uniform jacket, but I told him not to be silly and to have his meal – this was no inspection, nor was I trying to catch him out. Jessie offered me tea and fairly rattled the china, her hands were shaking so badly. Would that I inspired such fear and trembling in criminals, or even my own officers!

As Murdoch ate, I informed him of the sad event.

"I hope Margaret's fine," he said. "She and Jessie here are a sort of neckit," by which he meant 'connected', or related, but not so closely as cousins. Apparently Mrs. Murdoch's mother was a Donald, as was Margaret Morris's mother before she married Walter Dr.ennan. Murdoch's eyes narrowed when I mentioned McArdle's name, so I asked him what he was thinking.

"Well, I don't know. But every time he's in the Toun, something bad happens to the Morrises. It cannae just be – what's the word, Sir?"

"Synchronicity?" I ventured.

"That's no' a word I've ever heard afore, so it isnae, that!"

"Coincidence?"

"The very same, Sir. I don't like coincidences because they usually turn out to have some hand behind them. A door left open three nights running? A clerk taking wages from the bank to the works sees the same man following him two paydays in a row? A fight always starts in the same pub? 'Coincidence' says some. 'In a pig's ear' says I!"

"Albert! Language in front of Mr. Bremner!" Jessie remonstrated in a stage-whisper, with an apologetic glance.

"It's all right, Mrs. Murdoch. I trust my Constable's instincts. He's the one who keeps order in this parish, after all. I'm just the office boy. Look, Murdoch, I can't believe there's any connection between McArdle and the Morrises' misfortunes," I added, recognising that I sounded like a penny novel of the more sensational kind. Not that I read these, of course, but Isabella had progressive ideas about literature at the time, and used to leave her books lying about, sometimes where the children or servants might find them. I had mentioned it to her on several occasions.

"Well, maybe aye, and maybe no," Murdoch mused. "But I was in India, and I've seen things that would make your hair curl. Men struck dead by a single look from a Swami. Snakes made to dance to a pipe. Women, whose..."

"Albert Murdoch!" Jessie stopped him. "Mr. Bremner, more tea and a wee slice o' Dundee cake?"

I took the proffered cake, largely to conceal my amusement at this domestic altercation. But Murdoch was right; what did we really know of McArdle? Was he even who he said he was? Did he reside with the regiment in Perth? He certainly seemed to have a copious amount of free time on his hands. I resolved to put our minds at rest.

"Very well, Murdoch. See what you can find out about McArdle locally. I believe his father was a fisherman who died in 1850 or so. His mother? No idea. His forebears come from Shetland. Try your luck down at Fishergate and around the Royal George. Meanwhile, I may well visit Perth."

Murdoch's mantel clock struck three-thirty. I rose to leave, but while I was putting on my top coat there was a knock at the door. Jessie opened it to the boy who had taken the telegraph message for McArdle. He was surprised to see me.

"Oh, Mr. Bremner, Sir, the club steward sent me to find Constable Murdoch. Could he maybe go to Playfair Place?"

"Why, what's happened?"

"It's Margaret Morris, Sir. She died about half-an-hour ago. And old Mrs. Morris has taken on something terrible. She's breaking things!"

It's fair to say that the Morris family wasn't wholly pleased to see Murdoch and me when we arrived at Young Tom's house in Playfair Place. Agnes had calmed down significantly, but it was clear that, in her grief, she had smashed dishes, dashed pictures from walls and beat herself about the head and chest. She was red-eyed with weeping, wringing her hands and rocking back and forth while her children, James, John and the recently-married Elizabeth, tried their best to comfort her. But there was no comfort in Agnes Morris. And what man would want strangers to see his mother in such a state? James, not yet twenty but suddenly thrust into the place of the man of the house, showed us to the parlour while his sister stayed with Agnes.

"Poor Ma," he said. "First auld Janet, then the babby, then Margaret. It's too much to bear. But why are you here?"

"It's all right, James. The Club Steward sent the boy for Murdoch. Maybe he thought there was a danger that Agnes would hurt herself. Maybe he just thought it for the best, your father being away. Anyway, it isn't a police matter, and I regret the intrusion."

Murdoch harrumphed. "Begging your pardon, Mr. Morris, but is the doctor still here?"

"They're both here, Dr. Moir and his son. I think they're in the scullery, washing up. There was blood. Oh, so much blood!" And James himself broke down, feeling safe to do so in the company of other men, all the women being in the bedroom, keening over Margaret's corpse. "She loved that girl like her own daughter. And a grandchild! It's what she wanted. It reminded her of wee Tommy." At the mention of the long-dead brother he never knew, he remembered his elder. "But Tom! He's away! He won't know!"

"David McArdle sent a telegraph to North Berwick. Did no-one tell you? I left a message at your shop."

"Oh aye. Someone did say, so they did. I forgot. I'm sorry, Mr. Bremner. I'm not right, myself."

"Never a worry, James. You just..."

But I was interrupted by Murdoch who re-appeared and coughed. "You'll excuse me, Mr. Bremner, but could the doctor have a word?"

I followed the Constable into the scullery where the elder Dr. Moir was putting on his coat. His son, a newly-qualified practitioner only twenty-one years of age, was making out the Cause of Death Certificate. "Aye, Bremner. I'm glad you're here, but I'm afraid I'm going to complicate your life a bit. I want a post-mortem on Mrs. Morris and the baby."

"Why? Is there something suspicious?"

"I don't know. That's the problem."

"That a baby is stillborn, then the mother dies, is tragic. But not uncommon, surely."

"You mean puerperal fever. But usually the mother takes a few days to die. In this case, she had a ruptured uterus, worse than I've ever seen. And the blood just would not stop. Plus, she was coughing blood at the end."

"Coughing blood? Just like..."

"Just like old Janet Morris, aye. Also, the child had blood in its lungs, even though it wasn't breathing in the womb."

"But Janet died of old age, surely."

"Bremner, I don't know if I should tell you this, but although Janet's death went down as old age, the cause was never certified. Tom had a quiet word with me in case it was tuberculosis, and I examined the immediate family and close neighbours. Not a sign of it, I'm pleased to say."

"What? You conspired to conceal a consumption outbreak?"

"Now, now, Bremner. If I'd found anything I would have notified the right authorities. And I felt, like Tom, that to start a contagion rumour unfounded would be worse. In the event, there was nothing to report. And this today, it isn't tuberculosis either. Some kind of a haemorrhagia, but of a type I've never seen. So, I'll certify the death as due to womb rupture and the child as stillborn from distress, but I'll still insist on an examination. That means a delay and, I'm afraid, it also means..."

"It means no burials until this is resolved, which will upset the family even more. I see. Well, do what you must, doctor. The police will co-operate, of course. Is there anything you need?"

"Transport for the bodies, but the undertaker will see to that. I have prescribed Mrs. Morris something for her nerves and to help her sleep. To be honest, I've given her enough to fell a horse. I think she will need it."

"One last thing, doctor – and I don't want to put thoughts in your head, but is there anything you haven't considered that may have an origin abroad?"

"Abroad? You mean a tropical disease of some kind? Possibly. But who would carry such a thing? Has anyone arrived here from overseas recently? A sailor perhaps?"

"Not a sailor, as such," I said, but decided to keep my further thoughts about McArdle to myself. "Don't mind me, doctor. Just theorising. But do keep an open mind."

"Well, I shan't be doing the autopsy. It will be Pettigrew, the new Professor of Medicine at the United College. But I'll be sure to mention it, if you think it best."

"It may be. Goodbye, Dr. Moir."

He made to leave, but stopped in the doorway. "You know, Bremner, now that you mention it, there was something strange. Not here, but at Janet Morris's cottage. I didn't go there until after she died, of course. She didn't hold with doctors. A good dose of turpentine cures all ills, was her view, or treacle and sulphur. But when I went there, I smelt something vaguely familiar."

"How so?"

"It took me a while to recall it, but I was in the Punjaub from '61 to '74 and I remember some horses dying of a mysterious disease. Alive one day, dead the next. And a strange, sweet smell in the stables. I detected something similar at Kincaple."

"You didn't recognise it?"

"I put it down to mould. The house was damp enough for it. Anyway, it's probably nothing."

"As you say. Thank you doctor."

He took his leave and Murdoch and I stepped inside. The Constable had been taking notes, which he now consulted.

"Aye, well. 'Tropical disease'. 'Never seen it before'. 'Recent arrivals from abroad'. Sounds like India tae me. 'Deed aye!"

"I know what you're thinking, Murdoch. McArdle! Has he brought some form of plague with him?"

"And maybe he has, Sir."

"In that case, how is it only the Morris family is affected?"

"We don't know that, Sir. They're the only ones we've noticed."

"Fair enough. But if McArdle was a carrier of some deadly malady, half the Black Watch in Perth should be down with it by now."

"If he's at Perth at all, Sir."

"As you say, Murdoch, as you say. And I shall find out. You, for your part, can investigate his local past, as we discussed."

"I'll get straight on to it, Sir, never fear," Murdoch said, saluting me and turning to go.

"Ah, one last thing, Murdoch." He shot to attention. "Dr. Moir said he smelt something similar when he was in India, am I right?"

Murdoch made a show of consulting his notes again, although he knew the answer well enough. "That he did, Sir."

"You're thinking there is some foreign poison at work. And McArdle was in India, yes? But so were you, Murdoch, so were you!"

And I left him steaming gently into his collar. Every so often it's good to show the men that their Chief Constable is still on his toes. It maintains discipline and affords me modest amusement. But there were more serious matters at hand. Not wishing the Morrises to arrive home unaware of the further sad turn of events, I arranged for a second message to be sent to North Berwick.

Figure 6 Black Watch Crimean War veterans
This photograph was taken in 1856 at Dover, about the time McArdle joined up. Pictured are:
Piper Muir, Private Glen, Private Mackenzie and Colour Sergeant Gardner, who later won the
Victoria Cross during the Indian Mutiny.

CHAPTER SIX

I kept in communication with the Morris family over the next two weeks. The Morrises, father and son, had just finished their game against the Parks – and had been victorious – when McArdle's telegraph arrived. A local gentlemen, hearing the news, had immediately put his steam yacht at their disposal. It took them all night to get back. Old Tom had received my second message while they were on board, but he had not told his son of it until they were within sight of St. Andrews. Friends had met them at the pier, and on receiving confirmation that Margaret and the baby had died, Young Tom collapsed in a state of total grief. His anguish veered from the horror of losing his family to recrimination and guilt that he had chosen to play at North Berwick instead of staying at his wife's side during the confinement. Many well-wishers told him that there had been no reason to suspect a problem. Further, had he been in Playfair Place, there was nothing he could have done. But he was inconsolable, listless and – a word we are taught us to use more and more nowadays but did not utilise much at the time – depressed. Dr. Moir examined Young Tom for signs of the mysterious illness which carried away his wife and child, but could find nothing and indeed could do no more than prescribe a nerve tonic and suggest an early return to golf and club-making.

The post-mortem of Margaret and the infant had shown widespread destruction of the blood vessels, especially in the lungs and internal organs; and the red blood cells – which, I am told, carry air around the circulation – were burst. No cause was suggested. At my prompting, a sample of Margaret Morris's blood was stored for possible further analysis. In all, it was over two weeks before the deaths could be registered and the mortal remains consigned to the earth. In the meantime, Murdoch had been diligent in ferreting out those who knew McArdle and his antecedents. He spoke to some who had attended The Madras College at the same time, found old fishermen who remembered the family and had even sought out past neighbours. His findings were most surprising, particularly in one regard.

During this time, I had occasion to visit Perth, an easy train ride from Cupar. My early engagement fulfilled, I went to the Queen's Barracks, where I might expect to find McArdle. I was armed with Murdoch's intelligence and intended to ask the man a few questions. In the event, I arrived just as a full parade was under way. There are few sights more stirring than a Highland regiment in dress regalia, and the 42nd is one of the most resplendent, with its scarlet coatees and diced Highland bonnets. The pipes were skirling and drums tattooing *Wha' Saw the Forty-twa* and *Johnnie Scobie* (which others perhaps know better as *'We're no' awa' tae bide awa'*). I enjoyed the spectacle, recalling my own militia days. McArdle had seen me, but as the senior officer in barracks at the time, he could not break away from his inspection duties. When he was free and the men dismissed, however, he greeted me cordially and invited me to his office for coffee, delivered by an ancient Private who looked grizzled enough to have fought with the Spartans at Thermopylae. That put one or more suspicions immediately to rest – McArdle really was a Black Watch captain at Perth, and his uniform clearly displayed his V.C. We exchanged pleasantries while the old sweat poured the cups, and when he was dismissed, McArdle quickly turned to the reason for my visit.

"Not that I'm unhappy to see you, Mr. Bremner, but to what do I owe the pleasure? Perth is a bit out of your locality, is it not?"

"I did have a social engagement here earlier, but I also wanted to let you know about the Morrises."

I briefly gave him the gist of the events after he had left St. Andrews on the eleventh. He knew of the deaths – Old Tom Morris had written to him – and of Young Tom's fragile state of mind. He would attend the funeral at the family's invitation, he said. I was more circumspect in revealing the autopsy results, which at the time had not been fully reported in their final form. But I did broach the issue of his foreign service.

"One possibility is a tropical disease of some sort – just a possibility, mind. And you are the only person we know of returned to St. Andrews from such parts in recent months. Have you or any of your men been suffering from particular illnesses?"

"There have been the usual colds and rheumatic aches that come with returning to Scotland from warmer climes. And one or two occasionally shake from the after-effects of old fevers. But anyone really ill would have been invalided home or discharged when he returned. There were none of the latter, except a few whose wounds militated against further service. And I myself have occasional bouts of intestinal hurry, no doubt a result of the inevitable bowel infections we all caught at various times. But nothing like the condition you mention. I'm sure Regimental Surgeon Clutterbuck would confirm this."

"Dr. Moir, the attending physician, claims to have seen a similar condition affecting horses in the Punjaub. Have you ever encountered such a thing?"

"I had little to do with horses. Infantry and cavalry rarely mixed. I occasionally had my own mounts, but I don't recall any such problem."

"I'm sure. And neither Dr. Moir nor any of the other medical gentleman of the town or the university can name the illness nor guess at its cause."

"Incidentally," McArdle added, "you might tell Murdoch – the reason for our parade today was a belated farewell to an old comrade. Brevet-Major Francis Edward Henry Farquharson, V.C. passed away on September twelfth at his home in Haberton. Murdoch mentioned that he was there at Lucknow when Francis displayed his gallantry."

"So he did. What were the details again?"

"It was the ninth of March 1858. Lieutenant Farquharson, as he then was, led part of his company to storm a bastion where there were guns. He spiked two of them, which meant that the positions taken and held during the night were secure from return artillery. The next morning he held an advanced position although severely wounded."

"You knew him well?"

"Old friends. Although he was younger than myself. In fact, he didn't reach his fortieth birthday."

This mention of yet another untimely death connected to McArdle, and around the same time, brought me back to the matter at hand.

"Tragic, to be sure. But on our more local concerns, I thought I might visit your friend Dr. McIntosh. He seems particularly well-versed in a range of scientific subjects and might shed some light on this."

"A splendid idea, Bremner! William does seem to know the oddest things across the spectrum of science and medicine. Do you go to the hospital now?"

"I thought I might."

"Then perhaps I could accompany you. I haven't seen him for over a week, and I could do with cheering up. If you allow me to change from my parade finery into my walking-out dress, I will be with you shortly."

"Can you leave your duties so readily? You seemed rather engaged when I arrived"

"Oh, we have a brand-new Sergeant-Major in John Barclay's place. It's not official until the twenty-fifth, but he's just itching to get his hands on the men. Plus there are twenty or so bone-idle Lieutenants with little enough to do. Let them worry about watching the shop for a wee while."

I had, in truth, intended to visit Dr. McIntosh alone, but on reflection, I felt McArdle's presence would be useful, although I could not vouchsafe to him the reason at the time. Ordering his Private to organise transport for us, McArdle excused himself to change and returned a few minutes later, just as a carriage and pair pulled up outside, driven by the same ancient. We mounted and were driven the ten miles or so to Murthly in the bright but crisp September day. On the way, McArdle inquired further as to how the Morris family was coping, on which matters I gave him as full a report as possible.

In my turn, I quizzed him about Perth. I remembered that in 1873 the Secretary of War, Edward Cardwell, has requested that a 'Localisation Committee' create Sub-district Brigade Depots.[13] This scheme paired one hundred and forty-one regular army battalions at sixty-eight numbered permanent depots. The idea was that one battalion would serve overseas while the other would remain at the depot to recruit, train and send drafts abroad, changing places at regular intervals so as to keep each battalion fresh. McArdle explained that in 1874 these depots were renamed, Perth becoming Infantry Brigade Depot 57, which the Black Watch shared with the 79th, the Camerons. They each had two companies there, under the command of a Colonel Harenc. Both regiments had therefore more or less kept their original territorial designation of 'Highlanders' while others, not so lucky, found themselves in counties with which they had no historical connection – or even in Ireland![14]

McArdle also took pains to point out to me various places of interest along our route – for example, the site of the battle of Ardoch, where the Celtic tribes united under Calgacus were routed by the Roman army, and the stone circles left presumably by the mysterious Dr.uids of which Caesar wrote. He told me of the cinerary urns unearthed when Murthly Hospital had been built some twelve years before. I complimented him on his antiquarian knowledge, but he laughed and admitted that everything he knew came from letters McIntosh and his sister had written to him, along with her drawings of the megaliths in this miniature Stonehenge.

I have never managed to get straight in my head all that business about Picts and Celts and Scots and which came first and who was who, so we discussed that for the remainder of the journey.

On our arrival at Murthly, I was surprised to see Dr. McIntosh in the grounds, wearing gardening clothes and engaged with a group of patients in digging and planting. When he saw us, his face displayed both pleasure at McArdle's presence and surprise at mine. McArdle briefly explained my purpose in Perth. McIntosh said that he had been told about Margaret's illness but not of the deaths, and he expressed his condolences to McArdle, adding

---

[13] The scheme was in fact initiated in 1872 but did not take effect until the Army Order of 17th March 1873 and was implemented from 1st April.

[14] In fact, the Black Watch had as its sub-district Perth, Fife and Forfar (now called Angus), so it was not really 'Highland' at all.

his wish that these be passed on to the Morris family.

As McIntosh escorted us to his office, McArdle commented on his appearance and activities. "Is it that they don't pay you enough as the Superintendent Physician, William, so you're the head gardener as well?"

"Now, now, Davie. You know fine well I encourage the patients to an interest in gardening and growing crops. It stimulates their minds and even provides them with skills they can use to get employment when they leave here, if they do. Many of them are simple, and do not get on well in the presence of others. Some are also just nervous of mass human company. So working quietly with plants and vegetables suits them. Did you see the large-set man who was holding those dahlias so carefully?"

We confirmed that we had.

"You would not think him capable of any violent murders, then."

I was aghast! "A murderer? And he's on the loose and in the open?"

"Indeed, Chief Constable. But whom did he murder? His errant, drunken wife who constantly tormented him by her liaisons with men, and two of her 'admirers'. She was, apparently, a lady of negotiable affections – a few shillings and a bottle of the demon gin would secure her company. Mr. Taylor found the three together at his home when he returned unexpectedly and, enraged beyond all sense, he dealt with them speedily. The judge called it insanity, and in truth it was. Her constant infidelities drove him to it. But who else will he now murder? His tormentor and her cup-bearers are gone. His cuckolding is over. The only job I had to do was to teach him to contain his anger. That I have managed, and he is not only good with delicate plants, he is the gentlest soul with the linnets and other birds he keeps in his room. He is a threat to no-one but he will be here for the rest of his life, thanks to a judge more concerned with expressing society's outrage than with individual justice."

"I see you have progressive ideas on the criminally insane, William," I said, not wholly comfortable with this.

"Ah, but think, Mr. Bremner: what is the criminal here? It is alcohol, for which women will disport themselves and which drives men to lust, all inhibitions fled. And what is the insanity? That we, as civilised men, allow the conditions to pertain in which strong drink is freely available and widely taken. In certain countries in Europe, that man would have been adjudged to have committed a crime of passion, and set free with the court's commiserations."

I was speechless. McIntosh, when passionately espousing a cause, was different from the man awkward and diffident in society. He continued.

"And from whence does mental instability arise? I do not use the word

71

'lunatic' with its superstitious overtones of the moon-struck, and the term 'insanity' is a legal definition, not a medical diagnosis. We are coming to better understand the origins of nervous problems. We have travelled far from chaining up and exhibiting the poor mad and we are near to a time when we will see their conditions as simply that – illnesses, like influenza, sugar diabetes and worm infestations, to be treated and dispatched. There are clues emerging as to the physical causes of certain states of mental incapacity. Charcot has made hysteria reveal its secrets as an organic disorder rather than some condition of the womb. Broca has found the portion of the brain connected with articulate language. Beard tells us that neurasthenia may make one susceptible to more severe mental illnesses. Bucknill finds that electrical stimulation of the skin and potassium oxide help melancholia. And it is fully thirty years since our own James Braid – no relation to our Edinburgh mycologist as far as I know – coined the term 'neurohypnosis' and used the mesmeric trance for surgical anaesthesia. Where there is a physical or chemical cure, there must have been an organic cause. But there are also new psychologies emerging which suggest that the various disorders of affect and the neuroses might be explainable in terms of early experience and family life.

"Are these just your thoughts, or do others share them?"

"Oh, I correspond with a bright young medical student in Vienna named Sigmund Freud. We write to each other mainly about the intersexuality of eels and the primitive lamprey, *Petromyzon*, but he also has an interest in psychiatry and I have sought to encourage him in this. Already he has had some quite startling insights."

But by now we had reached William's office, and such a Salomon's House it was! Stuffed animals and preserved sea creatures covered almost every surface. Glass tanks held young fish, snakes, lizards and other things I could not even name. On a chemicals table an alembic bubbled away. The walls were festooned with drawings and watercolours of exquisite execution. It was to these my attention was drawn.

"The work of your late sister?" I asked.

"Indeed, Mr. Bremner. I miss her so very much, both privately and professionally."

"Yes, I did not know of your loss until McArdle told me after his visit to Cupar. My belated commiserations to you and to the rest of your family."

A female voice from behind surprised me. "Thank you for your kindness, Mr. Bremner. And how pleasant to see you again after all this time"

I turned to see a tall, handsome woman in her middle thirties[15], but I recognised her right away. "Agnes! Agnes McIntosh. I have not seen you for years! You are well?"

"I am very well, thank you. And hello, Davie."

McArdle smiled and bowed, then kissed her hand. Agnes blushed slightly and I suspected there was perhaps a mild *amour* between the spinster and the dashing Captain.

"I gather you look after this gardening doctor here. Do you tend his zoo as well?"

At this she laughed. "William's collection and his Museum are his affair, although I confess to moving the dust around from time to time. And ensuring that he remembers to eat. On which note, it is almost luncheon time, gentlemen. Will you stay?"

McArdle and I agreed that we should be delighted and Agnes retired to oversee the preparations.

Dr. McIntosh had by now washed his hands and exchanged his gardening apparel for a more traditional frock coat. He indicated chairs for us opposite the desk at which he sat, and waited for us to speak. I told him of the unhappy occurrences at the Morris household and as much as I could of Dr. Moir's thoughts and of the autopsy. He asked a few pertinent questions, but mostly listened. At one point he rose to consult a book from his shelves for a moment. Finally, he paced for a few minutes, looked from his window, then sat again and spoke.

"I agree that the description of Mrs. Morris's condition does not appear usual. I can think of no tropical disease which would result in these symptoms, but it is not a field in which I am an expert. However, I am drawn to one possible conclusion. A toxin."

"You mean poisoning?" I said. "That had occurred to me. And largely because you said Professor Braid's mixture might lead to similar results. Is there a connection?"

"Actually, Mr. Bremner, I was thinking not of a chemical poison. Oh, I can imagine several which, in unlikely combination, might effect such a result. The mode of administration, however, would rule out their being given surreptitiously or taken by accident. I feel we can exclude Professor Braid as a

---

[15] Bremner has this absolutely correct, but from guesswork or knowledge of the family we cannot tell. John McIntosh and his wife Elizabeth Mitchell produced Margaret (1831-1920), Ann Barclay (1834-1915), Eliza Mitchell (1836-1916), William Carmichael (1838-1931), Agnes Mitchell (1840-1923) and Roberta (1843-1869). The two younger sisters were devoted to William.

potential poisoner. No, I was thinking more of a toxin of animal or vegetable origin."

"Ah! I see. But such as..."

"Well, as for animals, you will be aware that scorpions, some snakes, various spiders and many marine animals use venoms to paralyse or kill their prey. In the main, these affect nerves – the nerves of motion, or of breathing, often. But some act on the blood system, preventing clotting or in certain cases causing circulatory collapse."

"So could we be looking for an exotic spider or snake at liberty in St. Andrews?"

"Not an impossibility, Mr. Bremner, and one you might investigate. Although quite how one would hunt down such a creature defeats me, short of evacuating, emptying and minutely searching the Morrises' various houses and premises."

"Including the aunt's cottage?" McArdle interjected. "You imagine a spider or a snake making its way from St. Andrews to Kincaple specifically to bite a Morris?"

"Oh, come now, Davie. I have no doubt that she visited her family in the town where she might have been bitten. But even then, I consider it unlikely. Why, for instance, were just two women attacked by this mystery animal and not more victims? But I do bear it in mind."

"How would it have got here? "I asked, eyeing the various inhabitants of the glass cases displayed around the room.

McArdle saw my anxious glance and laughed. McIntosh blushed, and answered, "I assure you Chief Constable, my interests are purely in native fauna. There is nothing more exotic here than a stuffed viper and a few sea-urchins, although I will agree they were all poisonous in their own way when alive. But the British viper or adder will hardly if ever bite anything it cannot eat, except in self defence. Sea urchins are rarely fatal to humans. But if you are looking for an overseas origin, many ships bring intriguing creatures to our shores. The jute boats at Dundee, fruit shipments landing at Glasgow or Leith – all have on occasion, and more often than we realise, I suspect, carried a small stowaway or two. That is, after all, how the bubonic plague arrived here centuries ago. The plague lives in rats and is carried by fleas, both imported from the East on ships. One day we may discover the actual agent responsible. Goodsir in Edinburgh has demonstrated that infective diseases are caused by microscopic germs, and both Pasteur and Koch follow his reasoning. But I must say I was really thinking of a plant toxin."

"You were? How so?" I asked, thinking to myself how useful it would be to have the man on hand for police business of this kind

"Oh yes. There are many poisonous plants. Nettles, in a small way, are an example. Most beans are toxic, which is why we soak and boil them before eating. And everyone knows not to eat green potatoes or certain berries and mushrooms for the same reason."

"You mean, the victims could have eaten something, by accident or design?"

"Surely. But many plant toxins can be absorbed through the skin as well as inadvertently ingested."

"So the victims could even have brushed against something?" McArdle asked.

"They could, Davie. And you might know this – does the golf ball trade use any unusual plants or plant products?"

McArdle thought for a moment. "Well, there's gutta-percha for the new balls. It comes from the East. I suppose they use various oils and solutions in the preparation of it."

"Castor oil? Or flax oils, perhaps?"

"I have no idea," McArdle admitted. "When I thought of entering that trade it was all leather and wet goose feathers."

"I'm intrigued, Dr. McIntosh," I said. "Why castor oil? My wife gives it to our children for gripe."

"Yes, many mothers do. But the raw beans of *Ricinus communis* contain a particularly vicious, fast-acting and untraceable poison. Furthermore it may produce symptoms similar to those you describe in the three Morris deaths – diarrhoea, nausea, vomiting, abdominal cramps, internal bleeding, profuse sweating, liver and kidney failure, circulatory collapse, convulsions, rictus and ultimately death, sometimes within twelve hours. As few as twenty-five grammes of castor bean seed will be lethal to a horse and less for a human. Under an ounce will kill, I assure you. It is true that commercially-prepared castor oil contains little or none of the toxin, but I certainly would not be feeding it to children."

I made a mental note to tell Isabella and to scour the house for any bottles of the oil. Out they would go!

"As for other exotic substances, we should ask Old Tom," McArdle suggested.

"Indeed we should," I agreed.

"Mr. Bremner, would it be in order for me to visit Mr. Morris and explore this with him?" McIntosh asked.

"By all means, William "I agreed. "But I will have a Constable accompany you, as this is a police matter."

"Of course. And could I, with the family's permission, see the bodies?"

"If you do so quickly. They are still under my authority. Also, the man at the University who has the bodies intends to keep some organs for further study. You may care to look at his jars."

"Wonderful!" cried the doctor, with an enthusiasm I could applaud but could not quite share. "It is just a shame we cannot get some of Mrs. Morris's blood. But her body will be long exsanguinated by now."

I was pleased to inform him that, on a whim, I had asked for blood to be stored cold. He expressed his delight and approbation. They can be somewhat ghoulish, our medical friends, even if in a good cause.

At that point, Agnes McIntosh re-appeared to announce luncheon, which we took in the hospital refectory with the rest of the staff and the more sensible of the inmates. I confess I found it not wholly conducive to the appetite to watch some of the simpletons dribbling their soup, or the toothless vacantly masticating the bread for all to see. But McIntosh and the others seemed inured to it, and discussed plans for a new kitchen garden, while McArdle and I talked to Agnes about her family and times past. I noticed that McArdle asked for some food to be taken out to the soldier waiting patiently with our carriage.

As we rose to take our leave, I thanked McIntosh for his time and consideration and expressed my desire that he were closer to hand, in St. Andrews. To my surprise, he himself voiced the same wish and confided that he had recently applied for the vacant Chair in Natural History at the University, where he hoped to devote himself more completely to the study of marine life. But he was not optimistic about the chances of his success.[16]

After lunch, we arranged that Dr. McIntosh would visit St. Andrews the day after next – the Friday – and made to leave. Then, in a gesture which I confess was calculated to elicit a response, I stopped McArdle and said: "But don't you want to stay on a while longer?"

"Pleasant as it is to see William, I feel he has given us enough time from his duties. And Agnes is likewise busy."

"No," I said. "I thought you might wish to visit your mother."

I am not sure what reaction I truly expected, but Dr. McIntosh froze and McArdle held my gaze.

"Ah. I see you have been investigating me."

"Yes, and I cannot apologise or ask your forgiveness, as it is my function and my duty. But I have been finding out something of your history."

"Mr. Bremner, I am neither upset nor embarrassed that my mother is a charge here at Murthly. She gets good care from William and is comfortable.

---

[16] In fact, Dr. William McIntosh did achieve this dream, but not until 1882.

And it matters little if I visit her today or next week or next month. She doesn't recognise me and won't remember. But since you have been busy on my account, I will be happy to complete the picture for you. On the way back, please feel free to ask me any other questions. Then, perhaps, you'll do me the courtesy of explaining why I have come under your scrutiny."

We took a somewhat uncomfortable farewell of McIntosh and his sister and mounted our carriage, to a full array of salutes and stamping from the Private driving, to McArdle's annoyance.

"Thomson, you know I dislike all this foot-smashing-down that has recently pervaded the Infantry. I blame the Foot Guards. It is quite possible to be smart without stamping. Do you hear me, Thomson?"

"Aye, Sir," the Private agreed. "Perhaps ye'll tell the Parade Sergeant Major, though."

"Oh, I have, I have. And much good it's done. Now, Mr. Bremner. What would you like to know?"

"In front of…" I indicated the driver.

"Private Thomson dresses me and arranges my things. He has also seen to my wounds and on occasion told me when I was being stupid. He knows more about me than most, so I don't mind. Pray continue."

From what Murdoch had elicited, and the missing parts that McArdle provided to the puzzle, it seems that his story was this:

His father had been a violent drunkard of a man, mistreating his wife, who was not of strong mind to begin with. But in her simple way, she had loved her husband. Finding it harder and harder to get work at sea, as his temper and his habits became more widely known, he had taken to caddying to earn a few shillings, which he then spent mostly on ale and spirits. He often caddied while intoxicated – as did many of the second-tier caddies, although it was never tolerated in those of the first rank. One day, in his cups, he lurched too close to a golfer when he was on the backswing and took a heavy club straight between the eyes. It killed him instantly. Mrs. McArdle's mind was unhinged by the news and the sight of his gashed forehead. She could no longer work at fish-filleting and there was no money coming in other than Parish Relief. To help, the Morris family gave food, and Old Tom made sure that the young David McArdle got caddy work while not neglecting his studies. But this, in combination with the accident which had robbed her of her husband, got turned around in her sad mind so that, in some way, the Morrises were responsible for her situation. It mattered not that they were helping – she saw this as even greater evidence of their complicity is what she felt was a murder. One day she went to Tom Morris as he worked in Allan Robertson's shop and brandished a knife. Unable to reach him, she turned it on her own wrists. She was restrained, certified insane and confined in a hospital, where she became all but catatonic.

McArdle was by now old enough to make his own way in the world and, feeling no little shame, took himself to Leith where he entered into the Merchant Service. Some ten years later, when the Murthly Hospital opened, he was able to arrange for her to be transferred to the care of his friend Dr. McIntosh. But from the time of her certification to the present, she did little but mutter spitefully about Tom Morris. She recognised no-one and nothing and had to be helped even to eat. Her mind broken, she never again knew her son.

All of this said, we were back in Perth. McArdle instructed Private Thomson to drive us first to the station where I might take the Cupar train. He accompanied me onto the platform so we could have some final privacy.

"So, Mr. Bremner, I take it I am in some way a suspect in these deaths?"

"Well, when there was the possibility of some foreign disease, you were a feasible source. And you seemed to have been around the Morris family at each of the deaths. Moreover, we knew nothing about you other than what you had told us. It was our responsibility to dig a bit deeper."

"I accept that," McArdle said. "But I fear I have done myself little service."

"How is that, McArdle?"

"Look at it with your policeman's eyes. My father dead, my mother mad, all because – in her thinking at least – of Tom Morris. Who is to say I do not share her conviction, or may choose to avenge her sorrow? I have made myself an even stronger suspect. I have the motive. I have had the opportunity. But how did I effect the crimes? Did I bring a venomous animal back with me from Africa? Am I proficient with the poison-tipped blow-dart? Did I find some subtle magick in the mysterious East? And was my solicitousness at each Morris death merely a device to get me near the victim so I could remove any evidence of my involvement? I must be a stone-cold killer indeed, and a practiced one. In fact, I'm surprised you haven't also pegged me for the murder of Cock Robin.[17]"

"All a bit far-fetched, McArdle...", I started to say.

"No more so than William's plant poisons. So I feel I have only one course of action, Bremner."

"What is that?"

---

[17] A reference to a popular English nursery rhyme from 1744, thought of as a morality tale for children but actually a political poem about the downfall of Prime Minister Robert Walpole in 1742.

"To clear my own name, I must find your murderer, if murders there were, or a rational explanation of the deaths."

"I think you might best leave this to the police," I suggested.

"Forgive me, but even you will admit your men can be leaden-footed at times. They are just as likely to leave it unsolved and with a pall of suspicion hanging over me. I will try not to get in your way, Bremner, nor to impede any investigations of yours. Anything I discover I will share with you. I trust you will extend me the same consideration. Goodbye."

And with that, he turned on his heel and marched back to his carriage. It was only later, mulling on the train, that I realised he had started to call me by my surname only. Was this simply our increasing familiarity, or had he lost whatever respect he might have felt for me initially? Either way, our relationship was not the same and I regretted this. I also had grave forebodings about an amateur getting in the way of the police – especially one of McArdle's obvious determination and resourcefulness.

I half-remember thinking: 'The game is afoot', or that may be a phrase I encountered more recently in a similar context. I cannot be sure.

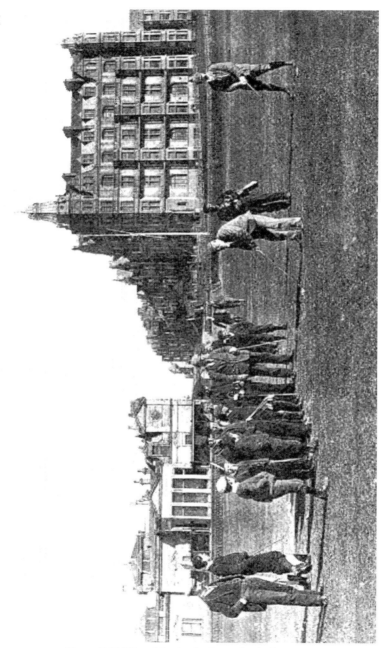

Figure 7 Old Tom Morris playing at St. Andrews
Note the difference in the Clubhouse from the later, extended structure

CHAPTER SEVEN

O n the morning of Monday 27th September I received a parcel of documents, sent on by Murdoch to my office in Cupar. These included his own report, along with a written summary from Dr. McIntosh of his examinations, plus a note from Captain McArdle. I can do no better than to reproduce these here in their entirety.

Murdoch's report

Constable A. Murdoch
Fife Constabulary
St. Andrews.

On Friday 24th September, 1875, as ordered, I met Doctor William McIntosh, Superintendent Physician of the Murthly Hospital, Perth. I accompanied him to the rooms of Professor J B Pettigrew, anatomist at the United Colleges of St. Andrews. Doctor Robert Moir M.D. was also present, as was Captain David McArdle of the Forty-second Highland Regiment, Perth. I noted that Professor Pettigrew and Doctor McIntosh were acquainted, both being Fellows of the Royal Society of Edinburgh. An examination was conducted of the mortal remains of Mrs. Margaret Morris of Playfair Place, wife of Mr. Thomas Morris Jnr., golf-club maker and her child, who had died on September 11th of this year. Doctors Moir and McIntosh had much medical talk. Doctor McIntosh has written a separate report which is attached.

Captain McArdle feels that he is under suspicion of involvement in these deaths and the death of Miss Janet Morris, aunt by blood of Mr. Thomas Morris Snr. He expressed his intention of investigating the deaths on his own account. I issued a strong caution against interfering in police work and obstructing the Constabulary in its duties. He replied that to obstruct a Constable a person would be best advised to stand between his bed and his dinner table. We had further words on the subject. Captain McArdle was permitted to watch the examination by the doctors, from a distance, but not to touch the bodies.

After the examination, Doctor McIntosh wrote some notes. He showed these to Doctor Moir, who agreed they were true records of the events and conversations, and signed them. Doctor Moir also expressed his intention to now certify the death of Mrs. Morris as rupture of the uterus. This will allow Mr. Morris Snr. to register the death with Mr. John Varley, the Registrar in St. Andrews. The business being concluded, Doctor Moir departed. I allowed Doctor McIntosh time to make a copy of his notes, which he kept for his own records. Captain McArdle waited for him.

Doctor McIntosh desired to ask Mr. Morris some questions concerning golf balls. At the shop, Mr. Morris was not there and he asked one of the ball-makers about gutta-percha.

My part completed, I saw McArdle and Doctor McIntosh out of the shop and they left together. Later that same day, Captain McArdle left at my house a sealed letter addressed to Captain James Bremner, Chief Constable of Fife, which is delivered, unopened, with this report and Doctor McIntosh's notes.

Albert Murdoch, Constable.

Signed at St. Andrews, Saturday September 25th, 1875 and despatched to Mr. Bremner at Cupar.

The report of Dr. William McIntosh

William McIntosh M.D. F.R.S.E.
Murthly Hospital
Murthly
Perthshire

Mr. James Bremner
Chief Constable of Fife
Cupar
September 24th, 1875

I must first express my thanks to Captain Bremner, Chief Constable of Fife, for allowing access to the bodies and permission to examine them, and to Dr. Robert Moir M.D. for his help and patience in this matter; and to Professor James Bell Pettigrew M.D. LL.D. F.R.S., Chandos Chair of Medicine and Anatomy at the United Colleges of St. Andrews.

Mrs. Margaret Morris, aged 30 years, was delivered of a stillborn infant at approximately 11 A.M. on September 11th, 1875. She died four hours later at 3 P.M., primarily from blood loss following a rupture of the uterus. Dr. Robert Moir M.D. was in attendance, as was Dr. John Wilson Moir M.D., who certified these deaths and times. I was not present at either of those events.

There is no doubt that hypovolaemic shock following uterine rupture was the ultimate cause of Mrs. Morris's death. However, there are puzzling aspects to her final illness. First, it proved impossible to staunch the bleeding. Second, she was also, according to Dr. Moir, exhibiting haemoptysis, epistaxis and petechiae immediately before her death. And third, her husband's great-aunt, Miss Janet Morris, had recently died, also showing haemoptysis before death. Janet Morris, being aged 92 years, was not considered to have died from other than natural causes, but Dr. Moir took the sensible precaution of examining her close friends, neighbours and relatives for any sign of contagious lung disease, such as tuberculosis. None was found.

I discussed with Dr. Moir the possibility that the death of Mrs. Morris might be attributed to the bite or sting of a venomous reptile, insect or marine animal. Such an injury could, in theory, introduce a toxin which might lead to such a circulatory disturbance. Together, we examined Mrs. Morris for evidence of a bite or other epidermal puncture, but none was found. However, there was evidence of inflammation and mucosal irritation around the lips, which, at the time, Dr. Moir had ascribed to Mrs. Morris biting her lips during her ordeal.

The corpse had been partly eviscerated by Prof. Pettigrew and the lungs and liver and spleen retained and preserved. The lungs showed considerable evidence of haemosiderosis, which accounts for the haemoptysis and epistaxis, as Prof Pettigrew had already noted. (Note added in margin: Dr. Moir suggests that I make clear these medical terms. Haemoptysis is coughing of blood. Epistaxis is nosebleed. Petechiae are small red spots on the skin. Haemosiderosis is bleeding in the lungs.)

The liver and spleen showed some evidence of capillary degeneration. I have, with permission, taken small slices of these organs for further microscopic examination.

There were no unusual stomach contents, although there was evidence of bleeding in the bowel. Her brain was not examined, except grossly, and showed no obvious pathology.

Chief Constable Bremner had caused a sample of Mrs. Morris's blood to be stored. This was helpful. Also, Prof Pettigrew had had the presence of mind to take a film of blood on a microscope slide immediately he received care of the body, and to fix it with a cover slip. He and I examined this by microscope and found considerable evidence of haemolysis (that is: the erythrocytes, or red cells, were mostly ruptured). This cannot be confirmed by any re-examination of the stored blood, as erythrocyte degeneration is a natural consequence of storage. However I have taken a sample of this blood for further testing. There is, according to Dr. Moir, no family history of anaemias, purpura or other blood conditions. There is also no recent history in the family of infections or contagion other than benign colds, influenzas, boils et cetera.

Next, we examined the stillborn infant. The child's body showed all the signs of massive circulatory damage, but the circulation and organs were well formed. The death was not due solely to the perinatal stress of the mother's uterine rupture and subsequent anoxia. There appears to have been the same systemic condition as the mother exhibited. But had this been of long-standing, the foetus would not have developed as it did, nor would the pregnancy have gone to term.

My conclusion, therefore, with which Dr. Moir concurs, is that Mrs. Morris suffered from an unidentified systemic condition acquired immediately before the onset of her labour. The only agent which could have caused this would be either a fast-acting toxin or a new and unrecognised contagion of particular virulence. As there have been no other cases of such a disease in the St. Andrews area immediately prior to Mrs. Morris's death and in the thirteen days since, the latter is considered unlikely

An animal bite or sting is also considered unlikely for the reasons given above.

We are left therefore with the possibility of a chemical poison or vegetable toxin. I consider a chemical agent difficult to administer without detection, and therefore suggest a concentrated and highly toxic plant product, such as the curare which certain South American natives use to tip their spears. I shall endeavour, by dint of further analysis of the blood and organs, to determine what I can and will report any findings.

I also enquired of the Morris ball-makers as to the exact process by which gutta-percha is made into golfing balls. Contrary to my earlier considerations, there are no suspicious chemicals, resins, oils or extracts used in the manufacture, and no other substances of a dubious nature are stored in the shop.

Signed   Dr. William Carmichael McIntosh M.D.
Signed   Dr. Robert Moir M.D.

Letter from Capt McArdle

Captain David McArdle
42nd Regiment
Written at St. Andrews
Friday September 24th

Mr. James Fleming Bremner
Chief Constable of Fife
Cupar

My Dear Bremner,
I trust you will have forgiven the somewhat abrupt manner in which we parted last week at Perth. I confess I felt at the time that I was being investigated without my knowledge and was uncomfortable with this. On reflection, I understand the reasons. In a police investigation, everyone is a suspect until eliminated. If your separate inquiries did not tally with my statements, you would have good cause for thought. And if a suspect knew of your activities, he might seek to interfere with them. On the other hand, I am still resolved to explore this matter on my own account. I encountered no little hostility from Constable Murdoch to the idea, but again I imagine he was simply carrying out his functions to the letter.
Even if not a suspect, I have no other status than a member of the public class and no rights in the matter beyond those of a friend of the Morris family. However, I feel I have some insights to share with you.
You will no doubt have received a report from William by now. After he and Dr. Moir completed their examination, we discussed the matter. William is firmly against any natural disease and Dr. Moir is baffled.
After Murdoch left us, I returned to Morris's in order to pay my respects and to meet Young Tom, whom I did not know until this time. He is a very sad man, and his father doubts the likelihood of his competing in the next Open Championship in October, if his spirits do not lift. To this end, I offered him a game and we played some holes together. But after six or so, he was evidently tired and also unable to concentrate.
He proposed that we have tea at his home and we repaired there. It emerged during my visit that amongst Margaret's last acts, she had asked to see a certain photograph in a silver frame. This is a picture of Young Tom taken at Musselburgh, and it had been left for her at the Morris shop in Pilmour Links on the day he had left for North Berwick. As she started to her labour, she asked to hold the photograph, and kissed it many times, saying she wished 'her Tom' was with her.

Now, this news came from Young Tom's sister, who is caring for him at present. When she told us, it became immediately clear that, contrary to everyone's belief, Young Tom had not left it for her or sent it. In fact, he knew nothing of its existence or origin. It had never been mentioned up to that point, so it was a surprise to him. I asked to see the photograph, and it was brought. Young Tom identified it as having been taken at Musselburgh about three months ago and pictured him with some other golfers. He does not remember the identity of the photographer, other than that he lives in Musselburgh and is quite well known.

I asked if I might borrow it, to show it to William McIntosh in case it provided inspiration in the case. I know little of photography but even I am aware that it uses poisonous chemicals in its processes. So I asked for a paper bag to carry it in and suggested that Young Tom and his sister immediately wash their hands in case of contamination. I shall take it to Perth and return it later.

Of course, your policeman's nose may twitch at this – if the photograph is the source of some poison, then I could have introduced it to the Morris house as readily as anyone, and on a day when I knew the two Toms were away.

And now that I have it in my possession, I could dispose of it or substitute it for another, could I not?

On the other hand, if I were the poisoner and the photograph the agent, why should I even mention it? In answer to that, because it may be reported by the Morris family at some future time and therefore I am deflecting suspicion from myself by mentioning it now.

Alternatively, one reads in certain lurid stories of master criminals who delight in dangling their genius before the police – perhaps I am in that category?

I fear that by taking his action I can only have increased my suspicion in your eyes. So be it.

If anything further emerges, I shall inform you,

Yrs,

David McArdle (Capt)

I was pondering these communications, when one of my officers knocked at my office door and entered.

"Sir, there are two gentlemen outside who say the must see you urgently. Names of McArdle and McIntosh."

I was stunned at this, and told the man to show them in without delay.

McArdle and his medical friend came in, both somewhat excited and breathless. McArdle spoke first.

"Bremner, we have news. Margaret and her child were definitely murdered! William has proof."

"What? How can that be? Who murdered them?"

"Oh, we don't know the murderer, Mr. Bremner," Dr. McIntosh said, "but I think I know how the deaths were brought about." And he put on my desk a small glass vial in which was a reddish liquid.

"What's this, William?"

"Mouse blood, Mr. Bremner."

"You're saying they were killed by mouse blood?"

"Of course not. But it proves something interesting."

The two sat down and McArdle nodded to William to continue his explanation.

"You remember that I took some tissue samples to examine by microscope. I did so, and it showed that the small blood vessels in each organ were catastrophically damaged. Also, all the erythrocytes…"

"The red cells in the blood?" I queried, to show I was keeping up.

"Indeed. The red cells were all burst. And I had a sample of Margaret's blood. There were two things interesting about this. First, it contained much more iron than is normal. Second, I found it had another property. I reduced it down to dryness and took up a concentrated extract. Next, I added a drop of it to some blood from a mouse. It burst the red cells almost immediately – that is what you see in the vial on your desk. Then I injected what remained into two living mice. Both died horrible deaths within minutes, bleeding from their noses and mouths. Examination of their lungs showed the same haemosiderosis as in Margaret Morris and her child."

"So even a small amount of her blood contained an agent so potent it could kill a mouse?"

"Yes," McIntosh confirmed. "Imagine how much she had taken, then. No wonder she bled to death and her womb ruptured."

"And the iron…?"

"That is a consequence, not a cause. The toxic agent also had the effect of changing the amount of iron in the blood – some of it from the destroyed blood cells, some perhaps moved from the spleen. But that is less important. It was the damage caused by the poison to the organs and the blood cells themselves. Not only did it burst the erythrocytes, it prevented the blood from coagulating. Normally blood will clot if left to stand in air. It is how cuts and wounds heal, at least in part. But that function also was interfered with by this substance."

"And so she bled to death. But how was this... whatever it is given to her?"

"Ah," McArdle said, picking up the thread from his friend. "You recall that I took the photograph of Young Tom to William, in case it had some poisonous chemical upon it? William immediately told me that there is no such poison that would be left on a photograph by the usual processes, but it did seem to be covered with something viscous. He washed it and the frame and again concentrated down the solution."

"Then I repeated my mouse blood test and I also injected it into a live mouse," William added.

"With the same results?"

"Exactly!"

"And you said, McArdle, that Margaret Morris had held and kissed the photograph?"

"She did, which may account for William's observation that her lips were inflamed. A good thing we all washed after touching it. The poison was still active."

"But what is this poison?"

McIntosh closed his eyes and thought for a moment. "Its nature eludes me. It is not any of the expected toxins, judging by its effects. And it is not any inorganic chemical that I can discern. It may be that it is so powerful, it exerts its effect at doses too small even to be detected by my admittedly crude chemistry."

"And where is the photograph now?" I asked.

"Safely locked away and securely wrapped, in my laboratory at the hospital. No-one else is at risk, I assure you. In any case, I may have washed away all of the toxin. But I felt it best to be safe."

"I agree with you. And perhaps you will keep it secure for the time being."

"Of course."

McArdle spoke again. "The question now is, did Janet Morris die the same way? William says there is little point in having her exhumed. We know she coughed blood. And there will be no blood left in her body that William could extract. Also, it would be extremely distressing for the family. But I happen to know that all her meagre possessions have been distributed among the Morris family and some friends, so perhaps these should be impounded and examined, too. We would not wish anyone else to inadvertently handle this poison."

"I shall see to that, right away." I agreed.

"And perhaps William and I should visit Kincaple. He is likely to find something that might elude a non-medical man, or a policeman."

I thought about this for a minute or two. "Surely, I can see merit in William visiting the cottage, but with a policeman accompanying him. I am not so sure that a member of the public such as yourself should be allowed. This is now a murder investigation, which is a very serious matter indeed."

"A serious matter you did not know was murder until I brought you the evidence. I think I have a stake in this," McArdle pointed out reasonably.

"Very well," I consented after a brief internal argument with myself. "But as with the autopsy, you are there strictly to observe. You will not touch anything or take any active part. I will give you a note for Murdoch ordering him to go with you and to keep a strict eye on you. If he feels you are interfering, he will ask you to leave. Is that clear?"

"I agree," McArdle said and looked at his friend.

"Yes," the doctor said.

"Good, then please take this note to Murdoch in St. Andrews." I wrote the note somewhat hastily, sealed it and handed it to McArdle.

"We shall leave immediately. Come on, William."

The two departed without shaking my hand. It occurred to me that if McArdle was indeed the 'master criminal' he had confessed to being half in jest, he was going to extraordinary lengths to incriminate himself. Or else he was laying a trail of red herrings that would stretch from Pittenweem to Cellardyke.

I know of what occurred next from Murdoch's later report. McArdle and McIntosh arrived at Murdoch's house and were told by his wife where he would be on his patrol. They found him and gave him my note. After looking at it, Murdoch fairly read the Riot Act to McArdle, telling him exactly what he would and would not tolerate. He was rather more deferential to McIntosh, who was acting on my instructions. Then they headed for Kincaple.

At the old aunt's house, they found a young family in residence. The mother had come to the door, with a babe in arms and two other young children peering wide-eyed from behind her skirts. Murdoch explained that they were looking for something connected with the death of the previous tenant, and the mother asked if she was in any kind of trouble. Murdoch reassured her that she was not, and they entered. The woman confirmed that when she and her husband had taken the cottage, it had been completely empty. They had had to borrow a few sticks of furniture from her parents. There seemed little hope of finding anything of interest in the case.

But then something happened which would probably not have been thought significant by a policeman alone – McArdle and McIntosh both noticed that the baby was coughing! William explained to the mother that he was a doctor and asked if he might examine the infant. The mother replied that she had no money to pay for his services, but he assured her that there would be no charge and she relented. After examining the baby's throat and nose and listening to his chest. William asked if he had ever coughed blood. Occasionally over the past few days, when the coughing had started, the woman replied, but not to any great extent. She had put it down to the damp autumn weather. Then William asked if they might see the room where the children slept.

In the bedroom there was a cot and a larger bed in which the two older children slept together. The parents had a recess bed in the parlour. McArdle pointed out that the cot was in the same position as Janet Morris's bed had been. Murdoch moved the cot on William's instructions and revealed a corner with wallpaper which had an obvious damp spot. Putting on his gloves, William pulled at the paper and it fell away, revealing a dark mould growing behind it. He tore the stained paper off and also asked for a kitchen knife so that he could scrape away some of the mould from the plaster. This he wrapped in the paper and carefully enveloped both in a sheet of newsprint the woman provided. He then examined every other wall in the house but found no further site of infestation. Finally, he told the mother, in no uncertain terms, to move her children immediately to the other room to sleep, and that when her husband came home, he was to remove as much paper as possible and scrub the walls with bleach and soap, wearing leather gloves and with a cloth over his mouth and nose. Then they should light a fire to dry the room thoroughly.

William left his gloves for the husband to use, with instructions to boil them afterwards. McArdle, it seems, gave her a few shillings to buy coal. She nodded her understanding and the three left the cottage.

By the Friday noon, my officers had contacted everyone who had received some memento or inheritance from Janet's cottage. In the main these were a china service, a few pictures and ornaments and some linen. He furniture had not been thought worth anything and had been disposed of, as had her clothes. Those who had eaten and drunk from the plates and cups appeared not to be suffering from any maladies and in any case, everything had been washed before use. As a precaution, it was all packed and taken away. I also had read Murdoch's report of the Kincaple visit which I found immensly disturbing. Taken together, they added up to only one conclusion – we had a multiple murderer on the loose.

That day I also received a further communication from William McIntosh. He had examined the mould with his microscope (he dearly loved that instrument! – I learned later that it had been crafted by our very own Sir David Brewster)[18] but could not as yet identify it. However, he was sure it was not native to these islands and could only have been introduced on purpose. The area of the wall where it had grown was not particularly damp so as to encourage growth in that one spot in preference to another, further suggesting its placement there was no accident or natural occurrence. But most surprising of all, he had made an extract of the mould spores, adding it to mouse blood.

It had had the expected effect! He also administered it to live mice and they succumbed. Clearly then, the mould was the source of the toxin. The older lady had inhaled the spores – possibly over a few weeks – and being old and enfeebled, it had been sufficient to kill her. Margaret, a much younger and healthier woman, would not have been affected so readily, and also it would be more difficult to introduce it to a busy household like the Playfair Place home than into the cottage of an elderly woman who was often not there as she visited her St. Andrews relations. Margaret required direct administration of the essence of the mould. The only sensible conclusion was that whoever had placed the mould in Janet's cottage had later learned to extract from it the active principle, which had then been introduced to Margaret Morris on the photograph.

This was shocking news indeed. We had a criminal of extreme ingenuity and no little technical ability. He could only be a medical man or scientist. It put McArdle out of consideration, unless he and McIntosh were in some way acting together. But for what purpose? I thought again about McArdle's poor, mad mother, she who was in the care of McArdle's close friend. Was this all about revenge? But if so, why were the two Morris women targeted and not Old Tom himself? Or had he just been fortunate to avoid an attempt on his life

---

[18] Sir David Brewster (1781 –1868) was famous for his contributions to optics, especially photography and microscopes, and for the invention of the kaleidoscope. In 1838 he became Principal of St. Andrews University and in 1859, at the age of 78, he was elected Principal of Edinburgh University, a post he held until his death nine years later. Brewster was also editor of Encyclopaedia Britannica for 22 years.

thus far? And in that case, if McArdle and McIntosh were the twisted perpetrators, why were the two so assiduously pursuing the cause? To allay suspicion? It hardly seemed credible.

I read deeper into William's report. There was much of a specialised nature concerning the mould which I confess I did not really take in. But he concluded by saying that he knew vaguely a man in London who was an expert on such matters and would write to him, sending also a sample and the drawings he had made from his microscope.

There seemed little more for him to do but to wait for a reply, which might take some weeks.

On the Saturday I was to play at St. Andrews. I took pains to visit Old Tom and found McArdle there. He too had a game. I took him to one side and asked if he had said anything to the family about our mystifying case. He said that he had not, as he felt that was the business of the police. I agreed and asked Old Tom if I might talk to him.

It is the unhappiest part of a policeman's lot to break bad news to someone, particularly when it concerns a death. But to tell someone, who has already grieved for lost loved ones, that there was a possibility of foul play, that is doubly difficult. Young Tom was also called for and I addressed them both.

"I regret very much that I must give you this news, and there is no way to soften the blow. It appears that both Janet and Margaret were murdered."

The effect on the father and son was devastating. Young Tom broke down immediately and wept for his beloved wife and the baby he never knew – as if he had not shed enough tears already. Old Tom was stoic, but a dark rage sat behind his eyes. He lowered his head into his hands.

"And now I must ask you," I continued, "if you can think of anyone – anyone at all – who would have wished harm to your aunt and to Margaret."

Old Tom said nothing, but his son wailed that Janet had not an enemy in the world and why would anyone bear even an unkind thought to his dear, dear Margaret who had never harmed anyone in her life.

It was McArdle who put into words what Old Tom was probably thinking. "You know, Bremner, they may have been the victims, but perhaps they were not the targets."

"I don't follow you," I said, genuinely perplexed. "You mean this outrage was aimed at someone else?"

"Oh no. Putting a mould into Janet's cottage and sending a poisoned photograph to Margaret – these were specific and carefully-executed acts. But what is the worst possible thing someone could do to another soul? Not kill him. Oh, no. It is worse by far to kill someone dear to him and to leave him alive to mourn."

Old Tom nodded silently in assent.

"And there may be enough people who bear a grudge against either of the Morrises. Business rivals, jealous professionals, someone who holds him responsible for some imagined harm. We even discussed my own mother."

I glanced at the elder Morris, who sighed. "Davie and I have talked about that. I know what she thought in her grief. And if you're thinking that he is carrying out some kind of revenge, I tell you I simply will not believe it."

McArdle spoke up again. "What we have here is a particularly twisted individual. And someone who knows a lot about poisons and medical matters. At least as much as William McIntosh, if not more. And a mould expert, which William is certainly not."

"I came to the exact same conclusion," I agreed. "I feel we have to question every medical and science man in St. Andrews. And goodness knows there are enough of them."

McArdle said nothing in response to this. But from later events I now know exactly what he was thinking.

I assured the Morrises that the police were giving this matter the highest priority and issuing them a stern caution to take care and to report anything suspicious, however trivial. I also asked them not to mention the suspicion of murder to anyone – even their own families – lest the perpetrator hear of it and be warned off or made watchful. I left for my club match and McArdle prepared for his – a game with three of his fellow Black Watch officers, I understood.

After my match, I returned to the Morris shop. It was the second of October and the Open Championship at Prestwick was a mere two days away. The Morris family had much to do. But I was heartened to see that they were concentrating on this – it would, perhaps, take their minds off their tragedy for a short while.

Naturally, Old Tom and I fell to discussing the likely outcome. He felt this was the most important Championship for many years and would be hotly contested.

"You see, the very first Open was at Prestwick in 1860, and it was professionals only. It was my idea, you know. With Allan Robertson dead, I though we should find out just who was the best golfer of the rest of us. Well, Willie Park beat me and I took runner-up by two strokes. The next year, gentlemen could play too. I won that and the next one, with Willie second both times, but in '63, Willie won again with me as runner-up, same as the first time. I beat our Andrew Strath in '64, Andrew beat Willie in '65, and Willie beat his brother David in '66. Then I won my fourth title in 1867. Young Tom was fourth after myself, Willie Park and Andrew Strath. After that, my lad beat me twice to second place – he was only seventeen in '68. There's some that think we arranged it that way, but I can assure you I played my best game and he still trounced me. He even got a hole in one, the first ever at an Open. He scored 154 the first year and 157 the next. The best I ever managed when I won was 160. Then in '70 he beat David Strath and Bob Kirk who tied second. He won by twelve strokes. Because Young Tom had taken the belt outright with three straight victories, there was no championship in '71, as you know. The big clubs – Prestwick, Edinburgh and the Royal and Ancient – subscribed for the Claret Jug and agreed on the rotating venues at Prestwick, Musselburgh and here. The 1872 was again at Prestwick and Young Tom beat David Strath again. On the course here in '73, Tom Kidd beat Old Daw Anderson's son, Jamie – Young Tom and Bob Kirk from Blackheath shared third."

"That's Tom Kidd who has caddied for me before, isn't it?" I remembered the '73 Open. "All that rain beforehand and puddles of water everywhere. The one-stroke penalty for taking the ball out of casual water made for some high scores."

"Oh aye! Tommy Kidd's 179 was one of the highest ever over 36 holes! He's a long hitter, our Kidd. His 91 and 88 beat Jamie Anderson by just one stroke. But it was good to see St. Andrews come one, two, three – even if the third was shared. Last year at Musselburgh, Young Tom was runner-up to Mungo Park. This year we're back at Prestwick again and the smart money is on Willie or Mungo Park, Young Tom and my man Bob Martin. Bob's a good caddy and a fine club and ball-maker, and I hope he wins it if Young Tom doesn't. But we'll see. The boy Jamie Anderson has a good chance as well."[19]

"And yourself, Tom? You don't fancy your own chances for a fifth time?"

He shook his head. "I'm fifty-four years old. I'm an old man. There are younger and better players. But Young Tom has a chance, if he can keep his mind on the game."

"So the betting will be lively, then."

"Aye. If Willie Park wins, it'll be his fourth time, the same as me and Young Tom. The Edinburgh men would dearly love that, but they wouldn't mind if Mungo won it again like last year. The Prestwick men – well, nobody from

---

[19] Bob Martin won in 1876 and again in 1885, on his home turf of St. Andrews, but Jamie Anderson took the Open three times in a row from 1877 to 1879, on the three different championship courses. The 'boy' Old Tom refers to was 33 years old in 1875!.

there has ever won it. Even when I was working there, I played for St. Andrews. So they'll be champing at the bit for one of their own to take it. Mind you, I did have a wee advantage seeing as I designed that course. I know every one of those twelve holes like I know my own name."

"And Young Tom?"

"He has a fair chance. He still holds the record there, you know. His 1870 first round score was 47. At the first hole he was down in three – and it's a 578 yard par 6."

Of course, I knew most of what he had told me – what golfer doesn't! – but it was good to hear him talk animatedly about the game he so loved and of which he was the greatest ambassador. I was sorry my police duties did not permit me to attend Prestwick. But I knew McArdle was going – not to play, as it transpired, but just to watch – and I resolved to get an accounting from him of the match as soon as ever I could.

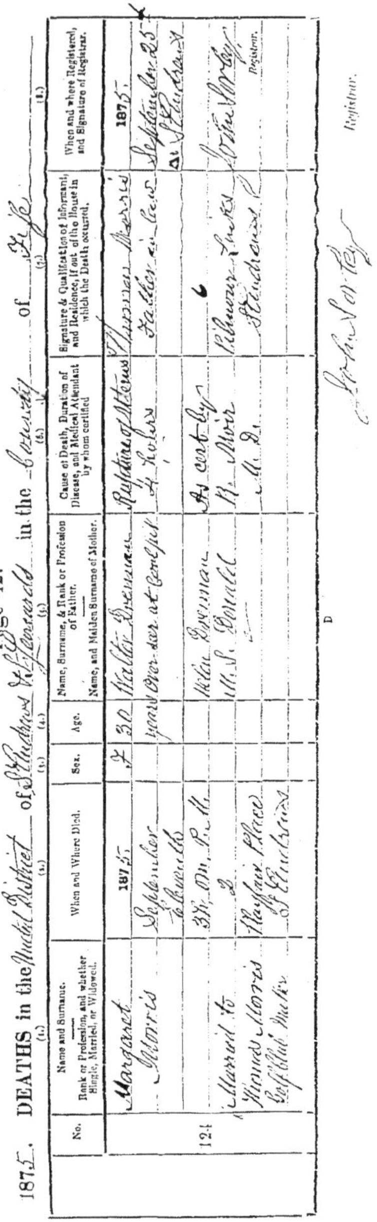

1875. DEATHS in the *District* of *St. Andrews Registered* in the *County* of *Fife*

Page 42.

No.	Name and Surname. Rank or Profession, and whether Single, Married, or Widowed.	When and Where Died.	Sex.	Age.	Name, Surname, & Rank or Profession of Father. Name, and Maiden Surname of Mother.	Cause of Death, Duration of Disease, and Medical Attendant by whom certified.	Signature & Qualification of Informant, and Residence, if out of the House in which the Death occurred.	When and where Registered, and Signature of Registrar.
124	Margaret Morris Married to Thomas Morris Golf Club Maker	1875 September Eleventh 3h. 0m. P.M. 2 Playfair Place St. Andrews	F	30	Walter Drennan Overseer at Coal Pit Helen Drennan M.S. Donald	Rupting of Uterus 4 hours As cert by R. Moir M.D.	Thomas Morris Father in law 6 Pilmour Links St. Andrews	1875 September 25 At St. Andrews John Sorley Registrar

Margaret Morris Married to Thomas Morris
Golf Club maker
1875 September eleventh
3h 0m P.M.
2 Playfair Place St. Andrews
F   30 years
[Father] Walter Dr.ennan Overseer at Coal Pit
[Mother] Helen Dr.ennan
[Maiden Surname] Donald
Rupture of Uterus 4 hrs
As certified by R. Moir M.D. Thomas Morris
Father-in-law
6 Pilmour Links St. Andrews
1875 September 25th at St. Andrews
John Sorley Registrar

Figure 8 Extract from the Deaths Register entry – Margaret Morris

CHAPTER EIGHT

I did not have the opportunity to speak to McArdle about the Prestwick game for two weeks. I was pleased that our earlier cordial relationship appeared to have been re-established, and had written to him at Perth asking him to visit us again at Sandilands and he had replied that Sunday the seventeenth of October was the first opportunity, his military and other duties being onerous at the time.

I had offered him a game at Cupar – we have a lovely little course here, which is said to be the oldest 9-holer in Scotland, that year being its twentieth at Tailabout Farm. I was keen to show the course to McArdle, as this might be the last season of its existence – the Club was struggling to come to terms with the farmer who owned the land and many of us suspected we would not be playing at Tailabout for much longer.[20] Some prefer the new course constructed in 1892, but it is too tricky for an old man, running as it does along the side of the Hill of Tarvit with sloped fairways and hard walking. I have fond memories of the first course and it was a fitting memorial to the great Allan Robertson, golf's first and greatest professional.

McArdle arrived at Cupar station and we drove to the course. During our play, I quizzed him incessantly about the Prestwick Open and in particular the fortunes of the Morris family on that day.

Of course, everyone knows the outcome of the 1875 Open Championship. Bob Martin, who worked for Old Tom at his shop, was narrowly beaten by Willie Park's creditable but not spectacular 166. Martin scored 168, Mungo Park 171, Robert Ferguson of Musselburgh 172 and St. Andrews' James Rennie 177. The two Tom Morrises had been four holes up with five to play and looked set fair to win, but Young Tom had completely broken down at that point. His collapse had, all too naturally, also affected his father, and both lost the remaining five holes, adding to their scores substantially. Otherwise, they could have come first and second.

---

[20] And indeed, Bremner was correct (although he is writing this from the perspective of 1902 when the outcome was well known to him). In 1876 Cupar Golf Club failed to reach an agreement with the land's tenant. They played for a time at a primitive course near Springfield House a mile to the west of Cupar, then Annsmuir opened near Ladybank and the Cupar club took their identity there. The golfing explosion of the 1890s encouraged the Cupar members to establish their own course and moved to its present site in 1892 close to Bremner's house at Sandilands. The present clubhouse was opened in 1907 and retains the original façade.

It was the last time Willie Park would ever win the Open, although his son took it twice in the 1880s[21]. Martin got his honour back the next year, 1876, beating David Strath of North Berwick at St. Andrews, in that memorable game where Strath refused to play off[22] and Old Tom landed fourth behind his old adversary, Willie Park.

But at the 1875 Open, while neither Morris was on his game, Willie Park was on the very top of his form that day, McArdle said. And he evidently thought the long journey to Prestwick less than worthwhile, just to see a St. Andrews man come second.

When McArdle had finished his recounting –on the ninth green, where he sunk a long and rather lucky putt to take the game by a single stroke – he paused in thought for a moment, then raised another matter with me.

"There is something else we might discuss, Bremner. You remember William sent the mould to a man he knows in London, as I believe he told you. He has now had a reply. He has written to you and you'll probably have it tomorrow, but I can give you the gist."

"Why didn't he just give you the letter to bring to me today?"

"Because he felt that it would be disturbing your Sabbath to be concerned with a matter of work, and he considers that he cannot take the responsibility on his shoulders for your being consigned to eternal perdition."

I laughed. "Then he wouldn't approve of this game. Golf on a Sunday."

"He doesn't approve of golf anyway, saying it's just 'a good country walk ruined' and a distraction from work and earnest contemplation."

"I wonder that you two are such good friends when you are so unlike. He disapproves of your golf, your whisky and your tobacco."

"And much else besides. But he has other virtues – tolerance of the weaknesses of others and an understanding of them. I believe he prays for me constantly. It may just be the saving of me yet."

"Anyway, what of his mould?"

"Ah. I wrote the name down because I would never remember it. I can barely pronounce it." He showed me a piece of paper with the words *Stachybotrys atra* written thereupon.

"And what on earth is that, when it's at home," I asked.

---

[21] Willie Park Jr. won the Open in 1887 and 1889, both after a play-off

[22] Bob Martin went on to win two Championships at St. Andrews in 1876 and 1885. In 1876 Martin was declared winner after David Strath of North Berwick was 'considered for disqualification'. After much discussion the competition was declared a tie and it was decided that there should be an 18-hole play-off at a future date. Strath refused to play under such conditions, so the next day, Martin walked around the course without playing and was declared Open Champion.

"It's the name for the fungus. Apparently it is well known in the Ukraine and other parts of Central Europe as growing on wet straw and killing horses. Anyone who breathes it in falls ill within days and often dies."

This rung a vague bell with me. "Horses. Horses. Why is that familiar?"

"Dr. Moir."

"Yes! He said that in his army days he remembered horses dying and a particular smell. Could it be that?"

"We should certainly ask him. I can tell you that Janet Morris's cottage did have a sickly, sweet smell when William exposed the mould on the wallpaper. William has managed to cultivate some of the mould on wet paper and doubtless Dr. Moir could be asked to identify the odour. But here is the strangest thing."

"What's that?"

"William's correspondent asked why we had written to him when we had a greater expert almost on our doorstep."

"Who?" I asked, intrigued.

"None other than Professor James Braid of Edinburgh."

"What? The potato rot fellow?"

"The same."

"Then we should consult that unlikeable man."

"Had I known all this, I could have asked him about it at Prestwick."

"He was at the Open?"

"Not playing. Watching, like I was. And most particularly watching the Morrises. I know he is having clubs made by them. Perhaps he wanted to see Morris clubs and bramble balls in play. Or perhaps something else was his purpose."

"Such as? What are you thinking?"

"I don't know quite what to think. But read William's letter tomorrow. Now, I believe you said Isabella was preparing fish for lunch."

"The best Arbroath smokies. Big and very juicy."

"Then we should not keep her – or them – waiting on us."

Back at Sandilands the children again pestered McArdle for war stories and he obliged. Isabella also inquired whether he had had time to re-acquaint himself with any of his old haunts in St. Andrews.

"Well, as you know, I left when I was a mere boy," he told her, "so I hardly had time to establish any 'haunts' as such. But, yes, I have been down to the Fishergate where I was brought up. I'm pleased to see the Fisher School has a decent new building on Kirkhill instead of sharing the mission hall. I met some fishermen I had known – Johnny Martin, Peter Cunningham, Tam Eye. I even met a lassie I grew up with. Joan, now Mrs. Clark, and she appears to have a decent business selling white fish from her barrow. And it was good to see that the fisherwomen still wear the traditional skirts and aprons and bright-coloured petticoats and they still sit outside their houses, gutting and net-mending and blethering. It fair took me back. There are still a few yells[23] down by the Royal George, so it looks like the fishing is thriving again. It took a bad knock a century or more ago, which is how my family came to be here."

"Oh? How so?"

"Well, as it was told to me, there was a bad storm in the bay one day in November 1765. Three of the five large boats were smashed to matchsticks and almost every man was lost. The fisher folk were always a superstitious lot – you know they can't bear to see a minister before they sail, and they won't hear the words 'orange' or 'pig' or 'stormy'. The tragedy – combined with the knock Scotland had taken over the Jacobites – persuaded a lot of the remaining families to look for work on the land. They turned their back on the sea because they felt the sea had turned its back on them. It had killed their men, destroyed their vessels and brought them an Italian dandy who fancied himself King Charles Edward Stuart[24]. Nothing would talk them back into the waters, it seemed. I think, too, the Press Gangs were about during the Seven Years War and anybody in a sea-side town who could sail a boat was a fair target. In any event, it was almost forty years until the Toun Council arranged for two yawls and a dozen men of the Shetland Fleet to remove to St. Andrews. My grandparents were among the families who came. That, and the new sea-trade meant that the harbour flourished again. Remember, Scotland was cut off from America and the West Indies for many years after the Revolution to allow the English a monopoly. But it looks to be in good heart nowadays. I see a lot of grain and potatoes going out, and a passenger packet boat to Leith. And a new lighthouse."

"And did you see many changes since your years away?"

"A great many! There are more trains coming, and more visitors too. Some of the hotels are away. But the biggest surprise was the Episcopal Church at the eastern end of North Street. Somebody's moved it!"

Isabella laughed. "Oh, that was something of a *cause célèbre*. It was only a few years ago – perhaps '69. It got shifted down the coast to Buckhaven, stone by stone."

---

[23] Small fishing vessels typical of the time and place

[24] This is "Bonnie Prince Charlie", the Young Pretender to the Stuart crown, whose emergence in Scotland led to the 1745 Jacobite revolt and its disastrous aftermaths. A dissolute drunkard to the end, he died in Rome in 1788.

"So I gather. I found our old house, though. As dingy and squalid as ever."

"At the Fishergate?"

"By the Royal George warehouse. Although that, too, has been turned into housing, I notice. Tiny but-an'-bens with a pub at each end. The smell of the gasworks on one side and that of the harbour on the other. When will somebody realise that people cannot be expected to live decent lives if they cannot have decent houses, food and water? I do believe the thing I craved most when I went away was not distance, but sunlight and fresh air."

"I'm sure you had plenty of that at sea, McArdle," I interposed, sensing a political turn to the conversation, something Isabella will never allow at table.

"Not a bit of it! Mostly sleeping ten to a stuffy galley!"

"In the army then? Abroad in the East?"

"Steamy barracks, foul water and worse food."

Isabella laughed again. McArdle was making light of his ordeals, but I knew from my own army days that a soldier's life was not all marching proudly about in the open air. Much of it was tedious, confined, noisome and frightening."

"So you finally came home to get decent weather?" I suggested. "I can hardly believe that, McArdle!"

"Oh, I'll grant you, when the wind blows off the bay and the rain comes at you horizontally, there are more clement places to be than St. Andrews. But then I remember swimming at the Step Rock as a boy and collecting mussel-scalps with William McIntosh and running about on the Scores. I see there's a bathing shelter there now, and a skating rink, too, I'm told, in the winter."

"And did you attend the Lammas fair this year?" Isabella asked. This, the last remnant of the five mediaeval hiring fairs, had become more of an entertainment and a market for general goods than a place for farm workers to fee their services for a year or a half-year. But it was renowned, even as far as Cupar.

"I did!" McArdle replied with enthusiasm. "And I was amazed to find it lasted the Tuesday as well as the Monday. The beer pavilion at the Queens Gardens did a roaring trade, from what I could see. I don't know if many farm workers got fee'd but a fair few got fleein', I would say! And there were booths, steam-engine rides and dancing. I ventured at a rifle gallery and came away with a china pot for three bulls-eyes."

We had more discourse on the many expansions and alterations to the Toun which had taken place in McArdle's absence, and he had noted the growing reliance on travellers, visitors and the holiday trade. The old Linseed Market might be away, but many an hotel was springing up in its stead.

McArdle left for Perth in the early evening, having agreed to a re-match the following weekend and I sat alone in my study, pondering the matter of the mould. The next morning I did indeed receive a communication from William McIntosh. It was not a letter so much as a scientific treatise, most of which was over my head. I give it here, as it may mean more to a better informed reader.

Letter from Dr. W. McIntosh

Murthly Hospital, Perthshire
Saturday, October 16th, 1875

To: Captain James Bremner
Chief Constable of Fife
Cupar

Dear Mr. Bremner
As you know, I despatched samples and drawings of the mould discovered in Miss Janet Morris's cottage at Kincaple to a correspondent in London. He had no difficulty in identifying it as Stachybotrys atra.[25] *This fungus was apparently first described by Professor A. C. Corda in 1837 who isolated it from wallpaper taken from a house in Prague. It is a member of the class* Deuteromycetes *and like its related species sporulates profusely, forming dark conidia, with asexual reproduction. A related genus,* Aspergillus, *includes the mould long known to cause the disease commonly called 'farmer's lung'.* S. atra *has rather unique phialides and conidial morphology – the conidiophores are determinate and macronematous; the phialides are large, ellipsoid and olivaceous; the conidia are ellipsoidal. The spores are not readily disseminated in the air but when dry and disturbed by mechanical means or movement of air, the conidia will disperse into the atmosphere.*
My correspondent considers that S. atra *produces highly toxic compounds as yet unidentified but for which he proposes the term 'satratoxins'.*
In the Ukraine and other parts of Europe there have been outbreaks of disease in horses and other domesticated animals characterized by irritation of the mucous surfaces of the mouth, throat and nose, plus shock (by which is meant a sudden and catastrophic blood loss), necrosis of the

---

[25] This fungus has since been renamed *Stachybotrys chartarum*.

skin, haemorrhage, nervous collapse, and death. The mould readily grows on hay, straw or grain fed to the animals in certain climatic conditions. It has been estimated that even a few milligrammes of the purified extract can cause death. Most outbreaks were associated with hay or feed that became infested during storage under wet conditions. This toxicosis can also be contracted by humans working with or near the contaminated hay or straw.

There are also records of exposure when infested straw is burned or from sleeping on straw mattresses. In humans the progression of symptoms is often a rash, dermatitis, inflammation of the mucous membranes of the mouth and throat, conjunctivitis, tightness in the chest, cough, bloody rhinitis, haemoptysis, headache, fever, fatigue, general malaise and the other symptoms we saw in Margaret Morris. Symptoms develop rapidly – within two or three days of exposure. In severe cases, pulmonary haemorrhage and haemosiderosis occur. The haemolytic effects have also been noted.

I therefore have no hesitation in stating that the mould in Janet Morris's cottage and the substance introduced to Margaret Morris on the photograph are the cause of their respective deaths.

My correspondent also informs me – and I regret that this did not occur to me – that Professor James Braid of Edinburgh, whom we encountered in Cupar, is considerably knowledgeable on Deuteromycetes and might be consulted with profit. I fear if I wrote to him and he remembered me, I would get short shrift. Perhaps this is an avenue which you might explore in an official manner.

I await your further instructions in this matter. In the meantime, I have destroyed the mould I grew on wet paper under glass in my laboratory as I feel it is a danger to the health of my staff and patients should it inadvertently be released. I have retained, secure, the original sample taken at Kincaple.

I remain,

yours sincerely,

William C. McIntosh M.D. F.R.S.E.

As might be imagined, most of this was beyond me: 'conidial morphology' indeed! But I understood the thrust of his conclusion. He certainly felt he had identified the agent of death. But as yet, no perpetrator had come to light.

At this point in my narrative, I feel it important to make it clear that my enthusiasm for McArdle's and McIntosh's mould hypothesis was less than wholehearted. In fact, my belief in both of them was waning. My officers had started on the arduous task of interviewing every relevant scientific and medical gentleman, every amateur naturalist in St. Andrews – but without revealing why they were being asked about moulds or mentioning the deaths, on my strict instructions. They were told to say, if pressed, that it was in connection with a public health matter, at the behest of the Board of Agriculture. Most of them took this with fairly bad grace. The unenviable task of asking eminent and erudite people otiose questions about fungus, on what appeared to be a trivial affair, was taking its toll. Not only were they reporting increasing irritation from those they questioned, they clearly felt it themselves. Some of them were doubting my wisdom in this, and it was especially galling to them that I would not share the reasons for this line of inquiry. I had kept any mention of murder away from my men, as I felt this should not be noised abroad until there we were on firmer ground.

Within the week I was making few friends amongst the intelligentsia, and even Provost Milton had been prompted to write to me, inquiring why police time (and the even more valuable time of the learned Professors and Doctors) was being wasted on what appeared to be an agricultural survey. Had my interest in rot become so wholly absorbing?

In my own thoughts, I was starting to come to the conclusion that this was all flummery. What if there were fungus on some wallpaper? It is common enough. What if a photograph became mouldy? They do. What if an old lady had died, coughing to the last? It is not an unusual end. Margaret Morris's uterine rupture and stillborn child? Tragic, to be sure, but in those days an all-too-typical sequel to what should have been a happy event. And the apparently mysterious and sudden appearance of the said photograph? Young Tom himself might have sent it. The evidence from the workers in the Morris shop was that it had been found there, wrapped, and with Margaret's name on it, not that it had been delivered by any person. Young Tom, frankly, was not completely compos mentis and the horror of the circumstances could have wiped the memory of a trivial love-gift from his head.

I was also now disinclined to take the mouse-blood stuff seriously. It smacked of alchemy and witchery and reeked of unlikelihood. I knew nothing of scientific affairs, but who was to say that this business of dropping one blood into another would not have the effects demonstrated, regardless of any toxic entity present? The autopsies were also less than convincing. Dr. Moir, though a fine man and a good family physician, was merely that. Had he been taken in and bedazzled by William McIntosh with his microscope, his medical Latin and his earnest manner? Pettigrew was probably keen to make his mark as a new Professor in St. Andrews and, like all Dissectors, in my experience, craved the new and the bizarre, the better to astound his fellows at the Royal Society and over College sherry.

Then there was William himself. He was not, by his own admission, an expert in any field touching this matter. In truth, he spent his time with lunatics, simpletons and ravers. Did he rave himself? Had his attack on Professor Braid at the Cupar meeting been equally unjustified and cavalier, arising out of professional jealousy?

Finally, there was McArdle – ah, McArdle! McIntosh was clearly in awe of his slightly elder friend – possible even in thrall. Was there undue influence at play? Would there still be a link with the mad mother? Was this, after all, some bizarre vendetta on the Morrises by a man who professed friendship and a lifelong debt to them? I wondered, not for the first time, why Captain McArdle, a soldier promoted rapidly and clearly on merit, and holder of the highest military honour his Queen and Country could bestow, should find himself in the position of a pen pusher. Recruiting, by Jove! He could have picked any assignment or billet he wanted, one assumed, and even been attached to a regiment of his choice. He had admitted to performing the some duty for the War Office, so he presumably had the ear of his superiors. No, there was more to McArdle's reappearance in Scotland than met the eye.

It was on the twenty-first of October that I received a letter – a short note, really – from McArdle, written the previous day, to say that although we had tentatively agreed a return match at some unspecified date, he would be unable to oblige me as he had a funeral to attend and then an army matter was taking him furth of Perth for a few weeks and possibly until Christmas.

I must own that I gave a sigh of relief. Much as I liked the man McArdle and enjoyed his society, I was disquieted by his persistent harping on about murder. With him away, the whole affair might die down. He might even come back with a clearer head and, with the benefit of distance and reflection, see that he was letting his affection for Old Tom Morris blinker his judgement. And if, perchance, he was in some way involved in the deaths, then his absence would mitigate against any further problems. My men could get back to their accustomed diet of domestic upsets, minor housebreakings, tavern brawls and complaints about fisher folk depositing their heads and guts in

Market Street under the noses of gentlefolk. So, all in all, McArdle was best out of the way. Sometimes it is better to concentrate upon the nefarious doings of the living rather than harp on the dead. And I had no Detective Officer on my force to take the matter any further.

It may seem callous, but the Morrises were buried and their deaths certified and registered according to statute. I was able to write to Provost Milton and assure him that the line of enquiry I had been pursuing on fungus was now at an end, and the matter put to rest. His learned friends could go back to their dusty books and dry arguments, free from any more police interest.

I say all this now, not because I seek to justify my own later actions, but because it may prove illuminating in the light of subsequent events.

But I did wonder at McArdle attending a funeral. Did death follow him around? Was he in some way implicated? Had I then known the identity of the deceased, and McArdle's purpose, my thoughts and actions might have been somewhat other than they were.

Figure 9 Young Tom Morris with his Open Championship belt

CHAPTER NINE

I t was indeed almost Christmas until I again saw McArdle. But in the intervening period I discovered a great deal more about the man.

November 1875 was a difficult month for Fife Police. Not least there was the fishing fleet tragedy. A storm blew up around three boats from Cellardyke and St. Monans. The vessels and thirty-seven men were lost. It was as if, by hearing McArdle talk about the 1765 disaster, we had wished another upon ourselves, one hundred and ten years later, almost to the day.

We should recall that 1875 had been a rather momentous year all round. The Alexandra Palace was opened. Henry Cavendish Jones persuaded the All England Croquet Club at Wimbledon to replace a croquet court with a lawn for tennis (and Isabella was at me to provide something similar in our garden). Gladstone was gone. Disraeli had bought us the Suez Canal with money from his Jewish friends, primarily the Rothschilds. Captain Webb swam the Channel. Women had a college of their own in Cambridge and – on a more modest scale – in Edinburgh[26]. The Fenian, Parnell, had begun his ravings about Home Rule for Ireland – thankfully, that nuisance John Mitchell of Tipperary was not allowed to take his seat in the Westminster Commons and forced a second election, which he again won, but died soon after.

The news from abroad was also unsettling. War in the Balkans was inevitable if the Turks could not tame Bosnia and the Serbs, which they did not. The aftermath of the Spanish Succession question – which had provided the excuse for the Franco-German War of 1870-1871 – continued to destabilise Spain. With Queen Isabel II deposed in 1868 and General Prim, leader of the Provisional Government assassinated in 1870, the Carlists rose again in the north. A rebel army reached the strength of fifty thousand by 1873, King Amadeo abdicated, the Spanish Republic was proclaimed and Don Carlos Calderón won Navarra and Catalonia, but failed to take Bilbao. By May 1874 the Spanish Republic was terminated and the young Alfonso XIII declared King. But when Don Carlos was foiled in his siege of Pamplona and he suffered defeats at Trevino in July and elsewhere, it looked like his forces would not last out the year.[27]

Worst of all, at least in prospect, was 'the war that did not happen'.

---

[26] Respectively, Girton College and the Edinburgh School of Cookery, precursor of Queen Margaret College

[27] After defeats by General Fernando Primo de Rivera at Montejurra on February 17th 1876 and the Carlist stronghold of Estella on the 19th, Don Carlos left Spain for the last time.

Smarting from the outcome of 1871, the German Chancellor, Bismarck, wished a further a war with France and to divide up the Balkans with Russia.

I mention all of this, not because I believe anyone knows or cares, now that we have entered the Twentieth Century and are at peace with the Boers[28] and Germany, but because it had a direct bearing on subsequent events in the McArdle story and it also set the scene for other happenings the next year, notably the fact that I, as Chief Constable, had to prepare for a Royal visit.

I discovered this – and more – when I was dealing with an altercation in Cupar. A squad of Black Watch men had alighted from a train at Cupar station, en route from Edinburgh to their Perth Barracks. Rather than wait for the connection at the platform, their Corporal had decided they might profitably while away the time by visiting a nearby hostelry. This in itself would not have been a problem – and the landlord would have appreciated the unexpected trade – had it not been the evening on which the Fife Mounted Rifles[29] had chosen to hold one of their regular meetings in the same tavern. Nonplussed at finding their accustomed berths by the ingle occupied by Highlanders, the Cavalrymen started some banter about 'dress-up sojers' – a reference to the full parade kit the Black Watch men were sporting. This was rejoindered by much chi-iking about 'part-time cuddy-men' and the like. It might have stopped there, but a Highlander spotted a helmet which had pride of place atop the bar gantry ever since 1860 (for this tavern was a home-from-home for the Old Fifes) and took it down, making much sport of the silver trim and the Thane of Fife and St. Andrews Cross helmet plate. A lewd translation which was apparently given of the motto *'Pro Aris et Focis'*, I leave to the imagination of the reader.[30] Finally, insult upon insult, the plume was cut and handed to a local doxy who pranced about with it, play-acting a horse's tail.

---

[28] Bremner is writing this just after the Second Boer War, which had begun in 1899, ended with the Treaty of Vereeniging in May 1902.

[29] Bremner is slightly off-target here. The Old Fifes comprised the Forfar Troop (raised in 1793) and the Fifeshire Light Dr.agoons (around 1798) which become the Fife Yeomanry Cavalry –a unit of seven troops under the Earl of Crawford –and gained the designation 'Royal' in 1814. In 1860 the Fifeshire Mounted Rifle Volunteers were created under the Earl of Rosslyn with the 1st Company at Cupar, 2nd Company at St. Andrews, 3rd Company at Kirkcaldy and 4th Company at Dunfermline. In 1870, by the time of which Bremner is writing, they had become the 1st Fifeshire Light Horse Volunteer Corps, under Lt-Col Anstruther Thomson based at Cupar, with a strength of 240 all ranks. The Forfar Troop became the Forfar Light Horse Volunteer Corps in 1875 and attached themselves to the Fife Light Horse, who were said to be 'stronger and more solidly organised'. Their informal name 'The Old Fifes' was used.

[30] Properly translated, it means 'For our altars and hearths' (Cicero). By an interesting coincidence, the same Thane of Fife cap badge was worn by the Fife Police and, from 1887 to 1906, by the Black Watch 6th Volunteer Battalion.

The ensuing *mêlée* was sufficient for the tavern man to call out the local police and, fortunately for the two constables involved, the Rifles' adjutant, Captain Crabtree, along with Sergeant-Major Coutts, arrived in time to restore some vestige of order. The Volunteers were ordered out and the Black Watch men were invited to spend the night courtesy of the Cupar gaol pending my attention to the matter in the morning. Fortunately, they went meekly and without demur, my constables having made sure they had paid the tavern-keeper for the beverage consumed. Meanwhile, a message was dispatched to Perth so that the regiment would not fear it had lost a party of deserters.

I was faced with this *fait accompli* when I arrived at my office next morning. I was also in receipt of a return message from the Adjutant at Perth to the effect that the alleged offences were of a sufficiently serious nature to require that he visit me during the day to discuss the matter and would I be so kind as to keep his men under close guard until his arrival. I – and my Cupar Sergeant, who was sporting a glorious black eye acquired during the altercation – agreed that this was in all ways the best plan and we left the Forty-seconders cooling their heels a while longer. I did want to send a strong signal that such behaviour would not be tolerated from the military.

In the afternoon I received Major William Wood and Lieutenant-Adjutant Andrew Scott Stevenson, come to retrieve their men. Captain Crabtree was with me. Lieutenant Stevenson was in uniform but Major Wood was not. Stevenson did most of the talking, and he could not have been more apologetic and reasonable over the affair.

It is my experience of military men that, when faced with the civilian authorities, they tend to bluff and bluster and make it clear that they were away fighting for Queen and country while the rest of use were tucked up safely at home. But there was none of that from the two Black Watch officers. I have no doubt that I could have merely had the soldiers escorted to the station and they would have gone quietly enough, with an effusive apology from the officers.

But Wood and Stevenson were the very souls of reasonableness, and fully accepted their men's faults. For my part, I allowed that the Volunteers had overstepped the mark and, had they greeted the Forty-seconders as comrades-in-arms rather than intruders upon their demesne, the evening might have ended in a spirit of fellowship rather than bowls of Cupar gaol porage. Crabtree was also at pains to admit that the Rifles were not without blame and perhaps had partaken o'er deeply of the amber fluid. Not for nothing were they occasionally referred to as 'The Fife Tight Horse'.

The affair amicably resolved, the Black Watch men were paraded from their cells and stood rather sheepishly in front of their officers. But the Adjutant would have none of that! He ordered them to attention and parade-marched them up the street towards the railway station.

I was as surprised as they were when they found themselves marching past the Volunteers, all at attention and presenting arms. The Black Watch men raised their bonnets and gave three 'Huzzahs!' in return salute.

Nonetheless, I had no doubt that their Corporal, nominally in command of them during the regrettable incident, would be on the receiving end of summary judgement back at the Queen's Barracks in Perth.

But I also had another item on my agenda – discovering more about the mysterious McArdle, and the ideal opportunity presented itself. Major Wood had remained, as he expressed himself desirous of speaking with me on another matter, and in any case he was going on elsewhere by a later train rather than returning to Perth. We repaired to my office for coffee.

"Mr. Bremner," he started. "It is fortuitous that I was able to visit you on this matter. It allows me to bring up another, more delicate in its nature. Had I visited you openly, it might have led to speculation. This is fine cover, though.

"Does it involve Captain McArdle?" I ventured.

Wood sat upright in his chair. "By the Lord Harry! Everything McArdle says about you is true! You are one step ahead of the march, are you not?"

It was now my turn to show puzzlement. "McArdle has spoken of me? I rather thought you might be here to speak to me about him."

"Indeed I am. However, what I have to say concerns you more. But why would you think I had come to talk specifically about Davie McArdle?"

I took a deep breath and plunged into an account of the troubling events which had beset St. Andrews, the Morris family and myself ever since McArdle's re-appearance in Fife. I finished by voicing my concerns that he might have played a larger role in these matters than simply that of an involved bystander and aspiring amateur sleuth. Major Wood listed with rapt concentration and, when I had finished, his reaction was the one I might least have expected.

He burst into laughter.

I could do nothing but look on dumbfounded as he wiped his eyes and tried to stop his shoulders shaking. Finally he spoke. "Oh, Mr. Bremner! That is definitely one for the Officers' Mess tonight! McArdle a suspected murderer. Yes, we'll have some fine sport with him when he comes back, indeed we will!" And he collapsed into mirth once again.

I fear my irritation was showing somewhat. "Come now, Major. You must admit he has been in St. Andrews rather a lot and at rather convenient times of late. And there is this mysterious 'funeral' he had to rush off to attend, just as it became clear that he might be leading us a merry dance with his moulds and murders and poisons and the like!"

Wood had by now subsided. "Very well, Bremner. There is indeed a reason for McArdle's frequency at St. Andrews and his newly-restored passion for the golf. You, or rather the Lord Lieutenant of Fife, will be receiving notification of this shortly from Sir John McLeod."[31]

"Concerning what?"

"Next year, you will be entertaining a certain Royal Person at St. Andrews. I am to start you thinking about the necessary arrangements."

I rose slowly to my feet. "What? You mean... Her Majesty, here in Fife?"

"Oh, no, no. Not the Queen herself. Although she will be nearby, at Balmoral, as is her practice in the summer months. But Prince Leopold is to be installed as Captain of the Royal and Ancient.[32] Most of the members do not know this as yet, although General Moncrieffe is in the Prime Minister's confidence on this, as will be your Members of Parliament very shortly. You are to begin your security preparations forthwith. The reason why I have been asked to speak with you is that your liaison in this matter will be one of our officers. The one best known to you."

"Oh, you don't mean McArdle! For goodness' sake..."

"Yes, McArdle," Major Wood answered with a chuckle. "The well-known master-criminal and arch-poisoner! What do you say to that?"

I was dumbstruck. Wood continued.

"And I'm sure your next question would have been: 'Why McArdle?' To answer that, you need only think about the funeral you mentioned. October the twenty-first I believe it was? Just think – what funeral took place that day, some distance north from here? Hmmm?"

When I realised the answer, I was even more dumbfounded than before. "No! Surely not! McArdle was never at the burial of John Brown's father!"

"Indeed he was. John Brown, Ghillie, Highland Servant and *confidante* to Her Imperial Majesty. His father passed away and was buried at Micras. Of course, the Queen could not attend the funeral itself in the kirkyard, but she watched it with field glasses. They were provided by the Black Watch officer she always requests to attend her when she is in Scotland – Captain David McArdle V.C."

---

[31] Lieutenant-Colonel Sir John Chetham McLeod, K.C.B. was in command of the regiment from 1868-1877. Lieutenant-General Sir Duncan Alexander Cameron, G.C.B. was nominally the regiment's Colonel 1863-1888 and was a General from 5 December 1874. He was indeed Governor of the Royal Military College at Sandhurst 1868-1875 and died in 1888.

[32] Prince Leopold (1853-84), later Duke of Albany, Queen Victoria's youngest son, was probably the most interesting and most intelligent of all the Queen's children, and the first royal to attend Oxford. He was also the first royal haemophiliac

"McArdle is known to the Queen? But…"

"Oh, he is more than 'known' to Her. He has Her confidence. In fact, after the funeral, he accompanied Her Majesty back to England and has since left for Europe bearing a personal message and a War Office commission."

"Message? To whom?"

"Ah, well now! I may be out of turn in telling you this, but if it helps turn your gaze away from McArdle the murderer, I see no harm in it. I'm sure you know that Her Majesty takes a keen interest in foreign affairs and the doings of European monarchs. Since she is mother-in-law or grandmother to most of them, she regards it as just keeping her eye on the family, I'm sure. For example, back in '64 it was Queen Victoria, not Her ministers, who kept us out of the Prussia-Austria-Denmark war. It is at Queen Victoria's insistence that we uphold Turkish hegemony in the East as a bulwark against Russia. Now she fears renewed hostilities between France and the Prussians, who control all of Germany. Since the German Emperor's son has married her daughter,[33] she has written to him. Rather a stiff note, I believe."

I was aghast, and said so.

"Oh yes. That jumped-up sailor Bismarck seeks a military alliance with Austria-Hungary and Russia against France. Of course, Wilhelm, Franz Joseph and Alexander have their Three Emperors' Treaty. Now Russia and Britain must make it very clear that should there be any movement by the other two against France, we would not tolerate it and would lend support. So an envoy carries a letter to Emperor Wilhelm in those terms, but couched diplomatically, as is the way with such things. However, McArdle is along for a number of reasons. First, he is the envoy's personal guard. Second, his German is creditably good, as is his French. I believe he also has a smattering of Russian. And third, he is to seek out Bismarck's senior officers and make it clear, in terms that no diplomatist could, that despite our political differences around the globe, Britain will tolerate no further loss of French power. Should it come to war, British regiments – doubtless with the Scots to the fore as usual – will join the battle. I think we can depend on McArdle to express himself robustly. In fact, I shouldn't be surprised if he offers a fist-fight with Bismarck himself to settle the matter!"

"But why McArdle?" I asked, still amazed.

"You mean, why does he have the Queen's confidence? I know the man better than anyone, and I couldn't say for sure myself. There was a time when he was detached from the regiment between '68 and the Ashanti wars. The

---

[33] Freiderich, the son of Emperor Wilhelm I, married Queen Victoria's daughter (also Victoria) the Princess Royal, and reigned for 99 days in 1888 as Emperor Freiderich III. Their eldest son became Kaiser Wilhelm II.

rest of us were languishing around in home postings but he was up to his neck in something or other in London. All to do with Fenian sympathisers in the army, I hear. McArdle is rather dark on that subject, as he can be on occasion. All I know is, that when he got his medal from Her Majesty at Osborne, she is reported to have said to him: 'Captain McArdle, this is as much for your earlier service as for your recent gallantry'. What do you make of that? And now, when Herself is in Perth or Stirling or Balmoral, Davie McArdle is called to the Presence. I think she just plain likes him!"

I finally found my voice.

"And what does your Colonel say about all this?"

"Oh, he's delighted, naturally. Anything that keeps the 42nd to the fore is a good thing. In fact, the regiment was Her Majesty's Guard at Balmoral this Summer, which was doubtless something to do with McArdle's influence. You see, there are changes around the corner for the army, mark my words. Some regiments may well disappear for ever. But with a Black Watch man in her thoughts, it is unlikely that Her Majesty will be Graciously Pleased to abolish us!"

Light was beginning to dawn. "I see. So when it comes to arranging for discreet security around the Prince…"

"McArdle will be just the man. So you'll be seeing a lot more of him. I believe you first ran into him on the links in any case, and the two of you are quite social."

The import of this struck me for the first time. "You mean, he engineered our meeting and our acquaintance?"

"Probably not. But it must have saved him making a more formal introduction. So I fear you will be rather stuck with Captain McArdle for the foreseeable future. Better not lock him up, eh?"

This was all getting a bit too much! "I really do think I might have been told all this by more official channels."

"Oh, doubtless you will be. But Sir John knew Lieutenant Stevenson was coming here today so he asked me to tag along, and told me the whole story in order that I might prepare you. He felt that, had it been announced to you by the Lord Lieutenant, you might have felt somewhat circumvented. This way, you can have your ducks in a row beforehand. In point of fact, it was McArdle who first suggested bringing you into the plot ahead of time. He says you are 'sound', if apt to flap around rather when in a sand-bunker."

I really did not know what to say. On the one hand, a vote of confidence from McArdle was rather a cheek on his part, I felt. But against that, I was glad to be apprised early of the Royal visit. There would be much to do. Had McArdle been playing me all along? Were his regular visits to Isabella's table merely a way to inveigle himself into my confidence? Or was he just what he seemed – a soldier pleased to be home and make friends, albeit with another agenda to serve? My confusion was now almost total.

"It seems rather hard to credit, I must say, that a mere Captain is charged with so much responsibility."

"Well, he has been offered Brevet-Major status, but as he always says – 'why take the pay of the rank below and the blame of the rank above?' I see his point."

"Yes, but there's also that matter of promotion from the ranks. He makes no secret of it – he's really an enlisted man who has jumped a couple of hoops!"

"Indeed," the Major said, and stood to take his leave. "Well, now you know as much as I do, Mr. Bremner. Keep it close for the present, but be ready for it all to burst upon you."

"I shall, Major, never fear. And again, I should thank you for your understanding in the matter of last night's rammy."

"And I yours. On this short acquaintance, I think I can say that McArdle was right about trusting you. And us jumped-up enlisted men stick together, you know!"

"What? You too? I mean…"

"Ocht, aye. I joined up in 1843 and I was Sergeant Major and Quartermaster when McArdle joined. Or maybe I was Adjutant by then. Half-pay Captain in '63 and not a Brevet-Major until five years ago. But I originally enlisted as a Private Soldier, just like Davie McArdle."

"Are you the one that fed him whisky to join him up?" I asked with a laugh.

"Aye, he blames me for that! You could say I owe him a favour for it. But then, he owes me a few as well. In fact, I retired about two years back, but I am occasionally asked to help out with affairs at the 57th Brigade Depot. Sir John felt that a matter like this was probably best not left to a – how shall I put it – more regular officer like Colonel Harenc, the Depot Commanding Officer. He would have the whole place in a state of high alert. Be only a matter of days before somebody coughed at the wrong time and got shot, just out of sheer nerves."

Then shaking my hand and calling me 'Captain' Bremner, as military men tend to do to retired officers, he took his leave of me. For my part, I felt I was taking leave of my senses. Ignoring my duties for the rest of the day, I went home and confessed of a headache to Isabella, who put me straight to bed with a hot toddy.

Whisky is tolerated at Sandilands when taken medicinally. It's all one to me.

Figure 10 The disputed helmet of the Fifeshire Mounted Rifles.
It dates from about 1860.

BRUCE DURIE

CHAPTER TEN

I have no doubt William McIntosh would have diagnosed my malaise as neurasthenia and prescribed a solid dose of healthy work to keep my mind active. I diagnosed it as too much going on for a simple County Chief Constable to cope with, and took a day off to play golf and restore my spirits. That, plus Isabella's constant ministering, brought me back to sanity and I was back at my desk within two days and fully in control again. One of my first acts was to send a letter to McArdle at Perth. I had no idea when he would be back, but it would wait for him. I suggested that he join us for the annual Fife Police golf match, always held on Christmas Eve, weather permitting, and a jolly time in the Clubhouse if rain prevented outdoor enjoyment. I trusted he would be back in time to take part as my guest. I also said that if he had no other plans for Christmas he was more than welcome to join us at Sandilands and mentioned Isabella's New Year party, to which we hoped he could come. We had also invited William McIntosh and his sister, Agnes.

I received a cordial reply from McArdle on the twenty-third of December informing me that he had returned and would be deeply honoured to get his clubs out with the Constabulary the next day. He was due two weeks' leave, he said, and planned to spend them at Rusack's in St. Andrews. *Speaking 'creditably good German' with the owner* I reflected wryly, but dismissed the thought as uncharitable. As for Christmas, he had already accepted a kind invitation from Tom Morris and his family to spend the day with them. But at New Year, wild tigers would not keep him from Isabella's salon and my cigars.

We met up at the appointed hour on the Friday, getting caddies and new balls from Old Tom Morris. I arrived just as McArdle was asking after the health of Young Tom. Apparently he had been playing, and had even won a challenge match offered by a Mr. Molesworth of England. Unwilling at first, Young Tom's friends persuaded him it was a good way to take his mind off things and afterwards he went as far as to say that it was mainly not to let down his many friends and well-wishers that he had entered into it. However, his father now told us, with the Yuletide season approaching, Young Tom had again slumped into a despair, and it would be understood if McArdle did not want to join them on Christmas Day with such a pall of gloom about the place. McArdle replied gallantly that he would not miss it for worlds, and perhaps the presence of a guest would bring the mourning lad around somewhat. Morris thanked him, and we headed for the first tee.

McArdle was paired with a Constable I had judged to be of sufficient standard, and they were up against my Kirkcaldy Superintendent, William Chalmers, and a Sergeant.

Murdoch, incidentally, not being a golfer, was nowhere to be seen, but he would join us for such revelries as there might be after the game. Meanwhile he was doubtless plodding his normal beat. Someone, after all, had to keep the peace while the rest of us were at play.

My foursome was drawn to play far behind McArdle's and we met up as we were on the fifth hole and his four were coming down the Elysian Fields on the Long Hole towards the fourteenth. McArdle and his playing partner had reached the green in two but Chalmers was deep in Hell Bunker and look likely to stay there for the remainder of December. I know it is un-Christian of me to feel delight in the misfortune of others, but Chalmers and I never got on and I regarded him as a most untrustworthy officer. Later events were to prove me correct in this.[34] Exasperated, he conceded the hole, to the chagrin of his partner. To add insult to the injury, McArdle tossed a ball down near where Chalmers had had his sand lie, and jumped in with lofting club, 'just to see if it could be done'. He gave a mighty downward thwack and the pill lifted out high and fast, landing a good ninety yards on, to the front of the green but with enough back-spin to prevent it rolling down the slope towards the rear. I most remember the look of black hatred on the face of Chalmers, and ventured to the Inspector watching with me that McArdle had better not so much as whistle on the Sabbath if Chalmers were in hearing distance, or else he could expect transportation to the Colonies.

Although match play (which is to say, the winner decided by the number of holes won), there was a prize for the least stokes taken on a round. When we checked the cards back at the caddie sheds, McArdle's pair had won it with a joint one hundred and seventy-five, despite Chalmers' misfortune in the bunker. Many professionals could not break eighty-five over the eighteen holes at that time, so the scores were rather good and merited the prize, which was for the winners to buy every other player a drink. Chalmers had torn up his card and left for Kirkcaldy, and so did not partake. The rest of the party made for the clubhouse to join those already home and dry, if dry is the word. We dealt with the first nip and the requisite toasts, then set about subsequent ales and spirits as best we could, every man for himself and De'il tak' the

---

[34] Kirkcaldy Burgh seceded from the Fife Police in 1877, and set up its own Force with William Chalmers as Superintendent. In September 1892, Chalmers was found intoxicated in Kirkcaldy High Street and suspended from duty. He died two months later, possibly at his own hand.

hindmost. I noticed that McArdle did not keep up with the more thirsty of my officers. In fact, he had often taken a drink in my company, but I confess I had never seen the man the worse for it. Clearly, he enjoyed it in moderation.

After exchanging pleasantries and some banter with my Constables – many of whom did not get to see their Chief Constable very often, let alone have him stand them a peg or two – I went over to speak with McArdle, and clapped him on then shoulder.

"So. High Germany, was it?"

He smiled. "Oh, don't think to astound me with your clairvoyance and omniscience, Bremner! Fine well I know that Major Wood put you in the picture about my jaunt."

I laughed. "As he did, McArdle, as he did! But I can't say it didn't come as something of a surprise. That, and… the other engagement up at Abergeldie! You're a dark horse, no mistake."

"Yes. I own I have been less than honest with you about the nature of my duties at Perth. I do indeed take a hand in recruiting and looking after the Brigade Depot, but I have other duties from time to time. I trust you will understand the reasons for the slight subterfuge."

"Slight subterfuge!" I exclaimed. "There you are, gallivanting with, well, You Know Who, and here's me seriously thinking you guilty of crimes beyond imagining! You might have said something!"

"It wasn't up to me to do so. But be assured, at no time did I misuse the friendship and society you have shown me. I would not have traduced the hospitality of your house and that of your good lady wife in such a manner. Shake on it?"

And we so shook. But I deeply wanted to hear more of his foreign escapades, so we drew off to one side away from the constabulary throng – not that they were sensible to much beyond their own clamouring for yet more to swallow.

I gathered, from the little he could tell me, that the diplomatic mission to Emperor Wilhelm's court looked like having had the desired effect. His secondary task, as I now knew, had been to convince the German High Command privately that incursions on France or French holdings would bring Britain and Imperial Russia down on their heads in a most unlikely, but nevertheless persuasive alliance. War, it seemed, was avoided once more. Disraeli could concentrate on the problems in Suez and Egypt without worrying over disputes closer to home or in Bulgaria and the Balkans.

"So you enjoyed your convalescent sea-voyage then?"

"That was the best part," McArdle laughed. "As you know, an army Captain has equivalent rank to a naval Lieutenant and far, far below that of a ship's Captain. But an official envoy is automatically a Vice-Admiral for protocol purposes. The officers didn't know whether to salute me or throw me overboard. In the end, I solved the problem by dining with them and the Petty Officers rather than with the Captain and the Diplomat. Then they found out I had been in the Merchant Service and we all got on fine."

"And did you manage three rounds with Bismarck?"

Here, McArdle let slip an interesting addendum, which I did not fully understand until the next year. It was a simple enough, almost throw-away remark.

"I didn't meet him, which is probably just as well. I fear Chancellor Bismarck has no great love for me," he said, "and nor should he after our previous two encounters. I might have come back bearing a Heidelberg scar."

I let it go at that, as it seemed deep water at the time, and subsequently proved to be so.[35] The discussion then moved to other matters. But I could see that McArdle had something on his mind. Finally he brought up again the question of Professor Braid.

"I have to say that while abroad I thought long and hard about the deaths and the part played by the mould. I was more convinced than ever that Braid was the malefactor. So I visited him at his home in Musselburgh two days ago."

"What? You have been to see him? How?"

"Again, subterfuge. You remember that William had the mould identified by a colleague in London. Did he tell you who this Londoner was?"

"If he did, I've forgotten."

"Then he obviously didn't tell you. You would have remembered the name of Professor Huxley."[36]

"What? Darwin's bulldog?"

"The same. William does seem to know the most extraordinary people. It comes of being extraordinary himself. He and Huxley have had many a colloquy about marine invertebrates, it seems. Remember that Huxley's first post was as a Navy Surgeon, and that he surveyed the sea life of Australia while aboard H.M.S. Rattlesnake. I visited him at the School of Mines,[37]

---

[35] This is one of a number of cryptic references to McArdle's involvement with Chancellor Bismarck, not further elucidated upon in this collection of Bremner's writings. Further searches may bring other journals to light.

[36] Thomas Henry Huxley (1825-1895), indefatigable naturalist, scientific educator and champion of Darwin's theories of evolution by natural selection, was one of the towering intellectual giants of the Victorian era. It says much of William McIntosh that they were in close correspondence

[37] Now Imperial College, London.

taking a letter from William. This laid out our theory about the poisonings and I bid fair to say he was fascinated. Also, he has a particular dislike for Professor Braid – mind you, I have yet to meet anyone who doesn't. So he agreed to help us in a charade. Together we constructed a letter of introduction to Braid, setting me up as an amateur naturalist who had spent some time in the Crimea. I have enough knowledge of the place second-hand from my fellow officers to get away with it. I put to him the puzzling case of horses dying from infested straw and mentioned that Huxley had suggested the mould he and William had identified."

"Braid took the bait?"

"More than took it! He was onto it like a mongoose taking a cobra – showing off his knowledge, expounding on the nature of the toxins involved, suggesting remedies. The man has a deep knowledge of it. And he has more besides."

"What?"

"He has it growing in a sealed glass cage in his hot-house at Musselburgh!"

"No! So he has access to this monstrous toadstool?"

"And its extracts. He didn't show it to me, so he's not making it known that he has it. But I recognised it from the wall at Kincaple and from drawings Huxley showed me. But, I fear, short of bearding him with our suspicions and hoping for a full confession, there seems no way to tie him to the deaths. You're the policeman, Bremner. Any ideas?"

I had to confess, ideas had I none. If it was any small consolation, I reassured McArdle, I no longer held him and McIntosh under suspicion. He allowed that this was scant comfort and he would rather see the murderer of his old friend's family brought to book.

"As would I," I readily agreed. "But – you said it yourself – how to do it? What case do we have? What on earth would an eminent Professor be doing bumping off the nearest and dearest of some golfers?" (If this seems intemperate language and a rather brusque way of treating the horror of the facts, perhaps I may be excused on account of the surroundings and the circumstances. My deep sensitivities for the grief of the Morris family were, and remain, of the most sincere.)

"Well, we shall see," McArdle replied. "Inspiration may come with the New Year. Now that I have seen the man and his noxious fungus, I know that he is to blame. Perhaps he will tip his hand in some wise. Can you keep any eye on him from afar in any way?"

"Not without being fully frank with my opposite number at the Edinburgh police. And I cannot bring myself to do that on the evidence we have thus far."

"No, I see that. But just in case, I left myself with an opening to visit Braid again. I was only in his hot-house briefly but he clearly appreciates unusual flora as well as toadstools. I said I was expecting a crate of exotic plant samples being sent separately. In fact, Huxley arranged for me to collect specimens from Kew and to have them packed. I brought them with me and left them in storage. Oh, don't worry – there is nothing of a dangerous nature, just some unusual shrubs and the like. But it whetted Braid's appetite and, if needs be, I can revisit him."

"He didn't recollect you from Cupar, then? Or connect you with William?"

"He barely saw me at Cupar. And out of context, why would he recognise me? Also, I kept William's name out of any discussions for that very reason. Likewise, Huxley made no mention of him in the letter he gave me. As far as Braid is concerned I am just what I claimed to be – an ex-army man with a penchant for weird flowers and desire to learn at the feet of an authority." McArdle looked over at the clock on the wall. "Anyway, I must be off to Rusack's. I promised myself an early dinner and a hot bath."

With that we parted, agreeing to meet at my house on the New Year. I returned to Sandilands, but not before ensuring that all my men were off the premises and heading for their own homes. Christmas Eve high spirits is one thing, but drunken policemen loose on the streets is beyond the pale, even in Fife!

I should like to be able to record that Christmas Day went well and quietly. But as all the world surely knows, Young Tom Morris was found dead on that morning.

The news came to me by messenger from Murdoch two days later. The gist of his report was as follows:

McArdle had walked to Tom Morris's house on Christmas morning at the agreed time of ten o'clock, expecting nothing more than good cheer and a goose for dinner. Young Tom was not yet up, Old Tom explaining that his son had, about eleven the previous evening, said his goodnights, claiming tiredness, and had retired to his room. Young Tom had been staying with his parents, unable to face the emptiness of his own house. The family understood that the lad might want some time alone on this, the first Christmas without his beloved wife. He had said that he had a special bottle of Madeira sent by a well-wisher and that he would take a drop and 'just sit and think'.

At that moment, there was a clatter from upstairs. Hearing this, McArdle suggested to Old Tom that they go and rouse the younger Morris. Failing to get an answer on knocking at the bedroom door, Old Tom opened it. Young

Tom was dead in a chair, fully clothed, and with some cheese and a half-empty bottle of fortified wine beside him. His mouth and chest were covered with blood and a table was kicked over.

The horror felt by the family can only be imagined. McArdle, it seems, had to take charge and arrange for both Dr. Moir and Murdoch to be summoned. By the time the Constable arrived, Moir had certified the cause of death as a haemorrhage of the lungs, but added a query to this which appears in the Register of Deaths as a bracketed question mark, thus: *Pulmonary haemorrhage causing Apnoea (?)*. He was of the opinion that Young Tom had not been dead long and must have died quickly, as the noise heard was probably his death-throes. The time of discovery was not long after ten A.M., so Moir certified this as the time of death and so it was recorded when Tom's brother James registered the event with John Sorley four days later.

When Murdoch appeared, he was less than pleased to see McArdle at the scene of yet another Morris death and ordered him off the premises, telling him to keep to Rusack's hotel where he would see him later and take a statement.

By the time Murdoch left the Pilmour Links house, the rest of the Morris family had arrived and were consoling the parents and each other. Murdoch headed up Abbotsford Crescent for Rusack's and his appointment with McArdle.

What transpired next is rather glossed over in Murdoch's official report, but I know from other sources and from later conversations that words were exchanged, voices raised and, possibly blows struck. McArdle's version is that Murdoch more or less accused him of complicity in the death. McArdle told him not to be stupid – how could he have done any such thing when he had spent the day before with me, passed the evening quietly in his hotel (as witnesses could bear out) and had not been at the Morris household until just before the death occurred?

Matters got heated, and whether Murdoch attempted to restrain McArdle or not, I have no idea. It seems, though, that Murdoch was knocked to the floor. McArdle then said that if Murdoch wanted to catch the real murderer, he should accompany McArdle on the Monday to Musselburgh where he would learn the full facts. If, after that, he was not satisfied, McArdle would submit himself to police authority. But he asked that I not be informed just as yet.

He also showed Murdoch the Madeira bottle he had taken from beside Young Tom's body without anyone noticing and suggested Murdoch note the details on the label then have it wrapped securely and dealt with in a certain way.

Somehow, he talked Murdoch into this highly speculative, not to say unorthodox course of action. He was right to believe that, had I known about it, I would certainly have stopped either of them taking on any such foolhardy venture – Murdoch by direct command and McArdle by locking up if necessary. But that is exactly what they did.

Later on the twenty-fifth of December, McArdle sent a telegraph to Professor Braid announcing that the promised specimens were due at Leith that morning and that he wished Braid to be the first to see them. He would therefore be at Musselburgh by twelve noon on the twenty-seventh. I knew nothing of this until Murdoch's report reached me, arriving after they would have left. That crafty man had delayed sending it until he knew it would not reach me until the Monday morning. Clearly McArdle had talked him round.

Reading the report, I was flabbergasted. Of course, I was again dismayed to find McArdle implicated in another death. But I was even more perturbed that he had inveigled Murdoch into some madcap scheme to expose Braid. And where had the bottle gone? I might be evidence. If this hare-brained enterprise backfired, it would rebound on me, there was no question of that.

I apologise for that rather scanty description of the events surrounding the death of Young Tom Morris, but the next part of the narrative is known to me in greater detail as Murdoch reported it faithfully and almost verbatim.

As I was later to learn, McArdle, with a still-suspicious Murdoch in tow, set off early on the Monday by steamer. At Leith, McArdle did collect a small crate, but it was not straight from a ship. He had left it in storage some days previously, as he had told me. It contained the exotic plant specimens secured for him by Huxley from Kew Gardens. This they took as they travelled to Musselburgh.

Braid lived in a large but slightly decayed house just west of the Musselburgh golf course and set in substantial grounds bordering the River Esk where it entered the Forth estuary. McArdle noticed the unevenness of the land typical of the area, honeycombed as it was by old coalmining tunnels.

At Braid's house, they found they were expected. McArdle did not introduce Murdoch but made it clear by implication that he was a servant or porter. Braid therefore ignored Murdoch, as the upper classes tend to do with lackeys. This left Murdoch free to observe and remember.

Braid examined the plants and expressed himself delighted with them. McArdle suggested that, as he was wont to travel a great deal and could not hope to care for them, nothing would give him greater pleasure than Braid accepting them to add to his own collections or to pass on for propagation to others as he saw fit. Braid readily accepted and together they moved the box to his hot-house – exactly where McArdle had wanted to be. In fact, Braid was the very soul of bonhomie and produced a bottle of port.

"Do you take port wine, Captain McArdle?" Braid, without waiting for a reply, poured two small glasses. None was offered to the 'manservant' Murdoch, who would have refused in any event, being there in an official capacity, although Braid did not know this. The wine imbibed, Braid turned to his hot house specimens. There were plants of every variety – flowers, shrubs, succulents, bulb plants and tubers – but almost all appeared to be suffering from various kinds of rot or mildew. Some dwarf trees has spectacular fungi growing from them. The whole place smelled of damp earth and mushrooms and McArdle could feel himself staring to sweat from the heat and excessive humidity the growths obviously required. "I seem to remember we discussed an obscure but interesting Deuteromycete on your last visit. Have you any interest in fungi, Captain McArdle?"

"To the extent that I like a mushroom with my bacon. And I spent a good deal of time in India and Africa cleaning it off my webbing after the rainy seasons."

"Ah. But what of these specimens of mine? I'll warrant they're somewhat more remarkable – and more important – than your breakfast variety."

McArdle followed the Professor's pointing finger to where it indicated some leaves covered with a blackening mildew.

"This, for instance, is late blight."

"And what is late blight, Professor?"

"Not a farm man, I see. But if your livelihood had ever depended on potatoes, Captain McArdle, you would know it all too well."

"It's a potato fungus?"

"Well, actually no. It was once thought to be a fungus, and many still casually refer to it as such. But in fact it is now regarded as a water mould, or, to be even more precise, an oomycete. They are free-swimming spores with flagella, and they absorb their food from the surrounding water or soil. Or they may invade the body of another organism for their food. They are quite important in the decomposition of decaying matter. But some are parasites. Their greatest import for us are the many species of water mould which attack cultivated plants. I would go so far as to say they have recently had a major impact on world history – two, as it happens!"

Braid was clearly eager to say more. Once on his subject, Murdoch felt, the professor could go all day, and probably did. He was talking to McArdle, but somewhat absently, attending to his specimens like a mother hen to her brood.

"*Phytophthora infestans*, this organism here that causes late blight, is a

127

parasite of the potato. It followed its host across the Atlantic, but not until some 30 years ago. It likes cool and damp conditions, which explains why, during the summer of 1846, it wiped out almost the entire potato crop of Ireland!"

"The potato famine," McArdle said.

"Indeed. The great Irish potato famine. One of the most disastrous food crises since the plagues of Egypt. I believe over one million died and the same number or possibly more left Ireland for the New World colonies."

"Better watch it doesn't get out around here, then, Sir. I can't imagine the potato farmers of East Lothian being very pleased with you if it did."

"Ah, Captain McArdle. I am much more careful of these specimens than to allow such a thing, I assure you. And of the others."

"The others, Sir?"

"Oh yes. I have collected other species of *Phytophthora*. There are those that will destroy eucalyptus, the avocado, pineapples and many other tropical crop plants. Not that the pineapple is much at risk in Scotland, eh?"

"I fear not, Professor."

"But over here, Captain, over here I have my current obsession. And, I might add, the main provider of my modest livelihood. Behold *Plasmopara viticola*." Braid had moved to a grape vine plant, which was clearly suffering from a blight of some sort. It had a downy mildew of brown patches on the leaves with a white, frosty growth of cotton-like fungus on the underside of each. The grapes themselves had rotted brown and looked like deflated snuff bags.

McArdle peered at the specimen. "The name *viticola* suggests grapes, right enough," he said, suspecting it was time to show some evidence that his ignorance was not as total as the Professor might have imagined. "Is this the 'Noble Rot' I have heard about?"

"Quite the scholar, Captain McArdle, but not, if I may suggest, as knowledgeable on fungi as in Latin! The 'Noble Rot' is *Botrytis cinerea* which, if husbanded correctly, creates wines such as Tokay and Sauternes – deliciously sweet and smooth, but retaining sufficient acidity not to be cloying. Legend has it that in 1650, an attack by the Turks on Hungary delayed the grape harvest. When collected, a fungus had grown on some of the grapes, which were kept separate. When they were tasted, the result was a pleasant surprise. But no! I speak of an insidious parasite of the grape, not a happy accident. Indeed, this specimen of *Phytophthora* is the very parasite that bids fair to destroy the French wine industry even as we speak."

"And the French have asked you to investigate it, Sir?"

"Not directly, no. But there are enough Edinburgh gentlemen with speculations in vineyards and wine importing interests to be concerned, and to have sought my modest talents in the hope of a resolution. Not to mention those whose interest goes little beyond a concern that their supply of after-dinner claret will not dry up overnight!"

"Is that likely?"

"All too likely, Mr. McArdle. The French have also lately suffered from aphid infestations."

"Aphids, Sir? Greenfly?"

"Specifically, a particular *Phylloxera*, often called the Grape Louse. It is something like our greenfly, as you say, but lives on the vine roots. These *insecta* love the vine almost as much as the aforementioned gentlemen oenophiles enjoy its fruits, and for much the same reason. The insects seek to grow fat on it, as do our merchant importers." Braid allowed himself a small chuckle at his small joke. "To this end, the French growers were persuaded to bring over resistant American vine stocks. Inferior, to be sure. I fear the Americas will never produce a wine of any distinction. But their vines brought a new and a different hazard. They introduced, accidentally, it must be said, *Plasmopara viticola*. I played some small part in suggesting an admixture of hydrated lime and cupric sulphate, which has since come to be called the Bordeaux mixture. Not Braid's Mixture, note. There will be no posthumous fame for this humble botanist in that specific. A certain M. Millardet will forever have that singular honour, I fear."

"Any special reason for that, Professor Braid?"

"Ah, well, it is not the custom of our French neighbours to bestow a name on a thing if that name be not of French origin. I do sometimes feel that, ever since their Little Emperor was thwarted in his desire to control Europe – an ambition your regiment did much to spike, I believe – and having no colonies or empire to speak of, they would rather now turn up their collars against the rest of the world and feign it does not exist."

"You may be right, Sir."

"Not that Millardet knows what he's doing. He thought only to stop pilferage, would you believe. He treated his vines with this miraculous mixture simply to allay theft. I can claim in all modesty that had I not suggested he look for its fungicidal properties, he would not now be pursuing it with such vigour."

Braid was examining closely the grape vine. McArdle could tell that the professor was also holding back a certain amount of ill-suppressed rage. But he breathed deeply, forced a smile and turned again to McArdle.

"But, to compensate for any lack of historical distinction I have been honoured academically, and I have also been privileged to have a hand in applying this very compound to the control of pests in potato cultivation, late blight included. Your potato farmers in the Howe of Fife, and those in the Carse of Gowrie to the north, are no strangers to its use, and I have been rewarded most handsomely. Not that worldly recompense is an end in itself, but it comforts an old man in his twilight."

"And have you visited Fife, Professor?"

"Oh, indeed. I am often in Cupar or Ceres overseeing certain testings of this and other chemical compounds on the fruit and crops there."

"Do you ever come to St. Andrews? For the golf perhaps?"

Braid shot McArdle a furious glance, then composed himself. "I am no stranger to that fair town and its University, Captain. I have been honoured to present lectures there on several occasions. But play golf on that heath scrub? Never! It is fit for sowing beets and fattening rabbits, nothing more!"

"That's very strange, Sir."

"Is it so? And how would that be?"

"Well, Professor. A keen golfer like yourself. To visit St. Andrews and not play the Links – it seems unusual. What is more, I believe I have seen you there myself. I am also under the impression that you are having clubs made by Tom Morris. Or perhaps I am mistaken."

Braid turned back to his plants and clutched a small digging trowel. McArdle noticed his knuckles were white with the pressure of his grasp. He had, in effect, accused Braid of lying.

"And do you play, Mr. McArdle?"

"I was born in St. Andrews and I live near there now. So it's more or less compulsory."

"Do you play on the Rabbit Warrens?" He meant the St. Andrews Links.

"I do. But I'm not a member of the Royal and Ancient yet."

"I shouldn't bother, if I were you. Really, it is neither Royal nor Ancient!"

"Why do you say that, Professor?"

"Come, come, Captain McArdle. As you well know, the Honourable Company of Edinburgh Golfers has been playing since at least 1744 – ten years before your precious St. Andrews club was going. We wrote the first set of rules."

"Really? I thought that was the Gentlemen Golfers of Leith."

"The same, Sir, the same. We adopted the new appellation when we came to play at Musselburgh. I'm sure you know how the 'Royal' thing came about?"

"I'm sure I don't, Sir. Perhaps you'll enlighten me."

"Oh, St. Andrews wasn't Royal at all until some 40 years ago – 1834 I believe – when they talked silly old King William into becoming the patron. Got him befuddled on whisky, I'm told, and sprang it on him. He was too far in his cups to say no, as he should have."

McArdle said nothing, Something he had learned in his years dealing with senior officers in the Black Watch, he later told me, was that the least you said, the more forthcoming was the other party. Something to do with a blowhard not liking empty silences, just as nature is said to abhor a vacuum.

Professor Braid continued fiddling with his fungus-rotted plants and did indeed break the silence.

"We have hopes of the Royal Warrant ourselves, McArdle. Did you know that?"

McArdle remained quiet.

"Oh yes. The Musselburgh Golf Club has asked His Royal Highness the Duke of Connaught if he might graciously consent to become our Honorary President. Once 'Royal' – and we are most certainly 'Ancient' – we shall see who controls golf.[38] How will your rabbit warrens weather that storm, McArdle?"

"I couldn't say, Sir, I'm sure. It possibly won't make any difference at all. But I fear I must ask you again, Professor. You claim never to have played at St. Andrews, but I can name you at least one specific day when you were there. And Tom Morris will attest that you have visited his shop on numerous occasions. You are a liar. Why is that, I wonder?"

If McArdle had wanted to provoke a response from this, none was immediately forthcoming. Braid continued to examine his plants, then moved to a wooden bench where an alembic was bubbling over a Bunsen burner. McArdle decided it was time to make a more direct challenge.

"In fact, Professor, I also know of Braid's Mixture. I was at Cupar last July when you presented it to the Farmers Society meeting. I was sitting beside a certain Dr. William McIntosh who all but accused you of stealing the formula from the French and claiming it as your own. Perhaps you remember Dr. McIntosh."

At this taunt, Braid spun on his heel, the sharp trowel still in his hand. "That amateur? McIntosh, you say? I did not trouble to remember his name, as I do not trouble to dignify his ridiculous assertions with a response. The man clearly knew little of fungi and even less of chemistry."

---

[38] In fact, HRH the Duke of Connaught did accept the invitation in 1876, and held the position of Honorary President until his death in 1942; his son, HRH. Prince Arthur, was Honorary Vice-President from 1912 until his death in 1938. The title 'Royal' was added to its name 21 years later

"Do you think so? Well, I can tell you that Dr. McIntosh is a very old, very firm friend of mine and I would trust his word over that of any other man I know. I can also tell you that he is sufficiently well-versed in both fungi and chemistry to have collected and identified *Stachybotrys atra* from the cottage of Janet Morris and to have extracted the toxic essence of it. He even devised a test for it – haemolysis of mouse blood, I believe. And I know that you have cultivated that very fungus. I can see it over there under glass – a wise precaution given the toxic effects of its spores. Professor Huxley has helped Dr. McIntosh identify it. I suggest you have found a way to harness its essence and that you have used it or its extract in at least four murders in the Morris family so far. Doubtless, you plan more."

Braid froze, his face a contorted mask of hatred and rage. He spluttered, the spittle flying from his tightened lips. "Who are you? You come to me with this ridiculous assemblage of uninteresting plant life and what purports to be a communication from Huxley, in all likelihood a forgery. Then you proceed to insult me. Who are you, Sir?"

McArdle looked at him levelly. "I am merely a friend of the Morris family. But I am working closely with the Fife police on this matter. Constable Murdoch here can verify it."

Braid composed himself, possibly aware he had said too much in the presence of a police officer, then he bridled, and drew himself up to his full dignity.

"I have never been so affronted in my life! First you come to my home on a pretext, and now you make these…these…ludicrous allegations against me. I will thank you to leave at once. If you do not, I shall call the police. The Chief Constable of Edinburgh and the Superintendent here are close associates of mine. They will agree with me that you have no right to make such vile accusations against a prominent – yes, prominent – citizen! Nor will they take kindly to the involvement of another police force, probably in an illegal manner!"

And with that, he reached for a hand bell and rang it violently. A moment later a manservant appeared, wearing a leather apron and gloves. He had clearly been gardening just nearby the hot house. He was large, with a boxer's nose and ears. Braid lifted a claw-like hand and extended a finger at McArdle and Murdoch.

"Byng!" he ordered. "See that these… I hesitate to call them 'gentlemen'… are removed from my house and grounds forthwith!"

The man moved towards McArdle. Murdoch meant to interpose himself between the Captain and the burly handyman-gardener, whose domestic duties clearly extended further than mere rose pruning. But McArdle put out a hand to calm Murdoch and stay his move.

"We are leaving, Professor. A final word, though. I know you placed that fungus in the cottage of Tom Morris's aunt. I also know you introduced the toxin to Margaret Morris on a picture, killing her and her baby. And I know you murdered Young Tom by a similar means. I admit there is no direct proof as yet, but I will find it, never fear!"

"Again you accuse me of these imagined crimes? Stuff and nonsense about photographs and an old woman's damp cottage? I have no doubt that Morris's daughter-in-law was syphilitic and his son a drunkard who finally drowned his grief. And as for the old woman, I have never even been to Kincaple. Now leave at once!"

McArdle and Murdoch left, the man Byng shadowing them every step of the way until they were out of the grounds. The gate was firmly shut behind them.

Murdoch, who had said nothing during the whole episode now gave voice to his feelings. "You know, Captain McArdle, I think I have had just about enough of you! Any chance there was of catching that villain has been thrown away! He knows we're on to him, so he can dispose of any evidence and cover his trail. I feel it is my duty to inform Mr. Bremner that your interference in this matter has destroyed any chance we had of bringing the man to justice! Amateurs have no place in police affairs."

McArdle grinned and aimed a well-natured punch at my Constable's chest. "Oh, put your high horse away, Murdoch! Do you not realise what just happened in there?"

Murdoch's brow furrowed, but he gave no answer.

"I certainly intended to enrage him. I didn't reckon to have the same effect on you. Now, I'll buy you a wee dram for Christmas and then we have a couple of appointments, you and I."

"Eh? Where?"

"Musselburgh High Street, and a certain wine merchant. But first the telegraph office. I hope you can write a good description of that Byng fellow. Come on!"

And McArdle was off, leaving a very puzzled Murdoch to follow in his wake.

The 27th of December being a Monday, I would normally have been at work, but I was spending the time at home with my family. It was, after all, only two days since Christmas. Most of Scotland did not celebrate that festival much in those days – many people worked both on Christmas Day and the day after, saving their energies for our own, more pagan merriments at Hogmanay the week after or for Hansel Monday, which marked the Old New Year. But Isabella, with her finer sensitivities and Christian upbringing, liked to make much of the Yule time. The children got presents and we even had a small fir tree erected and decorated in our drawing room, as we had done ever since the birth of our eldest. I blame Prince Albert, dead these fourteen years already but still casting his German manners about the place.

Murdoch telegraphed me later that same day from Edinburgh. It arrived in the late afternoon along with his report of the death and the occurrences at St. Andrews on Christmas day, both of which I received at my office. The import of the message was that McArdle and Murdoch would visit me the next day – there was no possibility of a return from Edinburgh that evening – and would present me with startling new evidence. The reader may well imagine my shock and horror. Young Tom! Another Morris death. And McArdle up to his neck in it again. Clearly I had much to say to him and to Murdoch. I spent the evening turning the facts over and over in my head yet again. Oh yes, I would have much to say to that pair the next morning!

Murdoch and McArdle duly arrived at 11 o'clock on the Tuesday morning, expecting to find me there – as I was – but not expecting my other visitor. At 10.30, my door had burst open and the Lord Lieutenant of Fife had strode in, his face the very mirror of fury. He had berated me soundly without pause – almost without pause for breath! – for most of the intervening half-hour. Now that McArdle was here, he was clearly going to get both barrels as well.

"Ah! So this is the trouble-maker!"

McArdle looked from me to my other visitor. I felt I should make introductions. "This is Captain McArdle, as you have gathered. And Constable Murdoch. I would like you both to meet Lieutenant-Colonel Sir Robert Anstruther, Member of Parliament for Fife and our also our Lord Lieutenant.

McArdle, though somewhat surprised and in no doubt that Sir Robert was not in a sociable mood, extended a hand. "A pleasure, Sir."

Sir Robert did not take his outstretched hand in return. "No pleasure at all, Sir, as you will shortly find out! Bremner, you tell him. I haven't the patience!"

"Sir Robert received this morning, by special messenger, letters from, amongst others, the Principal of the University of Edinburgh, the Director of the Botanic Gardens, also Edinburgh, the Chief Constable of the same, the city's Lord Provost and its M.P. Have I left anyone out, Sir Robert?"

He glared at me impatiently, by way of answer.

"You will understand that Sir Robert is ultimately my superior. He has had brought to his attention, by the letters from these fine gentlemen, the facts of your visit to Professor Braid. The good Professor appears to have spent the rest of the day after your sojourn in his company, pounding on the doors of practically everyone he knows, decrying your name to highest heaven. He wants blood."

"Bremner, this is not a matter to be taken lightly! There are serious charges in these letters! Tell him!"

"Indeed I shall, Sir Robert. But perhaps first we will do McArdle the courtesy of listening to his explanation. We shall also ask Murdoch here for an official statement. Then, if there are police issues, I assure you I shall prosecute them without fear or favour. But I ask you to remember that McArdle visited this Braid with my knowledge." This was not strictly the case, except in that I knew subsequently, and I carefully had not used the word 'permission'. "So any contumely that falls on his head will also land on mine to some extent. I trust that is clear."

"Oh, very clear, Bremner. Very clear indeed. And I assure you, in turn, that if there are consequences of this, you shall be sharing in them."

"We understand each other, then. Proceed, McArdle, if you please."

I knew that Sir Robert was capable of bluster and had a fine, high temper, but was ultimately a fair man. What had engaged his spleen was being woken early to a series of extremely angry letters from men he could not but take seriously. This reflected on him as much as on myself or anyone else. McArdle did not know the man, so I expected he might be cowed by the Lord Lieutenant's rage and rank. But McArdle was made of sterner stuff. He had, after all, faced down the wily Pathan and the fierce Ashanti. I gathered instantly that he would not be put off his stroke by someone he probably considered to be a self-important popinjay and a bravo. Calmly, he sat down without being invited to do so, and began to speak.

"Mr. Bremner may have told you some of this already, in which case my apologies for any repetition. If not, I expect you to hear me out. That is the way amongst officers of my regiment. The same may not have been the case in the Grenadier Guards."

Oh, one hit for McArdle! He evidently did know of the man, at least by repute, and had already got his measure to some extent. Sir Robert fumed, but kept silent for a reason I did not realise immediately, although I came to understand it later in our conversation.

"You will know that Tom Morris, the professional at St. Andrews, has suffered terrible tragedies this year. First his aunt died, then his son's wife and stillborn child, and now his son. For a reason I do not yet understand, they were all poisoned by this Professor Braid. The methods?" He began to count off on his fingers. "One: an obscure fungus found in the house of the aunt, which is not native to Britain but which has known poisonous properties. Two: a toxic extract of the same fungus introduced to Margaret Morris smeared on a photograph of her husband, which she was almost guaranteed to handle during her labour and his absence. Third: Young Tom Morris poisoned by the same agent, introduced into a bottle of Madeira wine by syringe."

"What?" I was taken aback by this new intelligence. "When did this come to light?"

"I was there when Young Tom was found dead. The bottle was by him. I removed it secretly, partly in case it affected anyone else in the family, but mainly to have Murdoch send it to William McIntosh – a medical friend of mine and the mainstay of this case, Sir Robert – who has not only confirmed the poison in the wine, but has examined the cork minutely and finds a narrow hole imperceptible to the naked eye but consistent with the path of a syringe needle. He worked on this yesterday while Murdoch and I were in Musselburgh, then sent a telegraph to me at the office there, where I had told him I could collect it."

Sir Robert was not mollified. "All very well! But what has this to do with Braid? You made very serious allegations against him and he has raised a hue and cry against you. There had better be some direct proof!"

"Oh, I assure you there is. Yesterday, at his home, I purposely angered him. I have no doubt that is clear from the same feeling conveyed in these letters. He is a vain man and prone to temper when challenged, as Mr. Bremner can confirm. My friend Dr. McIntosh once took him to task on a point of science and also on a point of honour. Braid almost had a fit."

"I saw that, myself," I interjected, keen to support McArdle, but Sir Robert threw up a hand to prevent any further interruption from my direction.

"Next," McArdle continued, "I intentionally drove Braid to order us from his house. I hoped he would call a suitably violent employee or servant, and indeed such a one appeared, name of Byng. The reason was that I suspected such an individual would have played a part in this affair. For one thing, it is unlikely that Braid would have personally purchased the photograph which he later poisoned. He could be identified. Equally, he may not have bought the wine he sent to Young Tom Morris. Someone else must have acquired these. We knew the photographer in question had a business in Musselburgh, so we set out to visit all the likely premises and on the third, we struck gold. A local man called John Spence of Bridge Street in the Fisherrow – Murdoch has his statement – identified the photograph. I had it with me. William assures me it is free of all toxic properties now, as he has cleaned it thoroughly with a range of solvents. The photographer was initially unable to recall the purchaser, but when Murdoch read a description of Byng, he confirmed him as the buyer. We also visited Braid's wine merchant in Musselburgh. I knew the address because Braid had offered me a glass of port, and the merchant's details were on the label. Murdoch wrote them down. Naturally, he would not be so stupid as to obtain the Madeira with his usual order, but instructed Byng to buy a single bottle. The man would not be bright enough to go to other than a merchant whose place he knew. Again, Byng's description was confirmed to us. The wine merchant remembered, because the purchaser clearly knew nothing of Madeira and even mispronounced the word. And finally, of course, Braid is a fungus expert. Who else but a specialist could have grown, handled without risk and extracted the toxic mould, but a specialist? What is more, he has such a growth in his hot-house. I have seen it."

I thought McArdle had finished, but he was merely pausing to let the import of all this sink into Sir Robert's brain. Then he continued.

"But, you may say, all of this points to Byng, not to Braid. Even if Byng is of meagre wit, he may well have gathered enough of Braid's methods and practices to extract the toxin. Or, Braid may well claim, Byng took a known poison which Braid had prepared for a different and innocent purpose – the search for an antidote, perhaps or merely from scientific curiosity – and used it for his own ends. I have no doubt that if you investigate this Byng you will find a record of violent behaviour in his past. He looks the type. But there are four clinching details which makes it clear that Braid is the murderer."

"What's that? Proof?" Sir Robert asked, now totally rapt by this marvellous exposition of police thinking from a non-policeman.

"Proof of sorts. First, he knew that Janet Morris lived in Kincaple. I never mentioned it, nor did Murdoch. Why would he know the residence of an insignificant old woman, especially in a tiny hamlet that most Fifers don't even know exists, let alone a lofty Edinburgh Professor? Braid must have been there. And why? Only one reason to plant the fungus where it would grow. Next, he brought up the poisoned photograph. I said 'picture' but he knew it was a photograph. Further he made reference to Young Tom 'drinking himself to death'. And last, when challenged by Dr. McIntosh at Cupar, Braid claimed to have no interest in grapes or wine, yet he freely confessed to me that he had a valuable commission to investigate their spoiling by rot. The man is an out-and-out liar."

Sir Robert sat, stunned, for fully three minutes, during which time no-one else spoke, allowing the facts to sink in and mash. "Good grief!" he expostulated at last.

It was now my turn. "I see from Murdoch's telegraph that Braid also claimed never to have played at St. Andrews. I can attest to that being a lie. I have seen him there."

Sir Robert said nothing.

I asked Murdoch if he had anything to add. He merely confirmed that everything had occurred as McArdle had stated, and handed me a further report to that effect, plus Dr. McIntosh's telegraph and the Musselburgh photograph. The look he gave me left me in no doubt that he, too, had harboured doubts about McArdle's approach – even, possibly, his sanity – but now had no such misgivings.

If Sir Robert was anything, he was a shrewd politician. His thoughts now immediately turned to the letters he had received, and how to deal with them.

"Well, that is astonishing. If it is all as you say – and I think it bears much more investigation, this time from the Police, Bremner, not a gifted amateur – then we are left with the matter of how we respond to these."

He brandished each of the papers at me in turn – for emphasis, I imagine.

"The Principal wants you dismissed forthwith. The Botanics chap wants you certified insane. The Chief Constable makes a very persuasive case for merging your force with his own as you clearly have neither the manpower nor the ability to investigate a serious crime without taking on, as he says, 'irregulars'. The Lord Provost has already written to our Provost Milton suggesting a flogging is in order. And my fellow Member proposes to ask a question of the Home Secretary in the next Parliamentary session. All of them want McArdle hung, drawn and quartered and you, Bremner, removed from your position immediately if not sooner. I allow you considerable leeway as Chief Constable, but this is going too far. Too far! What do we tell them?"

"I propose we simply tell them the facts," I suggested.

Sir Robert gave an exasperated snort.

McArdle stepped in again at this point. "Sir Robert, I understand you. Perhaps too well. Your concern, frankly, is not whether Braid did it or didn't. I don't imagine you even care whether or not Braid is prosecuted and brought to justice. You are wondering how to reply to all these great and good men without making it clear to them that they have run around like asses on the word of a likely murderer. The embarrassment and political ramifications would be enormous. Is that not so?"

My superior finally looked abashed. "Now, come, McArdle. Little will be gained by putting these chaps at a disadvantage, and…"

"These 'chaps' wanted me – and worse, Bremner here – put at a disadvantage, did they not?. 'Dismissed forthwith' and 'Hung, drawn and quartered' wasn't it?"

"Well, I was paraphrasing, of course, but…"

"And if it needs explaining to these correspondents of yours, I will happily take the onus upon myself to do so. In particular, the Edinburgh University Principal. I suspect Sir Alexander Grant would give me a hearing, considering I saved his life in Bombay back in the '60s. If he had known the full particulars, he would not have written that letter."

Sir Robert was about to respond, but I beat him to it, adding to his misery in the process.

"I feel I can say the same for the Lord Provost," I told him. "Sir James Falshaw is a Wesleyan Methodist and a milder man you could not meet. He has been sorely misled. And as for Chief Constable Linton, I doubt he'll be in post all that much longer, for other reasons."[39]

Sir Robert came suddenly to realise that McArdle and I were not incapable of sticking up for ourselves and not without influences of our own. He retreated even more. "Of course, these letters may have been written in haste and, as you say, with an incomplete picture of the circumstances."

But McArdle was now in full flood. "I have seen three people killed – not to mention an innocent child – and watched a very old and dear friend brought to the brink of despair because of this madman. So if your concern is to spare a few high-placed blushes, I can assure you I will do everything in my power to see that their part in this is well-publicised. Any number of sensational journals and pictorial publications will take up this story, and they will bay for the blood of anyone they suspect is conniving in a cover-up."

Sir Robert's mouth opened and closed. But before he could formulate a reply, McArdle had lowered his voice to not far above a whisper and spoken again.

"On the other hand, if you will let Mr. Bremner here bring this to a speedy conclusion, the Fife police force will be covered in glory, and you will have the pleasure of replying to these friends of yours that you fully understand how they were taken in and hoodwinked by this lunatic Braid, and that you were apprised of the conduct of the investigations all along. Further, you can take the credit for encouraging Bremner to appoint me in a temporary capacity, knowing that I would be able to get close to Braid on a pretext, whereas a uniformed officer would merely have aroused his suspicions and put him on his guard."

---

[39] Thomas Linton lasted as Edinburgh's Chief Constable until 1878.

It took the noble Baronet a moment to answer, but when he did so it was in a far more conciliatory tone. "Well, you certainly are a bold fellow, I will say that for you!"

"They don't give the Victoria Cross for cowardice," I pointed out.

"The Victoria... You're that McArdle? I had no idea."

I simply had to add another piece. "And when a certain Royal Personage visits us next year, this very Captain McArdle will be our liaison with the military. I trust you'll be getting notification of this from the Secretary of State for War very soon. The suggestion was from Her Majesty herself."

Sir Robert could do nothing but murmur: "McArdle... Black Watch..."

"Yes, I shall be sure to give your regards to your son Ralph when I see him later today," McArdle added cryptically. "I think he is scrubbing the barracks floor. Again."

This was the last straw. Murdoch could not contain a chuckle and Sir Robert glared at him. I felt I should intervene.

"Murdoch was in the 42nd too, so he's doubtless scrubbed a few floors in his time."

"Good grief! Did everybody here wear the Black Watch tartan?" Sir Robert exclaimed, suspecting (with some justification) that we were ganging up on him.

But Murdoch got the last word in. "Well, I never did, Sir. I was a piper, you see. Black Watch pipers, drummers and bandsmen wear the Royal Stewart rather than the Government tartan. I'll get Captain McArdle to ask Her Majesty why, the next time he sees Herself, eh?"

Sir Robert took his leave of us, in a far less brusque manner than had marked his entry. Murdoch was still trying hard to conceal a grin, and voiced all our feelings at that moment. "Baronets, eh? What d'ye make of them? Just because somebody's great-granny bedded a king or his grandsire paid for a war in Ireland! Tchah!"

But there was a matter I did not understand. "McArdle, how did you know who Sir Robert was? And what was that about his son?" I asked, still confused.

"Ralph Anstruther is properly a junior officer commissioned in the Royal Engineers, but he is currently attached to the Black Watch at Perth while his esteemed father finds him a safe billet away from any serious trouble. I have no doubt he will one day be our Honorary Colonel, such is the way with Baronets and the like. I had the doubtful pleasure of inducting him into the regiment and of overseeing his training. I have even had occasion to reprimand and punish him. I am not impressed with the son and I am therefore unlikely to be overawed by the father."

"And whit's the boy like?" Murdoch asked.

"Ralph is a mere lad of seventeen summers. He has yet to understand that nobility is worked for rather than inherited, and that respect must be earned before it is granted. But I trust he will mellow."

I had no doubt that McArdle's 'mellowing' would be good for the boy. In fact, he turned out rather well, all things considered. When he inherited his father's baronetcy, he became Captain of the Royal and Ancient, about ten years or so back.[40] But we had more serious matter at hand. How could we finally bring Braid to justice? Now that he knew McArdle was on to him, even that avenue would be blocked.

But if I thought I had had as many surprises in one day as the human frame can withstand, there was another lying in wait for me.

"Incidentally, Bremner, when your officers questioned all the medical men and suchlike, did they interview the two Dr.s Moir, father and son?

"Well, no. In fact they were the only ones not questioned, as they were so closely associated with the case. Why? "

"Well, for a long time you have thought my appearance at or around the time of each Morris death was too much to be coincidence. Did it not occur to you that Robert Moir was summoned to Kincaple and gave us the first clue as to the fungus, that he and his son John Wilson Moir were both attending to Margaret and that it was Moir who certified Young Thomas as dead?"

"But they're the family's practitioners! What of it?"

"Tell him, Murdoch!"

My constable cleared his throat and consulted his notebook. "It may be something or nothing, Sir, and it isn't in my report. But I also noticed that they hadn't been put to the question by the men from the *other* parts of Fife..." (the implied criticism was not lost on me) "...so I looked into their backgrounds and did some extra checking after we left Braid's place."

I waited for him to continue.

"Dr. Moir the elder is not a native of St. Andrews, Sir."

---

[40] Sir Robert Anstruther, 5th Baronet, was M.P. for Fifeshire 1864–80 and for St. Andrews 1885–86, and Lord-Lieutenant of Fife. He died on 21 July 1886. His eldest son, Sir Ralph William Anstruther, 6th Baronet, JP (Fife) and JP and Deputy Lieutenant of Caithness, was born on 5 July 1858 and lived until 1934. He was Lieutenant-Colonel (commanding) and later Honorary Colonel of the 6th/7th Bn Black Watch, but as a Captain in the RE, he distinguished himself in the Egyptian Expedition of 1882 (medal with clasp, bronze star), the Bechuanaland Expedition of 1884–85 and in WW I (where the French awarded him the Legion of Honour). Like his father, he became Lord-Lieutenant of Fife. He was a Writer to the Signet (a Scottish solicitor) and was awarded an Honorary LLD by St. Andrews. Sir Ralph Anstruther was R&A Captain in 1891. Clearly, McArdle's influence on him had indeed been formative.

"I know that! He came from India last year. He told us at Kincaple. But what of it?"

"In fact he was born in Musselburgh, or rather Inveresk, just next door. He is the son of David Macbeth Moir."

"The poet?"

"Poet and physician, it appears.[41] Anyway, Our Dr. Moir has four sons and three daughters. The eldest, Dr. John Wilson Moir, was born in Musselburgh in 1854 when the practice was there. Three sons and, the daughters were born in Agra, Punjaub Simta, Haupper, Benarco – all on the North West Frontier .

"I know! Get on with it!"

"Agra, Punjaub, where was I? Ah, yes. All born in India between '61 and '74 when Moir was a Surgeon Major in the Indian Medical Service. The youngest, Robert, was born there only last year. So Dr. Moir and family are pretty recently returned themselves!"[42]

"We know that," I said, getting rather exasperated, I admit.

McArdle spoke again. "Surely. But we didn't know the Musselburgh connection. Furthermore, there is a vintner in Musselburgh named Robert Moir, doubtless a relative. In fact, that was the source of the Madeira. So if you're looking for recent access to tropical diseases, exotic poisons and fortified wine, a knowledge of Musselburgh photographers, a link to Braid and ease of entry to the Morris households – who would suspect a Doctor? – then turn your spotlight from me to them."

"Preposterous!" I exclaimed.

"No more so than suspecting me. And no more ridiculous, in its way, than suspecting Braid. I have a possible motive and ample opportunity, but no likely method. The Moirs have opportunity and possibly a method we understand nothing of, but no known motive. Braid has, I believe, motive and method we now understand, but what opportunity? Together, the Moirs and Braid have the whole packet. We should keep Dr. Moir in mind, that's all I say."

"I suppose so," I admitted, grudgingly. "But if our immediate aim is to entrap Braid, let us get on with that. What do you propose?"

What McArdle proposed was nothing short of astonishing. But then, McArdle was an astonishing man.

---

[41] David Macbeth Moir (1798 –1851) was born and practised medicine in Musselburgh, but is best known for his novels, poetry, (parodies of Tennyson, Coleridge and others) and as the most frequent and popular contributor to *Blackwood's Magazine* under the pseudonym 'Delta'.

[42] A further son, John E. Moir, was born at St. Andrews in 1876, in the family home at 46 South Street. Dr. John Wilson Moir lived at 127 South Street and by April 1881 had married and had a 7-month-old son.

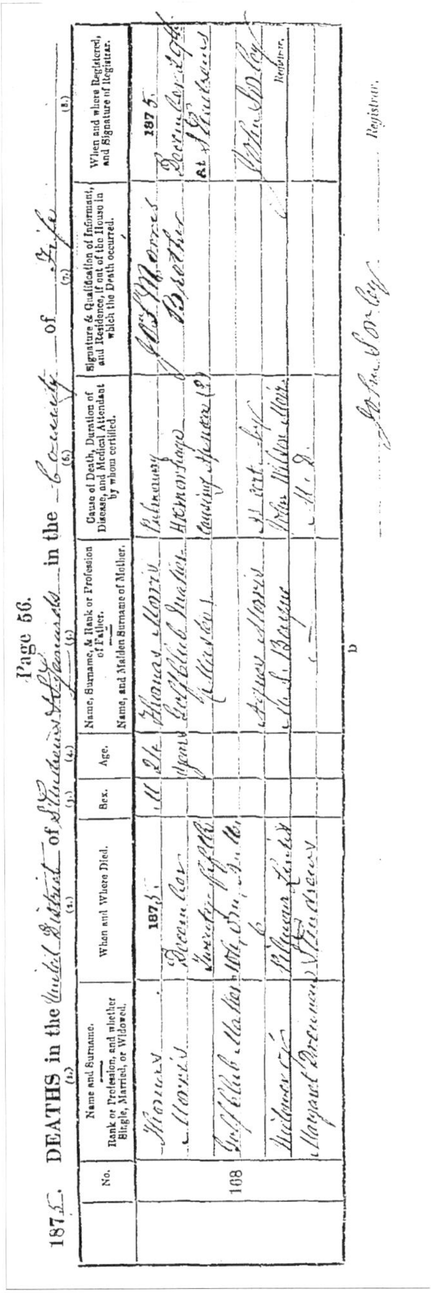

Thomas Morris Golf Club maker Widower
of Margaret Dr.ennan
1875 December Twenty fifth
10h 0m A.M.
6 Pilmour Links St. Andrews
M   24 years
[Father] Thomas Morris Golf Club maker
(Master)
[Mother] Agnes Morris [Maiden Surname]
Bayne
Pulmonary Haemorrhage causing Apnoea
(?) As cert. by John Wilson Moir M.D.
JOF Morris Brother
1875 December 29th at St. Andrews
John Sorley Registrar

Figure 11 Extract from the Deaths Register entry – Tom Morris Jnr.

CHAPTER ELEVEN

The plan McArdle had concocted to catch Braid was, to say the least, inventive. But it was also risky. For one thing, it required the co-operation of several others, in come cases knowingly, in some not. First, it necessitated that I write to Professor Braid. And second, it entailed the agreement and acquiescence of not only Old Tom Morris but also the President of the Honourable Company of Edinburgh Golfers!

As to the first part, I wrote – on McArdle's prompting – the most difficult letter I have ever had to compose. In essence, it stated that I had been instructed on the orders of Sir Robert Anstruther, Lord-Lieutenant of Fife, to apologise unreservedly for the embarrassment and inconvenience caused to Braid and for the slanders promulgated by McArdle. I assured Braid that the man McArdle was a maverick, in no sense acting with any authority of mine.

I even went to far as to hint that foreign service has blunted his wits and that I had made a recommendation to his regiment to keep him away from further excitement. As for his companion, he was a simpleton whom McArdle had suborned the better to play out his fantasy. (At no time had McArdle enlightened Braid as to Constable Murdoch's true identity or purpose).

Therefore, I wrote, I trusted that the matter could now be laid to rest and I took full responsibility for seeing that no such occurrence would trouble the learned Professor again.

That sent, by special messenger, the next step was to include Tom Morris in our plans.

McArdle and I hied ourselves to St. Andrews as quickly as was feasible and visited Old Tom together in order to run through our plot. We told him exactly what we thought Braid had done, and how, and why. We also enlightened him as to the contents of my letter of fulsome 'apology', intended to put Braid off his guard and make him think that he was immune from further suspicion should harm befall any other St. Andrews golfer. Tom had started our meeting full of grief for all his losses on the past few months, but he ended it coldly determined to bring the swine Baird to justice.

We had but hours to act! It says much for the fortitude of Old Tom Morris that he went through with the outrageous proposal, but assent he did. The plan we outlined to him was as follows:

An advertisement would be placed prominently in the main Edinburgh newspapers which would come out the next day. It would state that, given the death of Young Tom, and since Old Tom had not been able to play at the top of his game in the Open on October fourth last, the matter of who was the best golfer – the original reason for the Open Championships – was once again undecided. Moreover, the last match between the Morrises and the Parks at North Berwick (where they were playing when the news of Margaret's death had arrived) had not settled the matter. And further still, it was not clear which was the better club between the Honourable Company of Edinburgh Golfers or the Royal and Ancient, nor which was the better course – Musselburgh or St. Andrews. A challenge was therefore laid down for any doubt to be resolved once and for all.

The anonymous promoter would provide a purse of £1,000 for the best pair – one professional and one amateur gentleman – from each of the two clubs. A game would be played on Old Year's Day over eighteen holes. The winning pair would pocket the prize. Given that the Claret Jug was currently held by Willie Park and before him by his brother, Mungo – Musselburgh men both – the game would be played there. In the interests of fair play, the purse would be kept by General Moncrieffe of the Royal and Ancient, who would attend the game. The competition was to be played, caddied and spectated only by members of either club, the gentlemen of the press and other strangers being excluded. The players chosen from St. Andrews would be Tom Morris Snr. and, for the amateurs, Captain David McArdle of the Black Watch.

Before placing the advert – it was McArdle, of course, who arranged it, sending for Archie to go and telegraph the text and the fee to the newspapers in question – I had sent Murdoch to visit the Captain of Musselburgh and seek his collusion in the matter. Murdoch did not explain the true reason for our subterfuge, but suggested that we were close to breaking a gambling ring and that this wager would bring them out into the open.

I knew the Captain to some small extent. He was an advocate by the name of James Lutyens Mansfield who lived in some splendour at Chester Street, Edinburgh, with his wife, a coachman, four female servants and no children to worry about. He therefore played a great deal of golf. But he was also known for his hostility to the organised betting gangs which plagued the game at the time.

Mansfield had heartily agreed, replying that he and Willie Park would play for their side. Murdoch telegraphed 'Mr. Perth at Rusack's Hotel, St. Andrews' (the pseudonym McArdle had arranged to use for the purpose) when he had this assurance.

We had thought it likely that Willie Park would compete, when we first broached the subject with Old Tom. Any excuse to play his 'auld enemy'. In fact, the two men got on well enough together socially, but on the golf course they were better as adversaries and never won any match where they played together as partners. McArdle asked Morris if we should bring Willie into the plan and ask him to play along by losing the game.

But Old Tom smiled thinly and replied: "Willie never played a 'friendly' in his life. Every game is to win. Even in the days when he went a complete round with one club, he played to win."

"One club?" I queried. "What, driving, cleeking and putting all with the same stick?"

"Aye, Mr. Bremner. And 'stick' is right. It was nothing but an old, bent bit o' wood. But he could drive farther and putt straighter than anybody else wi' yon twig."

"But what did he do in bunkers?"

"Ah, well now. Willie has a secret wi' bunkers."

"Oh does he?" The golfer in me pricked up his ears. "And do you know it?"

"I do. Willie says the best way to deal with bunkers is not to get into them in the first place!"

"Better he thinks this match is for real, anyway," McArdle opined. "Less chance of our ruse being uncovered. It'll be a superior game, as well."

Old Tom spotted two flaws in our plot, however. The first concerned the rules of our 'wager'. "If Davie's to play, he'll need to be a member here. That's the rule you set."

"I have arranged that with Moncrieffe. He has fixed it for McArdle to be entered as a member on the books, pre-dated to last month."

Morris brought up his second caveat. "And Moncrieffe is really holding the prize purse? One thousand pounds? Has some benighted soul actually provided such a sum?"

"Well, not as such," I admitted. "The money does not really exist. Nor will it have to be paid to the winner."

"Oh, I think Willie will expect his cut if he takes the game."

"Really?"

"Indeed he will. And you know what that means."

"What?"

He clapped McArdle on the knee. "It means we'd better bluddy win!"

The scene was set, then. We earnestly hoped that the short notice would prevent knowledge of the wager being too widely disseminated and attracting undue attention. But we were certain it would be noised abroad amongst all the Edinburgh Golfers. And such was indeed the case. There must have been two hundred spectators ready to see the game. It should be remembered that the regular Park-Morris £100 match was considered extravagant and that the prize money for an Open was typically £11 or £12. A purse of £1,000 was unbelievable, as Old Tom himself had said.[43]

Morris and McArdle arrived at Musselburgh on the appointed day, ready for the one o'clock start time, with Tom Kidd and a golfing officer of mine as caddies. I travelled separately with Moncrieffe and two more of my officers who were Royal and Ancient members, bringing them into the plan as we went. Murdoch – who, understandably, did not want to be left out of the *dénouement* – was permitted to come along on the understanding that he stayed in a certain place until called for. It would not do for Braid to spot him and smell a rat. Also, Murdoch had another part to play in the drama to come.

And what did we hazard to gain by all this? To bait Braid with the presence, at one and the same time, of the object of his hatred (Tom Morris) and his pursuer (McArdle). It was our earnest hope that Braid, assured that he was under no suspicion, would throw caution to the winds and say or do something unguarded so as to indicate his guilt.

I had not officially alerted the Edinburgh police to our scheme, but hoped that a number of its uniformed Constables would be present, stationed there to control the crowd if things got out of hand. Murdoch had made sure the Edinburgh police knew of the match by leaving a copy of the newspaper advertisement in the Edinburgh police headquarters at 221 High Street. There would doubtless be many side bets that day, and in my experience, the prospect of large winnings and losses tends to lead to toping[44] beforehand and unruliness thereafter. Doubtless the local force would come to the same conclusion and arrange a strong presence. Ah, but would Braid see the notice of the game? We could only hope so.

On the journey south, in discussion with that knowledgeable man Moncrieffe, I gathered much about the history of golf in Edinburgh and at Musselburgh in particular, some of which I knew although some was fresh to me. I present it here in a digestible form, as it provides some insight into the likely state of mind of certain Edinburgh Golfers as to why they might regard themselves superior to the St. Andrews men.

It seems The Honourable Company of Edinburgh Golfers considers itself to

---

[43] £1,000 in 1875 equates roughly to £400,000 in 2003. However, we might note that the First Prize in the 2003 Open Championship at Royal St. George's was £700,000 (won by Ben Curtis) with £420,000 to the runner-up (shared between Thomas Björn and Vijay Singh).

[44] This is an interesting usage by Bremner. Did he mean 'tope' it its original sense of covering a stake or bet, or in one of its later meanings as accepting a toast or drinking hard and frequently?.

be the oldest club in Scotland (if not the World!) and Musselburgh the oldest extant course. Now, it is often said that the Royal Blackheath Golf Club was started in the Sixteenth Century when our King James VI went to be James I of England, taking many Scottish Gentlemen with him. Naturally they desired a golf club to play at. That being so, does golf in Scotland not predate the game in England? Indeed it does, and there are records of play from 1500 or so. Equally, the Dutch game of Kolf probably pre-existed our native game. I have even heard it said that the natives in India have played forms of golf, polo and even football for hundreds of years before that.

But we are discussing here the foundation of a 'Club' with members, rules *etc.*, not loose associations of gentlemen gathering irregularly to knock balls about. In any case, there is no written record of Blackheath as a club until 1787, although it seems they had a championship cup in 1766.

In Scotland, four Edinburgh clubs claim establishment prior to or around the same time as the Royal and Ancient – The Royal Burgess Society in 1735, The Honourable Company in 1744, the Bruntsfield Links Golfing Society in 1760 and the Royal Musselburgh Golf Club in 1774. My own club dates its inception from May 1754 (and its current name from 1854), although the Society of St. Andrews Golfers may well have existed in a less formal manner before that, meeting to play on the links and then to refresh themselves at Bailie Glass's tavern.

The Royal Burgess Society, for its part, played exclusively at Bruntsfield for over a hundred years, until removing to Musselburgh in 1874. The traditional inception date of 1735 may be rather later than it was in fact, but the actual foundation is obscured by the mists of secrecy which pervade and envelop any enterprise of the Freemasons, who founded the society.

It is also widely accepted that the Honourables played no small part in stimulating the development of golf at St. Andrews. Their Thirteen Articles were adopted almost verbatim by St. Andrews with changes to only four spellings and one penalty rule. The said Articles date from 1744 when the first competition was played for a silver golf club, presented by the City of Edinburgh, over the five-holer at Leith Links. John Rattray, the first winner, was declared 'Captain of the Golf' and his name appears on the Articles. These are the basis of the modern regulations everywhere.[45]

For the next twenty years the Leith competition was 'open', in that all golfers could play, but in 1764 the City of Edinburgh agreed to limit it to

---

[45] To this day the Royal and Ancient sets the rules for golf throughout the world – except, predictably, the USA and Mexico, who nevertheless work closely with the R&A to ensure some degree of consistency.

members of the Leith club. The Gentlemen Golfers built their 'Golf House' at Leith in 1768 (possibly the first clubhouse built specifically for such a purpose) rather than foregather at Luckie Clephan's tavern, and a fine building it was.[46] However, the Gentlemen Golfers did not become 'The Honourable Edinburgh Company of Golfers' until 1800 when legal issues required a standard name, and only subsequently was this altered to the present-day appellation.

Remember, too, that the beginning of the last century was a time when people had more on their minds than golf and the game declined in popularity. Napoleon was rampaging across Europe, which distracted the minds of many from games and pastimes, and a great number of gentlemen officers found themselves called abroad to fight.

In addition, there was a communitarian spirit abroad in the land. The common people preferred not to have their constitutional strolls on links like Leith interrupted by flying balls. Many golfing clubs simply disappeared around this time. The Honourable Company, short of members, indulged in heavy mortgaging of its properties. There was also some talk of misappropriation of club funds, and the club had unwisely acted a guarantor for the debts of others. In 1831, owing a few hundred pounds, an administrator was called in, who in 1833 sold off its earliest and greatest treasures for the paltry sum of £106.

Readers may have seen the famous portrait of William St. Clair of Roslin, now in the possession of the Royal Company of Archers, though how that near-bankrupt body bought it is a mystery.[47]

However, even this failed to clear the various debts, so the Leith clubhouse had to go, raising £1,130. No competitions were held from 1831 until 1835 as the Company hid its shame.

In 1836 the Honourable Company reformed at Musselburgh, which at the time was an eight-holer inside the horseracing track. The Musselburgh course was shared with several other clubs, so the Honourables additionally played the West Links at North Berwick during the summer.

They also took the sensible step of realising that the best golfer was not necessarily the sharpest administrator and so the habit and custom of declaring the winner of the Silver Club as Captain was abolished after 1837.

---

[46] The 1768 building was sold in 1833 and later demolished. The site is under the Duke Street building constructed in 1931 for the Leith Academy, later part of Queen Margaret College.

[47] William St. Clair of Roslin was Captain in 1761, 1766 and 1770-1771. One theory is that the Freemasons paid for it, as St. Clair was made First Grand Master Mason of Scotland in 1736. He abrogated his hereditary rights in favour of elected officials the same year.

Thereafter, the members elected a suitable person to oversee the club's finances and its proper organisation.

By 1865 their banking affairs were healthy enough to build a new clubhouse in Links Place, Musselburgh.[48]

So much for which is the oldest golfing club. My own belief is that the Royal Burgess has it, with the Honourable Company having the earliest set of codified rules.

And the claim of Musselburgh to be the oldest course? We have seen that its inception in an eight-hole form was before 1836.[49] I am told that Sir John Foulis, who has left our Antiquaries with many records of his golfing days at Leith Links, also played at Musselburgh in 1672. But Mary Queen of Scots is said to have played golf at Musselburgh as early as 1567. The Earl of Moray, in his 'Articles' to the Westminster Commissioners in 1568, accused Mary of golfing at Seton House only a few days after the murder of her husband, Darnley, which insouciance in bereavement he took as evidence of her implication in the act. If she did, then it was not at the present links, Seton House being some four miles to the east. There is a tradition that, losing a match there to Mary Seton (one of her 'Three Marys'), the Queen presented her lady-in-waiting with a necklace.

Even earlier, King James IV is supposed to have played at Musselburgh in 1504. However, equally valid claims for royal golf games are made for other courses, including Bruntsfield in Edinburgh and not a few in Fife.

Now, golf has surged in popularity again, due in no small part to the joint and several efforts of Old Tom Morris and the Prestwick Golf Club, and the annual staging of the Open Championship. We have seen that the 'Open', first played only at Prestwick from 1860, was held at Musselburgh in 1874, after the Honourable Company became involved in the organisation of the championship along with Prestwick and the Royal and Ancient.[50] So let us

---

[48] This 1865 building remains, although its current (2003) incarnation is as a children's nursery, address 6 Balcarres Road, Musselburgh. The Royal Burgess Golfing Society opened a new clubhouse at 10 Links Place (now 10 Balcarres Road) in 1875 but moved to Barnton, Edinburgh in 1895, and the building was bought by the Musselburgh Old Course Golf Club it in 1993 to be their clubhouse.

[49] Bremner fails to mention it, but he Old Links at Musselburgh was originally seven holes, with an eighth added in 1832 and the ninth or 'Sea Hole' in 1870 (which is now played as the fifth). In summary, no-one seriously disputes that Musselburgh is the oldest nine-hole course as no other ancient links had exactly nine holes, including St. Andrews with its original twenty-two.

[50] The Open was held at Musselburgh five more times –1877, 1880, 1883, 1886 and 1889 –the last being won by Willie Park Jnr. He and other notable Musselburgh golfers, including his father and the other Parks, are honoured on a plaque on the old Burgess clubhouse.

accept that Musselburgh is very possibly the oldest nine-holer[51], but that many others, including St. Andrews Links, can claim like antiquity, and leave the matter at that.

I should also record here that after the events described in these notes, the Honourables felt rather crowded at Musselburgh and resented sharing with other clubs. Their 400 members[52] jostled for space with the hundred or so of the Royal Musselburgh Club and similar numbers belonging to the Bruntsfield Links Society and to the Burgesses. Three of them had clubhouses at Musselburgh, cheek by jowl with each other. Therefore, the Honourable Company later moved to another racecourse in East Lothian, the Rt Hon Nisbet Hamilton's Hundred Acres Park at Muirfield. This did not come to pass until the May of 1891, but we might note that its original 16 holes were designed by Old Tom Morris, with the seventeenth and eighteenth added in December of that year. They expected the Open to move with them from Musselburgh to Muirfield, but it did not do so until 1892, the first year the play was extended from 36 to 72 holes. Not that everyone liked Muirfield – Andrew Kirkaldy, playing there that year, described it as 'an old water meadow'.[53]

I apologise if this somewhat lengthy discourse, of interest perhaps to none but historians of our game, has diverted the reader from the *res* of my account, but it serves, I think, to show that there was a feeling extant amongst the Honourable Company of Edinburgh Golfers that they had the senior club, played on the senior course, and held the honour of Musselburgh men taking the Open the last two years – Mungo Park on his home ground in '74, beating Young Tom by two strokes, and Willie Park at Prestwick in the year of which I write. But before that, St. Andrews men had had six Open victories in succession – and five of those were the Morrises, Senior and Junior. Old Tom Morris was regarded as the premier designer of golf courses and the Grand Old Man of the game, and had his eldest son not suffered the tragedy of his

---

[51] In 1925 the Royal Musselburgh also felt the Old Course too crowded and so, after 150 years, moved a few miles along the coast to rent Prestongrange House at Prestonpans, where they play to this day. The course was designed by James Braid (see page 115). However, they still use 'the world's oldest automatic hole cutter' (from 1829) and compete for 'the world's oldest golf trophy' (the Old Club Cup, played for continuously since 1774).

[52] This may be an overestimate on Bremner's part for 1875, but the membership had certainly reached this level by the late 1880s, so we may excuse his confusion.

[53] Andrew Kirkaldy, last of a dying breed of old-time rugged Scottish professionals, actually said "nuthin' but an auld watter-meddie', but Bremner has the sense of it correct. Incidentally, in 1879 Andrew Kirkaldy was runner-up to Jamie Anderson at the Open in St. Andrews and in 1891 was runner-up to his younger brother Hugh on the same course.

wife's death then the wickedness of his own untimely end, he would doubtless have dominated the game for some time to come. We hoped that this feeling of resentment beat equally strong in the heart of Braid, as his spiteful words to McArdle seemed to suggest.

We arrived at Musselburgh with just enough time for me to make myself known to Mansfield, their Captain, assure myself of his complicity in what he believed was our ferreting out of the wager-men, and receive his surety that he had told no-one else of the reason (as he supposed it) behind the challenge. As an advocate, he was only too keen to see the law upheld. He set off to find Willie Park and their caddies and meet his opponents at the first tee. Willie Park Jnr., then a lad of ten or eleven years, but later a great champion in his own right[54], caddied for his father and Willie's brother Mungo for their Captain.

Willie Park and Old Tom were entertaining the gallery with banter – good-natured to an observer, but doubtless spiked with a certain edge. Their many matches were already the stuff of legend and they were reminiscing aloud about famous battles of the past. I doubt, however, anyone was expecting as sensational an ending as was provided on this occasion.

There is no question that the Musselburgh course sits in impressive surroundings, with the Forth on one side and the looming presence of Arthur's Seat on the other. The nine holes weave in and out of the horse track. As I have explained, the game was to be played 'over four greens' as the term was in those days, meaning four complete rounds of nine and thus thirty-six holes in all. It was therefore the equal of an Open.

I had been scanning the crowd for signs of Braid – I trusted that while I would recognise him, he would not know me for who I was, having only seen me briefly at Cupar and not being introduced, and if he had spotted me at St. Andrews, he would think me only another Royal and Ancient member along for the sport. But I kept my Constable close to me and, when I espied Braid skulking close to Morris and McArdle at one hole, I indicated to my officer that he should move near and mark him closely. Braid's face was the very picture of venom! He had arrived after the game had started and, I later discovered, had not known about the match but came to play a round himself. Learning that this was a high-price challenge to his club's honour and that the St. Andrews men involved were Morris and McArdle, he must have been moved to near-apoplectic fury. The very result we desired!

---

[54] Willie Park Jnr. won the Open in 1887 and 1889, as Bremner must have known. In 1901, he laid out Sunningdale Golf Club and was the first professional to write golf manuals, entitled 'The Game of Golf' (1896) and 'The Art of Putting' (1920). 'Wee Willie' died in 1925 at the age of 61.– *Ed.*

McArdle played a steady game as did Mansfield, a fit young man of thirty-five or so, and by the twenty-seventh hole the scores were: Morris 120, McArdle 125, Park 121 and Mansfield 125. Old Tom and his partner were one up after three rounds! Willie Park fought back with his tremendous drives and accurate short putts. Tom Morris, to whom longer putts of six or seven feet held no terrors, was notoriously unreliable up close. He fell foul of this defect and foozled two short putts at the third (or thirtieth, in this game) whilst the two amateurs remained neck and neck, leaving Willie one stroke up. At the next, named Mrs. Forman's because of its proximity to the hostelry of that name, Tom again missed a short putt and Willie took the hole, two shots ahead with five holes to play. The Park supporters, who were in the majority by far, cheered and clapped enthusiastically and not a few aimed unnecessary insults at Old Tom.

Willie Park was, at the time, a man of some forty-two years old and roughly ages with McArdle. Old Tom was thirteen years his senior. It was therefore a surprise to no-one when Tom announced that he was in need of refreshment and walked off into Mrs. Forman's tavern. He also made it clear by his attitude that he felt irritated by the crowd. This was as we had arranged beforehand.

Willie, his partner and the whole gallery waited expectantly for Morris to return – five minutes, ten. The Musselburgh men were, not unexpectedly, showing impatience at the delay. However, I had warned Mansfield that such an occurrence was likely and for him to play-act along with whatever happened.

After fifteen minutes, McArdle walked over to his opponents and declared that he would go and see what the problem was, if problem there were. He entered Mrs. Forman's and re-emerged a few minutes later. He then announced in a loud voice to the assembly that Old Tom Morris was feeling rather put off by the undue and unsportsmanlike partisanship of certain of the spectators. However, he would try to talk him round, if everyone else would keep away and allow them the place to themselves for few minutes more. The Musselburgh Captain agreed (realising this was part of our 'plan') and Willie nodded a surly assent.

It was then I looked to my Constable, who in turn was sticking close to Braid. I saw the Professor detach himself from the body of the crowd and slink away to the rear of Mrs. Forman's place, thinking himself unnoticed. In truth all eyes were on the front door (those that were not clamouring for refreshment at the serving-hole in the wall!). At a nod from me, my officer followed Braid, but at a discreet distance. Moments later he returned to whisper to me that Braid had climbed in through a rear window, which he had opened with a large clasp knife.

Just then, McArdle re-emerged from the tavern's depths and held up his hands to quiet the crowd. He opened his mouth to make an announcement but paused, as if waiting for something. Just at that moment a shout was heard from within the building and McArdle dived back inside. This was the signal for McArdle's caddy (a policemen, readers will recall) and my other officer to leap to the doorway and bar anyone else's entry save mine. I ducked under their arms and flew inside. What I saw, I shall take with me to my dying day.

Braid had Old Tom Morris supine across a table, a knife at his throat. Murdoch – who had been secreted there for such an emergency – had sprung from his hiding place in a press and was grappling with Braid while McArdle was on the floor, lying amongst the smashed remains of a wooden chair. I bid fair to say that if I had not reached Braid there and then and helped Murdoch pull him away, his maniac's strength would have wrenched his right arm free of Murdoch's restraint and he would have finished off Morris for good! I shouted for my Constables, who flew in and held Braid fast. He was kicking, bucking, screaming inchoate oaths at Old Tom, who was gasping to regain his breath. Murdoch and I immediately bent over McArdle, fearing him dead. But, to our relief, he was merely stunned and came to as we peered at him. Murdoch shouted to Mrs. Forman (who, I might say, had watched the entire episode from behind her bar, paralysed with fear) to fetch a towel soaked in water. Jolted to her senses, the good woman looked at Murdoch, looked again at McArdle's prone figure, saw Morris lying across one of her tables clasping his throat and Braid struggling and spitting in the grasp of my two men, and promptly buried her face in her apron before fainting to the floor.

I heard Murdoch mutter, "I'll just get it myself, then," and he reached behind the bar to do exactly that. Applying the wet cloth to McArdle's brow brought him around. As McArdle revived, I asked Murdoch what had transpired and he enlightened me.

"I was watching Mr. Morris the whole time, Sir, as you asked. I had already asked all the other patrons to leave as there was police business in hand, and all the staff except Mrs. Forman, who was serving the outsiders. Seeing Mr. Morris was alone, Braid took his chance and rushed in from the back. I had heard him prise open the window. But instead of rushing straight for Mr. Morris, as we imagined he might do, Braid lifted a chair as if to strike him with it. I jumped from the closet, but he saw me and aimed the chair at my legs. Caught me a good one, he did, and I went down. Mr. McArdle appeared, but Braid was behind him because of his swing at me and he had time to crash the chair down on the Captain. Then he jumped on Mr. Morris with his knife out and open. I had just enough time to get to my feet and pin his arms. My, but he has the strength of five, that madman!"

"Madmen often do," I agreed. "But we pulled him off together, eh?"

McArdle was now vertical again and rubbing his temples with both hands. "Well, Bremner. It seems I was of little use after all. " Then he went across to his old friend. "Tom! Tom! Are you all right?"

The elder man was now also on his feet. "Ocht, I'm fine. Just a wee bittie shaken. I'll be richt as rain soon enough."

"But he nearly cut your throat, Tom!" McArdle exclaimed. "I never meant to put you in such direct danger. How can I apologise enough?"

"Acht, he'd never ha' cut my throat, Davie lad," Morris replied. "There's ower much o' my beard in the way!"

McArdle looked stunned for a second, then the two of them burst out laughing. I joined in, as men are wont to do when a moment of high danger is suddenly passed.

Meanwhile, Braid had calmed and my men were keeping him close pinned against a wall. I went over to him.

"So, Braid. We have you. Attempted murder of Mr. Morris, assault upon a police officer and grievous injury to a member of the public. You would probably have done away with Mrs. Forman too, as the only witness. And doubtless we can now prove your guilt in the murders at St. Andrews."

He glared at me. I have never seen such dark evil in any other man's eyes, and I hope I never shall again. "You?" he spat. "And who are you?"

"James Bremner, Chief Constable of Fife, at your service."

Even in his raving madness the man had wits about him. "Oh, 'at my service' is it? And I suppose these are your policemen? Then you can do me courtesy of having them unhand me. Your police force has no jurisdiction outside of its own Burghs and your arrest of me is therefore illegal. Furthermore, I have your written assurance that I am not under suspicion for these ludicrous charges of murder."

"A ruse, Braid. And you fell for it."

"You will answer to this, Bremner." And he spat at my feet as he struggled in his captors' grasp. "Unhand me, or I shall see every one of you answer to the Court of Session!"[55]

It was Murdoch who provided the answer to this insane challenge, as he arrived back with two uniformed Edinburgh men in his wake. "You know, Mr. Bremner. The Professor is correct. You have no jurisdiction here. You are no more than an ordinary citizen, and nor am I. Which means that we have just

[55] The Scottish equivalent of the High Court

156

THE MURDER OF YOUNG TOM MORRIS

made a citizen's arrest, eh? And as mere citizens..."

I caught his drift. "As mere citizens, we are not bound by the rules of police behaviour concerning the apprehension of suspects, is that what you were about to say?"

Murdoch grinned. "The very dab, Sir."

"In that case," I started, and without finishing the sentence, I swung my fist and delivered Braid a healthy blow to the chin. His knees buckled and he went down.

"The very dab, aye!"

"Murdoch, you're repeating yourself."

"Well, it bears repeating," he said as he hefted Braid and handed him over to the Edinburgh officers. "Here you are, boys. And as for Mr. Bremner's fisticuffs..."

The officer holding the dazed Braid's right arm behind his back looked at his colleague as replied, "Fisticuffs? No idea what you're talking about. You, Jimmy?" His comrade shook his head in negative assent. Sometimes justice must obey the spirit of the law, rather than its letter.

As the Edinburgh men were about to remove Braid from the premises, McArdle stepped forward once more. "Just a moment, gentlemen. We can't emerge yet. There are hundreds of people out there and the sight of a police captive, especially a member here, might incite a rush to see what was going on. Somebody could get hurt in the crush."

"You're right!" I exclaimed. "But what's the answer? They're all out there, waiting to know if Tom will play on."

"I think I can resolve this," McArdle said, and added mysteriously, "It might also resolve another matter."

He exited and I heard him address the waiting crowd in a loud voice. "Please, everyone, may I have your attention. Mr. Morris was taken slightly unwell. It is not serious – merely fatigue – and he expects to continue momentarily. But as a precaution, is there a doctor amongst you?"

The reader might imagine my surprise when McArdle re-entered with William McIntosh!

"What?" I exclaimed. "How..."

"I had William waiting near the front of the crowd. He came separately from the rest of us. My apologies for not informing you, but it was rather a last-minute thought."

"But why William?" I asked, now utterly confused by McArdle's actions (and not for the first time). "Surely any doctor could check over Tom and see he's all right."

"Oh, I'm all right," Old Tom said. "In fact, I feel years younger and lighter now that swine's caught."

"But you might not have been all right," McArdle answered. "And if Braid had got up to any of his poisons trickery, I wanted to make sure someone was here who might know what to do. But there is another reason for his attendance."

I opened my mouth to ask for an explanation, but was forestalled by a voice from the doorway.

"Are ye not well, Tom?" Willie Park said, bustling his way into the premises.

"Naethin' wrang wi' me," Morris replied.

Any other man might have surveyed the scene, taken in the broken furniture, the police presence, the sight of a man held captive and disarray all around and perhaps inquired as to what was going on. But Willie Park merely looked levelly at Morris and said, "Well in that case, are we playin' this game off, or what?"

"I told ye," Old Tom said to me as he rose. "Nae 'friendlies' for Willie Park!"

"Just a moment," McArdle said. "Mr. Park, there is more going on here than I could have explained to you earlier. But I think continuing your match would be a good idea if it gets the crowd away from this place. Give me a second to confer with your Captain." He strode outside, returning a few minutes later. Willie Park spent the time tapping his foot and staring at his pocket watch in obvious impatience.

McArdle returned and spoke to us. "Mr. Mansfield knows something of what has occurred here, but not the full story. However, he is now aware that there is a man in custody. For the benefit of the crowd, he is now announcing that, as he and I are tied, and all the interest is in Morris and Park, the two of them should play out the match one against one for the prize. Is that agreeable to yourself, Mr. Park?"

Willie grinned and put his watch away. "Oh, indeed," He grinned. "I aye liket best to play against Old Tom."

Morris laughed as he clapped Park on the shoulder and the pair of them exited, arm in arm, to a tumultuous cheer from the waiting crowd. We heard the noise recede into the distance and the gallery gathered around the fifth tee in anticipation of the remainder of this needle match.

Meanwhile, we had Braid to contend with. "I assume," I said to the Edinburgh officers, "that you can detain this miscreant until I formally request his delivery to me at Cupar by warrant?"

"Aye, Sir. We can that."

"Good. Constable Murdoch will follow on, with your permission, to explain matters to your superiors and discharge any paperwork. Yes?"

Murdoch and the two Constables nodded their agreement.

"Good, Then we shall just wait a few minutes until you can leave unobserved."

"There is another matter. Or two," McArdle said, stepping forward. "Murdoch, you saved my life and Old Tom's as well. Braid fairly got the better of me with that chair. Had he killed Tom, he'd have been upon me next and I would not have been sensible enough to put up any sort of a fight. I owe you a great debt. My life, in fact."

Murdoch sucked his moustache then looked up at McArdle from under his brows. "And I owe you an apology. I always thought you were deep in this matter and after yon visit to Braid, I dam' near arrested you myself for obstruction of police business. Now, I know you were right all along."

"Then will you shake on it?" McArdle asked, extending his hand.

"I will not!" Murdoch announced. "You deserve better than that." And instead of taking the proffered hand, he stood to attention and delivered the smartest military salute I have ever seen a man give. Then he spun on his right heel, stamped once and marched out of the tavern at parade time, humming 'Hieland Laddie' as he went.

William McIntosh, meanwhile, had not been neglecting his physician's duties. Seeing Mrs. Forman swooned behind her bar, he had administered *sal volatile* under her nose and brought her around, checking that she had sustained no contusions or abrasions in the fall. Now she was sat on a chair and calling for brandy.

"She's fine," McArdle observed. "But that's not why William's here, really."

"Old Tom's all right, too, " I reminded him.

"Yes. But perhaps one of the officers will now search Braid – carefully! – and put anything they find on this table."

One Edinburgh man did so while the other held Braid fast. He was by now cuffed and could not put up much resistance. In fact, now that the fight was out of him, he looked no more than a frail, embittered old man. The Constable laid his finds out as they emerged. There was a fob watch, some coins, a set of keys, a pocketbook, a kerchief, a notebook and pencil – plus a syringe full of a milky-white fluid.

"Ahahh!" McArdle exclaimed, picking up the syringe with his own kerchief and examining the wicked-looking needle attached to it. "Might I suggest that this is given to Dr. McIntosh for examination? He will, of course, share any results with the Edinburgh police surgeon and enter the syringe and a report in evidence. He has some expertise in this matter. In any case, it is not directly germane to the occurrences here today. You have the clasp knife as an intended weapon. Is that agreeable?"

The two officers looked one to the other, not used to taking decisions of this magnitude and quite certain that whatever answer they gave, somebody would criticise them for it. I decided to help them out. "Gentlemen, I shall take full responsibility and I will write you a receipt for it," I said, to their evident relief.

"I only need the contents," William McIntosh said, ejecting the liquid into a phial which he stoppered, then handed the now-empty syringe to the policemen with a caution to keep the needle covered. McArdle solved the dilemma by fetching a cork from the bar counter and showing the needle deep into it before handing it to the constables. Right enough, it was further evidence of attempted murder, or would be when we knew what it had lately contained.

As it happened, one of my men had had the presence of mind to go and find another Edinburgh policeman and ask that a carriage be summoned to the rear of Mrs. Forman's, which was off the links and not likely to be noticed. The carriage had arrived and Braid was bundled into it, a broken reed compared to the whirling Dervish of minutes previously. William McIntosh expressed his desire to return to his laboratory as soon as possible, but McArdle prevailed on him to wait until the end of the game, so that they could travel back together. McIntosh agreed, but would not stay in Mrs. Forman's, regarding all such places as dens of iniquity and debauchery. And who is to say he is wrong? He went off in search of tea at the clubhouse while McArdle and I caught up with the game.

"Braid must have gone home for that knife and the syringe," I mused.

"More evidence of intent. Doubtless the solution is a poison, perhaps the same one he used on the others. I imagine he intended to make Tom drink it unknowingly, or even to inject it into him, then slink away, leaving the corpse of an old man dead, presumably, from exhaustion. Murdoch scuppered that, though."

We headed for the two professionals, who were on the final 'Sea Hole'.[56] On the previous hole, the local man had, unusually for him, landed in the infamous 'Pandy' or Pandemonium bunker after an unlucky bounce, and had added substantially to his score. On the same hole, Old Tom, by contrast, had hit a long drive and landed his second at the foot of the plateau'd green. This left a three-shot hole for the match and the prize, but Morris was one ahead!

---

[56] This hole, copied by many other courses, is now played as the fifth, in case anyone wishes to recreate the momentous game.

At the last tee Willie Park, possibly out of rage, overshot the green with a tremendously powerful stroke, not even pausing at the top of his back swing as was his habit. Morris, holding the club tight and in his customary hunched stance, took things slightly easier and baffed a long, high shot which thudded onto the green not three inches from the pin. Park had the honour of the second shot, being the further away, and lofted a beautiful lob which landed just beyond the hole, but then spun backwards – and knocked Tom's pill a foot further away, rolling up to lie tight beside it.

Consternation reigned! The two balls were touching, and neither one was closer to the hole than the other. At this point in the game, Old Tom was one stroke ahead. But who would have the honour of the first putt? And which ball would be removed? Here, it seemed, two Rules of golf were in contention. One Rule states that if two balls touch, the first should be lifted so that the second may be played. But which was the 'first' ball? The one nearer the hole? Neither was nearer than the other. The one played most recently? That was Park's. The one first on the green? That was Morris's. Another rule holds that a ball must be played honestly for the hole, and not upon the other ball. But neither could be hit without disturbing the other.

If Morris lifted his ball and Park's putt went down, this would leave Morris with a short putt which he might not make, given his weakness at the close game. If, on the other hand, Park lifted his and Tom sank the putt, there was no way Park could win the match. Neither man would give way on the point.

The stillness was absolute within the gallery. I could have heard a needle drop. Morris and Park surveyed the situation but said nothing to each other; there was nothing to be said – each knew the rules and both understood the position completely. It occurred to me at that moment, as doubtless it occurred to everyone else present, that a crucial element had been omitted from this 'grudge match' – an agreed referee. Now, a referee could be called for, but only from amongst Musselburgh or St. Andrews men. And which would the other party trust? This had all the makings of a riot!

For fully three minutes both professionals stood on the green examining the situation. A yard-stick was called for at Old Tom's suggestion and Park's agreement, and brought from the clubhouse. Both players agreed that it yielded no new information – their distances were equal. The crowd was starting again to be restless. A susurrus began, doubtless fomented by the many side-bets which were restring on the outcome. Whichever way this went and whatever the outcome, the mood was likely to be ugly.

It was McArdle who provided the solution. He moved over to where the Musselburgh Captain was standing and observing the position – he as much at a loss as anyone – and spoke something into the man's ear. There was a nod in agreement and the Captain stepped forward onto the green. He had a brief conversation with both players, and walked back to speak to McArdle. A further nod, and Mansfield addressed the assembly.

"It seems we have an impasse. Neither player is prepared to concede the lifting of his ball. The Rules are unclear on the situation. Mr. Morris is a stroke ahead at this point in the play. It is therefore suggested that all four original players tee off again at this hole. As the leader in strokes, Mr. Morris shall have the honour of first play."

Morris and Park started off back to the tee. McArdle signalled to his caddie, as did the Musselburgh Captain to his, and their sticks were brought from the clubhouse to the ninth. Moncrieffe came over to stand beside me, his eyebrows raised in question. I told him briefly all had gone as planned and that Braid was in captivity. "Good," he said. "Now we can get back to thinking about golf for a change!"

All four players were now at the tee. Morris drew back and hit a stroke that was the twin of his earlier one from the same place. The ball landed inches from the pin. The crowd – even the local denizens – applauded this display of golfing mastery. Not to be outdone, Willie Park took an iron and smacked a high shot towards the hole, landing it an equal distance from Morris's ball but on the farther side, the backspin bringing it to a sharp halt. McArdle, as Morris's partner, played next. His was a creditable shot to the front of the green. Musselburgh's man played an equally long hit, which bounced before the green but slightly to one side, whence it rolled up to lie to the right about ten yards out.

McArdle would play first, being the further away by some six feet, and then Mansfield. McArdle surveyed the green, which looked flat but, as all golfers know, could conceal many a swerve, dip and contour. His putt snaked towards the hole, looking at first as if it would range to the left but finally, on losing its pace, curving inwards towards the pin and stopping short by about three inches.

The crowd sighed with one collective breath. As the Musselburgh man addressed his putt, a voice cried out: 'C'away the Golfers!'. Whether this came from a local or a visitor was not clear, but I believe the reaction of that good and honest man, Mansfield, would have been the same whether he thought it to be the one or the other – he paused, stood upright and said: "Unsporting behaviour, from whatever camp, is not tolerated at this Club!" There was scattered applause and some 'Hear! Hear!' in agreement from the crowd. Then Mansfield bent himself again to his stroke and sent it dead straight towards the flag, where it nestled up close by about a hand's span.

Both of these balls were closer than those of the professionals, who therefore had next turn to putt. At equal distances, Morris, as the first away, had the preference. There was a tense moment amongst those who knew his game, that he would not make the trivial distance with any accuracy, but he did, and a tremendous roar went up from the spectators. Willie Park, who excelled in the short game, sank his putt with barely a glance at it, stepping forward to drop the ball in with hardly a moment's hesitation. Applause erupted.

This left the Musselburgh Captain to play from a position of one stroke behind. His five-incher would not go down only by a miracle – and it dropped dead-centre into the four and a quarter inches provided.[57] This left McArdle with a tiny putt to take the match. There was no possible way he could miss it. He stepped forward with his wooden putting club, addressed the ball, tapped it – and it stopped right on the lip of the hole!

The gallery went berserk! How could he miss such a minuscule putt? The screaming and the shouts of 'No! went on for what seemed like ages. McArdle breathed deeply, tapped the ball with the head of his club and bent to retrieve it from the hole.

One expects clapping and tumult at the end of a golf game, especially one so close-called as this one had been. But there was not a whisper from the crowd. As the import sank in – a draw! – cries started to arise for 'Play-off' and 'Re-match' and suchlike.

At this juncture General Moncrieffe stepped onto the green and raised his arms to quiet the clamour. When order settled, he spoke. "I hold the purse in this contest, on behalf of the anonymous promoter. Had there been a clear victor, I should have awarded it without question. But the stipulation in the challenge was for thirty-six holes. I cannot in all honesty hand over this generous sum if the conditions are not adhered to. Thirty-six holes have been played – we cannot count the first unfinished business at this hole which prompted the current resolution as it was not completed. But there is no provision for additional play nor for a re-engagement. Nor is there a provision for a prize share. The challenge specifically referred to a 'winner'. I therefore have no option but to declare the match a draw, but without prize."

A policeman develops a certain sixth sense about a crowd – when it will go peaceably, when it will disperse with grumbling and when it will riot. But I could not, even with all my many years' experience, predict which way this mob would turn. Given the preponderance of Musselburgh supporters, I have no doubt that, had there been an uprising. Morris and McArdle might have been torn limb from limb, followed closely by anyone identified as supporting

---

[57] Musselburgh set this as the standard diameter hole, still used everywhere to this day.

the Fife side. It therefore came as a blessed relief when Moncrieffe again raised his arms for quiet.

"I am as aware as anyone of the unsatisfactory nature of this outcome. Therefore, I have a suggestion. Let us agree, as sportsmen and as fellows of good will, that Mr. Park and Mr. Morris are equal champions of this hallowed game, Hercules and Achilles, Atlas and Perseus, Hector and Paris – titans both. Let us further agree that the Honourable Company of Edinburgh Golfers and the Royal and Ancient Club of St. Andrews have pedigrees of equivalent standing and will continue to co-operate like true brothers in the promotion, regulation and advancement of this finest of sports. And let us finally reach a concord that, amongst golf courses wherever played, now and for the ages to come, Musselburgh is pre-eminent as to nine holes and St. Andrews the acme of the longer links. What say you, gentlemen?"

For a few seconds there was deathly hush, then, as if on a gunshot, a massive cheer erupted from the mass, with caps flung in the air and loud Huzzahs! exclaimed.

But Moncrieffe was not finished. A final time he called for silence.

"And I further pledge that whenever these two foremost exponents of this empyrean diversion we call 'golf' shall meet to contest for the honour of *magister ludi*, the prize money shall not be lacking. I will see to that from my own purse if needs be. But as for the thousand pounds unclaimed today – I humbly submit that the most fitting use for it, the Promoter permitting, should be as a contribution of a memorial to that Olympian of the fairways, gathered before his time like a Spring blossom wind-blown ere its season, and sadly missed by us all – Mr. Thomas Morris Jnr.!"

No-one, however hard of heart, could have resisted Moncrieffe's oratory. The crowd, as one, shouted 'Young Tom! Young Tom!' and before anyone could nay-say it, both Morris and Park were hoisted aloft willing shoulders and carried away towards the clubhouse. Doubtless they would raise a glass or two to the memory of Young Tom now his shade was avenged.

McArdle, Moncrieffe and myself were left standing alone on the green, watching two hundred backs and two head-high champions recede across the links.

It took a moment for any of us to speak. It was Moncrieffe who broke the silence. "So, Bremner. I imagine you'll count this day a success. From a police perspective, that is."

"Certainly we have the villain Braid to rights. I am grateful you went through with the charade that finally unmasked him."

"Charade?" Moncrieffe replied. "What charade? There was a game, conducted according to the rules set, and there will be, as announced, a memorial to Young Tom Morris. I see no 'charade' in any of that!"

"But the prize money that never was…"

"An irrelevance! No winner, no prize. Nothing has happened that is in contravention of the law of the land or – more importantly – the spirit and regulations of golf. You heard me mention the permission of the Promoter of this occasion. Since there is no Promoter, there can, *ipso facto*, be no permission. But Young Tom shall have a fitting memorial in St. Andrews, even if I have to hew it myself from the rock at Stirling Castle and drag it to Fife by hand and horse. What say you. McArdle."

"I agree with Mr. Bremner – without your part in this, all would have been lost at the beginning and an unfortunate disturbance would have ensued at the end. You had faith in us when others might have cried off. I am in your debt."

"Indeed you are, McArdle, and therefore I crave one single boon of you."

"Name it!"

"Tell me, honestly, was that penultimate putt a fluff, or was it meant to square the game?"

McArdle looked levelly at Moncrieffe for a moment or two, then spoke. "Many games have been squared today, General. Old Tom Morris might rest easier in his bed and Young Tom lie easier in his grave. Bremner here has an arrest and Sir Ralph Anstruther has vindication. Braid will face the gallows and I – well, I can always play another game of golf. I fancy this half-course is do-able in thirty-nine rather than forty. What do you say, Bremner, General? Will you both hazard at a game with me here sometime?"

"Only if you play honestly to win," I suggested.

"Oh, I always play to win, Bremner. Always!"

And with that, we aimed for the clubhouse, to collect Tom Kidd, Dr. McIntosh and my officers, ready for our journey back to the East Neuk.

But I will say this," McArdle added as we reached the edge of the course. "I figure that a professional-amateur mixed pairs tournament could catch on."

Moncrieffe pondered for a moment. Then he announced, "No, I don't believe it. Where would we be if gentlemen and professionals played alongside each other rather than in competition? Before you know it, we should have actors and comic singers and parliamentarians standing shoulder to shoulder on the fairways with royalty and clubmakers, as if all were equal."

"And are they not?" McArdle asked.

"Most assuredly not!" Moncrieffe replied. "Give me a decent wood-turner or ball-moulder before an M.P. or a Prince of the Blood any day. I know which I'd rather share a round with!"

Articles & Laws in Playing at Golf.

1. You must Tee your Ball within a Club's length of the Hole.
2. Your Tee must be upon the Ground.
3. You are not to change the Ball which you Strike off the Tee.
4. You are not to remove Stones, Bones or any Break Club, for the sake of playing your Ball, Except upon the fair Green and that only within a Club's length of your Ball.
5. If your Ball comes among watter, or any wattery filth, you are at liberty to take out your Ball & bringing it behind the hazard and Teeing it, you may play it with any Club and allow your Adversary a Stroke for so getting out your Ball.
6. If your Balls be found any where touching one another, You are to lift the first Ball, till you play the last.
7. At Holling, you are to play your Ball honestly for the Hole, and not to play upon your Adversary's Ball, not lying in your way to the Hole.
8. If you should lose your Ball, by it's being taken up, or any other way, you are to go back to the Spot, where you struck last, & drop another Ball, And allow your adversary a Stroke for the misfortune.
9. No man at Holling his Ball, is to be allowed, to mark his way to the Hole with his Club, or anything else.
10. If a Ball be stopp'd by any Person, Horse, Dog or anything else, The Ball so stopp'd must be play'd where it lyes.
11. If you draw your Club in Order to Strike, & proceed so far in the Stroke as to be bringing down your Club; If then, your Club shall break, in any way, it is to be Accounted a Stroke.
12. He whose Ball lyes farthest from the Hole is obliged to play first.
13 Neither Trench, Ditch or Dyke, made for the preservation of the Links, nor the Scholar's Holes, or the Soldier's Lines, Shall be accounted a Hazard; But the Ball is to be taken out teed and play'd with any Iron Club.

John Rattray, Capt

Figure 12 The "Leith" Thirteen Articles of golf from 1744

CHAPTER TWELVE

M ansfield had taken McArdle, Moncrieffe, McIntosh and myself back to
Edinburgh in his coach. The two Constables were to travel with
Murdoch to the city and return home after the various administrative affairs
were attended to by them and the Edinburgh police. Morris and Kirk would
make their own way back after the celebrations. Our party travelled as far as
we could together by train, with Moncrieffe heading for Falkland, myself for
Cupar and the other two bound for Perth. It was early on Old Year's Night, so
there were already revellers on the streets and in the train carriages.

The line we were on had been part of the old Edinburgh Perth & Dundee
Railway, absorbed by the North British in 1862, as so many smaller
companies were. I remembered – and was telling my fellow travellers – that
even before this, it had been the rather grandly-named Edinburgh & Northern
Railway, although it reached neither Edinburgh nor the North, but rather was a
link between them, running as it did from Burntisland in Fife to Tayport,
between 1847 and 1850. The E&N had also acquired the Edinburgh, Leith &
Granton Railway, which had a ferry terminal for the crossing. Thus, it
connected the train ferries which traversed the Forth and Tay rivers in the days
before the two bridges, and was a shorter route to Dundee than the more
circuitous one through Perth. From a somewhat grandiose terminal at
Burntisland, with workshops and a locomotive shed, it steamed via Kirkcaldy,
Falkland Road, Kingskettle, Ladybank, Cupar and Leuchars to Tayport.
Ladybank was the junction for the line which joined the Scottish Central
Railway at Hilton near Perth.

I mention this so that it will be clear that we were all together as far as the
Falkland Road station. In normal circumstances I would have continued with
Moncrieffe, getting off two stations further up the line at Cupar while he
continued on to Leuchars and changed again to the St. Andrews Railway, still
independent at that time.[58] On this occasion, however, the General was
spending Hogmanay in company at Falkland but was invited to Sandilands the
next afternoon for a party. He would drive to Cupar, he told us, and hoped to
see McArdle and McIntosh there too. I confirmed that they were already
invited, along with Agnes, McIntosh's sister. He left us, and I was grateful to
spend a final few minutes with the other two discussing certain details of the

---

[58] The St. Andrews Railway was absorbed by the North British in 1877. The line became part
of LNER in 1923, nationalised in 1948 and was closed in 1969.

case with which Moncrieffe need not be concerned. At the next halt but one, Ladybank, McArdle and McIntosh would dismount to await a train for Perth.

On the journey, William McIntosh had been examining the fluid taken from Braid when searched. In his medical bag he had various solvents and indicators, which he added by turns to small aliquots of Braid's milky liquid. He had set up a small spirit burner in the carriage using his up-turned valise as a makeshift table – much to the consternation of the train guard, until I explained who I was. The guard lit the oil in the pot-lamps above us, but watched suspiciously while William heated test tubes and peered at them intently. I shooed the man away with a shilling for his trouble.

As the train started off again from Falkland Road, William, who had not spoken for the duration of trip since Burntisland, sat back and exhaled. I gathered that he had come to some conclusion or other.

McArdle and I looked at him expectantly. He folded his arms and gazed back at us. "Well?" I enquired.

William collected his thoughts for a moment, then spoke. "I cannot be certain, and an experienced chemist should confirm this, but I think I know the nature of that fluid."

We waited another few moments. "WELL?" McArdle and I exclaimed at the same time. William McIntosh really could be the most exasperating man at times.

"Ah," he said. "I expected it to be the same fungal toxin as before, but it appears not to be. It has no effect on mouse blood. I brought some with me in order to make that very test. As best as I can determine, it is an extract of the castor bean."

"What? How do you know?"

"Three things – one, it contains traces of vegetable oil; two, the oil is of the correct consistency; and three…" He held the phial under my nose, "…three, it smells of castor oil!"

"But what…" It took a minute for this to sink in. "Ah, yes. You said once before that castor oil could be poisonous."

"Not exactly. The oil is removed from the pounded beans, leaving a pomace which contains the poison. This I imagine could be easily extracted with solvents like those I have used here. I have no idea of its nature, but I shall inject it into a mouse or two back at Murthly and see what effects it produces."

"I'm surprised there are any mice left at Murthly," McArdle muttered, but I hushed him, wishing to hear more about this second murderous agent Braid had brought to my attention.

"What do you expect to happen?" I asked.

"I am not entirely sure, but I think I have read that it produces results similar to tetanus or botulism, only much more quickly. Anyone finding Mr. Morris dead would imagine he had suffered some kind of seizure leading to muscle rictus. I doubt if anyone would have found a needle puncture, even if they had looked. A scratch would probably have sufficed"

At that precise moment, our carriage corridor door opened and a voice said, "Exactly correct, Dr. McIntosh. But at least he would have died with a smile on his face!"

It was Braid! And he was holding a pistol. McArdle made as if to lunge, but the revolver was pointed directly at him.

"Pray don't be stupid, Captain. Of course I intend to shoot you, but I would rather not do it here on the train. A quiet spot near the next station will suffice. For all three of you, starting with you, Bremner. I owe you for that strike to my face."

"So you did plant the fungus in the old woman's cottage," McArdle conjectured.

"A preliminary experiment, but a successful one," Braid confirmed.

"Then you perfected an extract to put on the photograph and in the bottle," McIntosh added.

"Much more elegant, don't you agree? And I could be reasonably sure the woman would kiss the glass and the boy Morris would drink the Madeira. Had they not, the attempts would have gone undetected and I could have essayed another method later. But I had no need to. So predictable, the lower classes. And had Morris shared his bottle around in the spirit of Christmas, I might have obliterated the entire family at a stroke."

"You're mad!" I ejaculated. "Mad!"

"Am I? If this McArdle, whoever he is, had not poked his nose in, the Morris women's deaths would have gone unremarked. I will get to the old man eventually, and possibly his other two sons. I shall be able to employ more direct means. After all, there is now no need for me to operate in secrecy, is there? This pistol, for instance, will suffice. Then the unnatural stranglehold that St. Andrews holds over golf will be loosened forever. The Honourable Company of Edinburgh Golfers can take its proper place as the undisputed senior and true arbiter of the game rather than the rag-tag rabble of drunks and fishermen playing your coney lands. The organisation of the Open will fall to us – Prestwick's day is over. And there are plans for a new nine holes to complement our rightly famous older links and produce a championship course of unparalleled majesty. Musselburgh will be the home of golf forever!"

"I see now!" McArdle said, nodding. "Finally, I understand why you have embarked on this crazy pursuit. And I take it that the constant visits to Morris's shop to argue about the clubs he was making for you, was merely the pretext to deliver the poisoned photograph and the wine. I knew you were the villain in the piece, Braid, but for the longest time it did not make sense to me that it was just revenge or some insanely misplaced jealousy between two golf clubs. But it's more than that, isn't it? It's the land!"

"What?" I asked, astonished as ever by the twists and turns in this matter.

McArdle spoke to me, but kept his eyes steadily on Braid. "When I was in Musselburgh visiting this lunatic, I asked around about him. He is the scion of an old mining family. The coal is gone and the mineworkings shut, but the land his house stands on is hard by the western end of the Musselburgh Links and bordering the Esk. I have no doubt that it was Braid's intention to offer this at a good price, but still a large one, to the Edinburgh Golfers. With nine holes of their own and no need to share, they could then have eased out the two smaller clubs, taken over all eighteen holes and indeed had a top-class course. But first, it was important to diminish the influence of St. Andrews and the Royal and Ancient. Once assured of hosting the Open on a regular basis – as Prestwick used to do – the investment would be even more profitable. Do I guess right?"

"Almost," Braid admitted. "Except for one thing. The coal is not completely gone. There is still some just near the surface. I have neither the capital nor the inclination to dig it out."

"Ahhh!" McArdle said, putting his head back. "But a company of investors from amongst the Golfers could perhaps provide the funds, sell the coal, repair the land and end up with a handsome profit and a new links all at the same time!"

"With you as the main stock-holder, Braid, is that it?" I added, catching up at last. "And are the Moirs with you in this?"

"Who are the Moirs?"

"A vintner and his medical relatives," I explained.

"Never heard of them, except the Musselburgh wine-seller, if that's who you mean. I assure you, I had no accomplices in this. I needed none."

"Except Byng," McArdle added.

"Pshaw! The man is a lumpen mule. He knows nothing other than to do as he is told," Braid spat, then grinned. "Well, you may congratulate yourself on solving the case, Bremner. Your last case, as it happens. Now we are approaching Kingskettle, so please get ready to leave. And no stupid moves, or I will shoot you where you sit, be assured of that!"

"Just one more thing, Braid." It was William, who until now had not spoken at all. "How did you escape police custody?"

"Those boobies? It was nothing! You may have noticed that I am rather below average height and that my arms are long while my legs are short. Regulation police handcuffs were not made for my particular anthropometrics! How simple, then, to swing my shackled wrists under my feet and bring them to the front while the rather dim officer guarding me briefly spoke to his equally otiose colleagues driving the carriage. I strangled him silently with the cuffs, extricated the keys and leapt from the rear door. It was not locked. It's likely they didn't know I was missing until they stopped at Edinburgh. Honestly, Bremner, I am surprised you policemen can catch so much as a cold, let alone criminals. And people wonder why so many footpads and pocket-artists roam the streets!"

"Then you followed us here? On the train?"

"Oh, no. I was ahead of you. I took a train to Leith and boarded the ferry there. Then I waited at Burntisland to watch you disembark from the Granton boat. Sure of which train you would take, I stole a suitcase from the waiting room and busied myself arranging it in the guard's van while you found your seats here. Then I waited for that military buffoon you were with to get off. I had no wish to confront four of you, and he doesn't matter in any case. It was you three I wanted. Especially you. McIntosh!"

"Me?" William gasped.

"For that insult at Cupar! Suggesting a French tinkerer is any part my equal in matters of fungal diseases. The very idea of it!"

"I see," William said. "Then you will assuredly be most interested to observe this." He leant forward to his rack of small bottles and uncorked one, holding it up to Braid.

"What is it?" Braid hissed, his interest clearly piqued despite the drama of the circumstances.

"Oh, you'll recognise it if you smell it. But take a deep sniff. It is rather faint."

Braid took the vial, careful to keep us all covered with the pistol, gave William a suspicious glance then put his nose over the opening and inhaled. Nothing happened for a second or two, then he flung his head back and roared. "Ammonia!" His eyes instantly streamed – and that was McArdle's cue to action. He lashed out with his right leg and kicked the gun upwards. It went off, sending a bullet through one of the pot-lamps in the roof directly above Braid's head. Oil spilled out over Braid and caught light. He screamed and started firing wildly in his panic. Neither of the shots hit us – thank God!

– but one smashed into a bottle of William's, which was obviously a solvent as it too caught fire and splashed back over Braid, adding to the conflagration.

McArdle shouted, "Quick! The door!!

Grasping his meaning, I reached out and pulled the handle strap, opening the carriage on the opposite side from the corridor. McArdle, who was now behind Braid, lifted his foot again and delivered a mighty shove which launched the murderer from the carriage, a screaming ball of flame. The train was now slowing, coming into Kingskettle. We watched as Braid tumbled down the embankment, a blazing, tumbling mass.

Of course, other passengers had heard the gunshots and the shouts, and some had seen the fireball shoot out of the train from their windows. Now we were stopped at Kingskettle, and everyone had left the train in confusion and near-panic. It took me a few moments to restore order on the platform, from which, fortunately, no-one could see Braid's body on the other side of the train. I explained the noise and the fire as a flare-up of a faulty oil lamp which we had flung from the carriage, and everyone seemed to accept this. I even heard one man say to his wife: 'A good thing it wasn't gas-lit. There might have been an explosion!'.

I then sent the guard to fetch the local policemen from the village, which he did speedily, and I gave orders to have Braid's body wetted and covered, thereafter to be transported by cart to Cupar. Meanwhile William had slipped away unnoticed and returned to whisper to me that he had examined Braid's body and the maniac was indeed dead. McArdle said nothing but closed his eyes in what I suspected was a silent prayer of thanks. At last the horror was over.

Calm returned to the travellers, everyone re-boarded the train, and the next stop was Ladybank. There, McArdle and McIntosh took their leave of me to await the train for Perth and we agreed to meet the next day at my home. McArdle offered to telegraph the Edinburgh police, to tell them of their missing men and to advise Murdoch and the others there was no need to wait there – the matter was at an end.

As the train travelled on through Springfield, I mused that it would have been good to think that Braid might be tried, sentenced and publicly hung. But perhaps, in the long run, his death was for the best – a violent and horrible end to a cruel and evil man. And all for vanity and profit!

The train reached Cupar in time for me to hear the bells ringing out their carillons to herald in the New Year. I walked the short distance from the station to Sandilands – half a mile, if that – and was met at the door by

Isabella. She kissed my cheek and said, "I thought you were never coming home at all!"

"Oh, believe me, so did I," I agreed. "So did I."

"Happy New Year," she said taking my hand.

I gave hers a squeeze in return. "Yes, I rather think it will be," I agreed.

Figure 14 The memorial to Young Tom Morris.
This can still be seen at St. Andrews Cathedral burial grounds.

CHAPTER THIRTEEN

O n New Year's days, Isabella liked to hold what she called 'a Ball' at Sandilands. To be honest, it was no more than a small gathering, but we pulled the furniture back and there was room for dancing. On that particular year, we were graced by the presence of Sir Robert Anstruther and General Moncrieffe with their ladies. Both wished to make amends to McArdle (and to me? I like to think so) for their previous misgivings, and could hardly refuse the invitations. Isabella, of course, was thrilled by the status this afforded her party and the swank it would allow her in Cupar society all the way to Easter.

I had spent most of the day at my office. Starting early, I telegraphed Sir Robert Anstruther who came to see me post-haste. He heard my report, then left to communicate the gist of previous day's events to the Edinburgh gentlemen who had, just the previous week, been baying for my blood, and all but demanded their apologies by return. These had arrived on my desk by the late afternoon. Sir Robert and I then had a further conversation about a mutual acquaintance.

Now it was just falling dark. Our garden was lit by torches and, the weather being fair and mild, some guests lingered outside while others preferred the warmth of the interior. McArdle arrived, looking very handsome indeed in his dress uniform, along with William and Agnes McIntosh. The ancient Private Thomson was driving the coach by which they had travelled from Perth, and he was taken off to the kitchen to have some supper and a wee *deoch an doras* there.

McArdle was to stay with us at Sandilands that night, while the McIntoshes and Thomson were booked into the Temperance Hotel. I had no doubt that Thomson would find a way to break the obvious injunction!

McArdle presented Isabella with a charming piece of Meissen acquired when he was in Germany – figurines of a girl and boy on a sledge portraying, I believe, Winter from a series of The Seasons. They must have cost him all of twenty shillings.[59]

William McIntosh took little part in the merriment, preferring to examine the trees and shrubs in my garden. However, he kept the children amused with information and anecdotes about this plant or that bird, or the worms which tilled the soil for us, or the myriad of tiny creatures to be seen in a droplet of pond water, or the affairs of grey seals, or the habits of cormorants, or many

---

[59] They must be worth all of £4,000 in 2012.

other facts of Natural History besides. Then the children were bustled off for their tea and to bed while the adults got on with the serious business of celebrating the turn of the year.

Figure 13 The Bremner Meissen figurines

Agnes McIntosh spent a considerable time talking to McArdle and I saw them dance once. Isabella noticed, and nudged me, as if to say that she felt a match was in the air.

Over the *buffet*, I overheard Moncrieffe tell McArdle about young Archie the caddie and his progress at the Free School. The lad had already won a twelve shilling prize as Best Reader (and let it be further stated that in the next year young Archie gained the ten shilling prize for Best Attender and a further eight and sixpence for Best Behaved). Of course, he did not actually see the money, as it was given over to Forgan the clubmaker and held in an account from which the boy in question could be clothed. But at least this saved Archie's mother from having to find ready cash to pay for his garments, and I believe she herself received a much-needed pair of boots after Archie's earnest pleading.

The real reason for Sir Robert Anstruther's appearance at our *soirée* was a scheme he and I had been hatching together (although, of course, I allowed Isabella to continue thinking it was the fame of her *salon* that had drawn him). We withdrew ourselves from the party and gathered up McArdle, taking him to my study on the pretext of a cigar and a brandy away from the ladies and their delicate sensitivities to tobacco smoke indoors. An American has said, 'If I cannot smoke cigars in Heaven, I will not go', and I wholeheartedly concur.[60]

Sir Robert quizzed McArdle on some of the more lurid aspects of the previous day, not least the struggle on the train. 'All very Charles Reade and Wilkie Collins!' was his judgement, and he did not mean it opprobriously.[61]

Then we discussed other matters pertaining, not least the relief that we felt in never actually having confronted Dr. Robert Moir with any suggestion that he might be implicated. But finally, at my prompting, we got to the nub of the matter at hand. Sir Robert took the lead.

"I have received two rather interesting telegraphs, one from the University of Edinburgh, that fine seat of learning, if somewhat younger than our own, and a second from the Director of the Botanic Gardens in that same fair city."

"About Braid?"

"Indeed. Both about the late and unlamented Professor Braid, may his soul rot."

---

[60] It was Mark Twain, and the quote is slightly wrong.

[61] Wilkie Collins will be familiar to everyone as author of *The Moonstone* (1868) which was described by T. S. Eliot as 'The first, the longest and the best of modern English detective novels'. Charles Reade (1814-1884) may be less familiar but his novels *The Cloister and the Hearth*, *It Is Never Too Late to Mend*, *Foul Play* and others were superior to those of other Victorian 'sensation novelists'.

"What do they say?"

On Sir Robert's nod I picked up one of messages from my desk and offered it to McArdle, who read it with some amusement.

"You are welcome to read the other one as well," I said, "but as you would see, they say almost exactly the same thing. I could almost believe they were written in the same room at the same time."

McArdle finished reading and handed the paper back to me. "The Botanics appears to be going out of its way to distance itself from Braid. I quote: 'At no time did he occupy an official staff post here or was considered part of the establishment. Any facilities accorded to him were informal and honorary.' And the University?"

"Much the same. He didn't really work there, just gave a few lectures, his title of Professor was honorific and so forth, they say. And I imagine it's probably the case. He was apparently of independent means from his coal inheritance and needed no annual stipend, and I don't somehow imagine him as the sort of man who takes joy in the instruction of young minds. Doubtless they will now find it within themselves to expunge Braid completely from their institutional memories. "[62]

McArdle picked up the other communication, that from the University of Edinburgh, and compared it with the first. "Right enough, they do say as much. In fact they almost use the same sentences."

"Well, the Director of the Botanics is also Regius Professor of Botany at the University, after all. And both replies were probably drafted by the University Secretary, doubtless over sherry at Old College. You will notice, though, that the University points out that there is no actual proof of Braid's alleged involvement in the Morris deaths other than our report of a confession, and that any material facts which might establish his innocence have probably

---

[62] There is indeed no trace of a Professor Braid on the staff lists of either Edinburgh University or the Botanic Gardens at the time in question. It is more than likely that he was an independent worker with a tenuous attachment to both bodies. Or perhaps Bremner has chosen to alter Braid's true name throughout his memoir, either to protect the University from further scandal or possibly as a result of later pressure from elsewhere. Whether he was in any way related in any way to Dr. James Braid, pioneer of hypnosis, or James Braid the golfer is not clear. This Braid (1870 –1950) was born in Earlsferry, Fife, and was one of golf's great champions and course designers in the early 20th Century, occupying a position in the pantheon of golf no less than that of Young Tom Morris in his day. James Braid won his first Open in 1901 and over the next ten years became the first man to take it five times, coming runner up thrice. Braid was a great course designer (ironically, including Prestongrange, where the Musselburgh club moved – see page 100), bringing his farming background to bear on that courses were well laid out and properly drained. He helped found the Professional Golfers Association and was its first President.

died with him. And anyway, what would be gained by having it known that the Morrises were murdered? Best let the dead lie easy. It is also suggested that a memorial to Young Tom might be fitting, and that the University would use its influence to help achieve that end."

McArdle laughed. "A sea-change from their original position. Do you really think they would have made good their threats to have you removed from office?"

"They could have tried," I replied, and I had in fact considered the possibility at one point. "But then, we, the Fife Police, are independent, so they would have had a long, hard chase. This, in my view, is why local police forces are so much better than national bodies, controlled by government. In every other country I know – and I have looked into this – where the police are an arm of the administration, they tend to get used for political ends."

I hoped Sir Robert took my point and would interfere less in the future. And I can only add that recent events in Germany and the Balkans bear out my thesis.

"But all of our letter-writers – they got their way, in some respects," McArdle added.

"Oh?"

"With Braid dead, there will be no further enquiry. I doubt that any Edinburgh police investigation will go much beyond the bald facts of the events at Musselburgh. Even if it did, there might yet be interference."

"How so?" I asked.

"I took the opportunity while at Musselburgh to enquire as to the membership of the Honourable Company of Edinburgh Golfers and they gave me a list. Every one of the letters Sir Robert Anstruther originally received was written by a member. That doesn't mean they were all implicated with Braid in the affair, of course. Just that he knew them well enough to pester them. But I have been wondering if Braid didn't have an ally in his crazy plot. Someone who might shield him from retribution. Someone who also stood to profit from his coal-and-golf scheme. He hinted as much."

"Someone in the government, or the judicial system, I imagine," I suggested.

"Or the police," McArdle added, to my annoyance. "However, I don't think the Principal of Edinburgh University or the Lord Provost would involve themselves in such an enterprise."

"Indeed," Sir Robert agreed. "But your University man makes a valid point about the Morris deaths – I am not sure that we want to have these known to be murders."

"Because the family has suffered enough, you mean?" McArdle said, with infinite sadness in his voice and his eyes. "Do you know what Old Tom told

179

me? 'People say Young Tom died of a broken heart, but if that was true I wouldn't be here either'. I trust that he and his family can find some measure of peace, now that it's all over."

"Precisely. Inquests, exhumations, changes to certificates – why not let everyone continue to believe the facts as they are believed now?" Sir Robert suggested.

"There may be some merit in that," I concurred. "There is no more justice to be exacted, with Braid gone."

"So the world will continue to think that Young Tom died of sorrow at the death of his wife. That might well be a more fitting tribute to him than a lurid story about a vendetta. My God! What a thing to do, all over rivalry between golf clubs and a land purchase."

"So be it!" Sir Robert declared. "He should be memorialised for his life, not the manner of his death. There should be something permanent to mark his final resting place. Moncrieffe has also said as much to me."

And so it was to be. A memorial to Young Tom was unveiled in the Cathedral burying ground on 24 September 1878. It was subscribed for by 60 or more golf clubs, the Edinburgh Golfers prominent among them, and bears the thoughtful inscription:

> *Deeply regretted by numerous friends and all golfers, he thrice in succession won the Championship belt and held it without envy, his many amiable qualities being no less acknowledged than his golfing achievements.*

But back to our discussions. While we had our smokes – as I recall, the new *Romeo y Julietas* which had just started to arrive from Cuba that year – Sir Robert made the suggestion he and I had been considering that day in the aftermath of the Braid affair.

"Now look here, McArdle, I trust we've put behind us that recent business between ourselves. To be blunt, you and Bremner were right and I was wrong. I flew off the handle, and if I have not apologised sufficiently, I unreservedly do so now.

"McArdle said nothing, but raised his snifter to Sir Robert by way of agreement and salute.

Sir Robert nodded back, and continued. "I also gather from your Colonel that your duties in the Black Watch are not merely recruiting and the proper chastening of remiss young officers like my son and heir, God rot 'im. Apparently you have something of a watching brief here in Scotland, especially when a Certain Lady is on the loose at Balmoral and elsewhere."

"She appears to take comfort from my presence, at times. Not that I get very close to Her. Brown, her Ghillie, sees to that!"

"As you say. But it seems to me that your talents are somewhat wasted, to be only employed three or four weeks in the year, if that. So we have a proposal for you. Bremner? Perhaps you would be so kind as to enlighten Captain McArdle. Tell him what we have in store for him, should he be agreeable, of course."

I put the ash from my cigar and cleared my throat. "In brief, McArdle, Fife lacks a Detective. I have one Superintendent, four Inspectors, four Sergeants and fifty-five Constables. But there is no officer on my force with the necessary aptitude for plain-clothes detective work, especially where a certain – how shall I say – *individual* cast of thought is required. Other police forces have them, and I am persuaded that Detectives are a good thing."

"Yes, I believe that London is to have a Detective Force and has just taken possession of splendid new premises in Great Scotland Yard," Sir Robert added. "I heard all about it when I was last at Westminster."

"Oh, they've had Detectives in London since '42," I informed him, mainly to show that I was not behind in my knowledge of wider police matters. "But, yes, in October last, the Detective and Public Carriage Departments did indeed move into that new building. And London was by no means the first. The French have had Detectives since 1810, set up, as it happens by a criminal."[63]

I paused before delivering the clinching blow, which I freely confess was well below the belt and completely unworthy of me. "Moreover, Glasgow has had Detectives since 1820,[64] and James M'Levy of Edinburgh is well known, not least from his own rather dubious – and, I might say – immodest accounts of his incumbency at 221 High Street."[65]

---

[63] The Sûreté de Paris was born in 1811, in fact, when Eugène François Vidocq, police spy and informer as well as crook, made a deal with the French police to let him off a crime he had committed if he would establish a Detective force for them. He was the model for Victor Hugo's Jean Valjean and Inspector Javert in *Les Miserables*, Balzac's character Vautran in *Père Goriot* and Edgar Allan Poe's Auguste Dupont in *The Murders in the Rue Morgue* as well as the mysterious fugitive in Dickens' *Great Expectations*. He also gets a mention in Herman Melville's *Moby Dick*.

[64] Bremner's memory is slightly askew once again. Glasgow Police appointed their first detective, Lieutenant Peter McKinlay, in 1819. He established a Criminal Department in 1821, at least eight years before Peelers were introduced in London

[65] James M'Levy was a real detective in Edinburgh from 1833 and published stories of his own exploits in 1861. Conan Doyle growing up at that time, would doubtless have read M'Levy, and it may be no coincidence that he gave the address of Holmes the same number – 221 – as that of the Detective Office in Edinburgh's High Street. It is also worth noting that fictional Glasgow detective 'Dick Donovan', the creation and pseudonym of J.E. Preston Muddock

There are few things a Fifeshire man hates more than the idea that Edinburgh or London has something that the Kingdom doesn't. And as for Glasgow – well, Fife gave that proud place both of its Patron Saints!

The Lord Lieutenant took up the reins again. "So what we propose, Captain McArdle, is that the Black Watch let us have you as a Detective. I can make the resources available to Bremner and he can put the arrangements in hand. What do you say?"

Before he could answer I added more sugar to the pill. "It was your persistence and quick wits that brought the Morris business to its conclusion, McArdle. And I remember the way you dealt with the escaping thief, Bryce was it?"

"Joyce. But surely…"

"And dealing with Braid on the train, not to mention cooking up the scheme to flush him out. You're a natural!"

"Yes, but…"

"I dare say you saved a few lives, too," Sir Robert pointed out. "Who is to say whether Braid might not have worked his way through the entire Morris family and then started on other St. Andrews golfers?"

McArdle finally got a word in. "Mr. Bremner, Sir Robert, I'm flattered. And I confess I have been rather wondering how I would fill the weeks and months beyond royal duties. But the police – I know nothing of police work or police procedures."

"No, but Murdoch does. I will promote him to plain clothes and he can work with you. The pair of you shall be based at St. Andrews. Now, what do you say?"

"I say that I doubt the army will allow it!"

"Ahah!" Sir Robert exclaimed, slapping McArdle on the leg. (I happened to know it was the wounded one, but he held back the flinch remarkably well, all considered.) "We have you there! I have already communicated with Sir John McLeod and with Mr. Hardy[66] and I imagine they'll both see the merit of it. Not to mention, you'll be on hand when Prince Leopold arrives later this year."

McArdle threw up his hands. "Well, it seems I am surrounded! I imagine I should surrender. Do I have any choice at all in the matter? Or was my old teacher at The Madras correct when he said free will is an illusion?"

It is sufficient to record that, without much more hesitation, McArdle said yes, and we toasted his acceptance in slightly more brandy than Isabella

---

(1842-1934), was appearing in *The Strand* from July 1892, just after Conan Doyle's first series of Sherlock Holmes stories. Scotland does not lag behind England in detection, real or imaginary.

[66] The Rt Hon Gathorne Hardy, Secretary of State for War in Disraeli's second (1874) cabinet.

would have approved of, had she known about it. We had a second cigar each to seal the bargain while we discussed details. Then we went back to the party. Isabella was deep in conversation with Agnes McIntosh and they both looked at McArdle when he entered, and smiled. He smiled back at them ingenuously. But I know a conspiracy when I see one!

I should perhaps note here that the Edinburgh policeman whom Braid attempted to strangle recovered, although he was probably not the loudest voice in the Church Choir for a week or two. Murdoch was of the opinion at the time that the man had fainted from fright rather than asphyxiation. Murdoch himself had remained in Edinburgh that night, the toast of the local force as he gave them chapter and verse on the whole sorry business. Doubtless they had kept him well-lubricated to aid his voice and his memory.

Braid himself was soon a memory, and not even an official one. He is not recorded in the annals of the Great Poisoners or Serial Murderers, and perhaps that is also for the best. The public dwells over much on the lurid details of deaths and sensations, in my view. Trashy novels and illustrated periodicals abound, pandering to this fad of the macabre and the mysterious. I sincerely hope and trust that this memorandum does not fall into the hands of some penny-shocker hack who turns it into a cheap Detective thriller.[67]

But Old Tom's heartbreak was not over. On the first of November, 1876, his beloved wife, Agnes, passed away. No foul play this time. I suspect she had simply had enough of grief and loss – her firstborn son, her other son named for him, his wife, a grandchild and the aunt by marriage she was so fond of. On the Death Certificate, young Dr. Moir went into great detail about Congestion this and Degeneration that and Chronic the other. I believe she simply wore out.

The same year, 1876, Davie Strath left St. Andrews to be Keeper of the Links at North Berwick. I have told earlier how he tied for the Open at St. Andrews that year but lost on a technicality. Not two years after, he died while on a health trip to Australia. One by one, all Tom Morris's old golfing cronies and adversaries fell away.

Old Tom himself is still alive as I pen these words in 1902. Doubtless he will outlive me.[68]

By early February 1876, the administrative matters concerning McArdle's appointment to Inspector Detective had resolved themselves rather neatly to

---

[67] Oops!

[68] Bremner was correct. Old Tom Morris even outlived all his own family. He died in 1908, a few months after being injured falling down the stairs at the Royal and Ancient clubhouse.

the satisfaction of all concerned, but not without many exchanges of correspondence between myself, the Colonel of the 42nd, the War Office and my own superiors on the Police Committee. In the end, matters were arranged in this manner: McArdle would remain at his Captain's rank and on the Reserve List, for which he would receive half-pay;[69] the remainder of his pay would be made over to me, to help defray the cost of his appointment at a full Inspector's salary paid in addition to his army draw, the other portion of which would be met by a slightly increased vote from the Burghs within the Fife police area (at which idea, might I say, only the Burgh of Kirkcaldy cavilled, doubtless stirred up by Superintendent, Chalmers); the other Burghs appreciated the economic logic of spending more to save more, and that having a Detective Officer on the force would, in the end, be an advantage; McArdle would receive no accommodation benefit, affording me a modest sum to hold for engaging Dr. McIntosh if and when required; and Murdoch's pay-rise would have happened in any case within a year or so.

Thus, the War Office and Her Majesty retained the particular services of McArdle when needed. Without additional cost, I had an extra and valuable officer and one more plain-clothes man (whom I would have to replace with another constable for the St. Andrews beat, but that was a different matter). McArdle and Murdoch both ended up slightly better off than they had been. Further – and this was perceived to be a great benefit in the Murdoch household – Mrs. Murdoch no longer had to polish uniform buttons and cap badges. St. Andrews, in the person of Provost Milton, was determined to show its gratitude by providing a small house for McArdle (down by the end of North Street near the Fishergate area he knew so well from his boyhood) and Moncrieffe persuaded the Royal and Ancient to give him a permanent membership, which Moncrieffe paid for personally, saying he would win it back by betting on McArdle in matches. Whether he would place him to win or to lose, Moncrieffe did not elucidate.

For my part, I would always back McArdle to win.

Any game, any circumstance, any matter at all – McArdle was the sort of man who would come out the better in the contest.

Of that, I had little doubt.

---

[69] Before 1871 a Regular Army officer had no entitlement to a pension on retirement and most either sold their commissions or moved onto half-pay, a retainer paid until and unless the officer was called up again.

APPENDIX

added by Chief Constable Bremner

Lest anyone should think that I have embellished or – worse! – invented any of these events above recounted (and, no doubt, pricked by my policeman's conscience to provide as much documentary supporting evidence as possible) I have obtained from the Registrar at Cupar copies of extracts from the Register of Deaths pertaining to the Morris family. I present them here.

I also include something which was published in 1876, a year after the affair in question. A certain Mr. George Bruce, a St. Andrews man of some distinction, fancied himself a poet and tragedian, and had published at his own expense a weighty volume of his works entitled *Destiny and Other Poems*. It included a eulogy on Young Tom and also a short textual description of the great golfer's life and death. The text is erroneous in some small matters, but it serves as an almost-contemporary account from a man who knew the Morrises well, both on and off the golf course.

As to the excellence or otherwise of Mr. Bruce's poetic efforts, or whether he indeed deserves the epithet 'The McGonagall of St. Andrews', it is not for me to judge. [70] But much can be inferred from the somewhat vainglorious portrait of himself included in the book and the fact that no publisher would take the volume on under conventional business terms. However, George Bruce's own opinion of his own work was uniformly high.

---

[70] The reference is to Bruce's exact contemporary, Dundee-based William Topaz McGonagall (1825-1902), self-proclaimed "poet and tragedian", who has achieved lasting fame as "the worst of writers, of them all". Even a cursory reading of Bruce's poetry confirms that he could give McGonagall a run for his money.

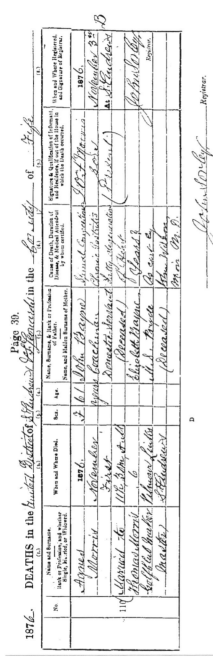

Agnes Morris (Married to Thomas Morris Golf Club Maker Master) 1876 November First 11h 30m A.M.
6 Pilmour Links St. Andrews
F   61 years
[Father] John Bayne Coachman Domestic Servant (Deceased) [Mother] Elizabeth Bayne [Maiden Surname] Pryde (Deceased)
Spinal Congestion Chronic Gastritis Fatty Degeneration of Heart Years?
As cert. by John Wilson Moir M.D.
J.O.F. Morris Son (Present)
1876 November 3rd at St. Andrews
John Sorley Registrar

Figure 15 Extract from the Deaths Register entry – Agnes Morris

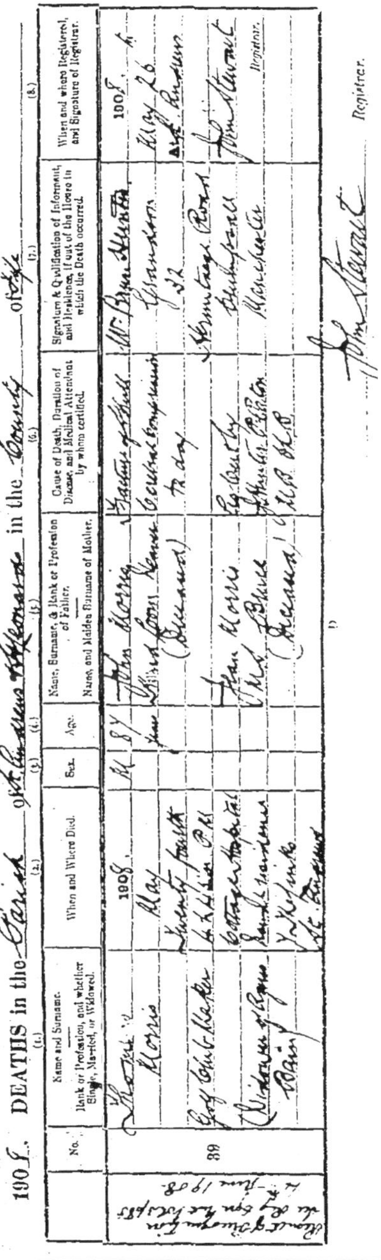

Thomas Morris Golf Club maker
(Widower of Agnes Bain)
1908 May twenty fourth
4h 45m P.M. Cottage Hospital Usual
residence 7 The Links St. Andrews
M   87 years
[Father] John Morris Hand Loom Weaver
(Deceased)
[Mother] Jean Morris [Maiden Surname]
Bruce (Deceased)
Fracture of skull Cerebral compression 42
days
As Cert. by J Hunter P Paton M.B. Ch.B.
Mr. Bruce Hunter
Grandson
32 Hermitage Road Crumpsall
Manchester
1908 May 26 St. Andrews
John Stewart Registrar

Figure 16 Extract from the Deaths Register entry – Tom Morris Snr.

IN MEMORY OF YOUNG TOM MORRIS

THE CHAMPION GOLFER OF THE WORLD.

from *Destiny and Other Poems* by Mr. George Bruce

As a golfer,
>He was a man—take him for all in all.
>We shall not look upon his like again."—*Hamlet*

HE'S gone,—cut down in Summer's sunny prime,
A flower—which bloomed upon the links of Time,
And yet—not gone, for Time's undying pen
His name inscribes amongst her noted men.

As one,—so young—so fair—so mild and true
Whose fame still onward like his "tee shots" flew,
When, from the golfing world,—a stripling, bore
The triple triumph from the peaceful war!

There was a spirit in his mild blue eye,
Which shone triumphant, like the azure sky
When lit by Phoebus on a summer's noon,—
But, clouds—not evening hid its fire too soon!

Yes! in it lurked a latent—innate fire
Which neither years nor skill could quench or tire—
Which shone on Friend and Foe with equal ease
Nor lost its lustre in his wish to please.

All foes he beat—but One—an unseen foe
Whose silent footstep tripped, and laid him low.
When, with his father—on North Berwick green
Success flew smiling o'er the cheerful scene.

But, like the juggling witches on the blasted heath
The hour of Triumph was heralded by Death!
Which came and grinned with a malignant leer
And blanched his spirit with the hue of Fear.

At one fell swoop, Death's cold and icy hand
Hurled into dust the prop which made him stand—
His better self, who, spirit to him gave—
And unborn Hope,—both,—shrouded for the grave.

He played again, but ah! his wonted style
Was gone —or flickered like a lamp, a while,—
Around their grave his wounded spirit flew
With wearied wing, to rest beside them too.

And ah! too soon his yearned for wish was given
To meet her spirit in the aisle of Heaven!—
Where Death no more shall snap the cords of Life
Nor feelings wither with departed wife.

189

Where Hope, again, shall flourish—evergreen,
And Love eternal gild the happy scene—
Where Worth and Goodness shall for ever dwell
With those who merit it, by living well!

Too soon with Thee the purple stream ran dry,
Its fountain dried up with an unheard sigh,—
Too soon for Golf the city's anxious breath
On one deep whisper, murmured Tommy's death

The star of golf bath left its earthly sphere
Nor soon its equal shall again appear,
Nor one with such a steady lustre shine—
So "far and sure "—alas! young Tom, as thine!

Figure 17 George Bruce, from *Destiny and Other Poems*,
trying his best to look like Alfred Lord Tennyson!

IN MEMORY OF YOUNG TOM MORRIS.

The subject of the foregoing sketch was Young Tom Morris, a young man of an agreeable, cheerful disposition, who had the rare virtue of speaking ill of none, a great golfer, and a general favourite with all, lie died very suddenly en Christmas morning, 25th December 1875, through the bursting of an artery under the right lung. He went home about eleven o'clock on Christmas eve in his usual health. He was heard rising in the morning as usual, but, not coming to breakfast, his room was entered, and he was found dead, apparently having slipped quietly away. He was a native of St. Andrews, that famous centre of golf, and after going through an unparalleled course of success, both in England and Scotland,—at the National Scottish game,—he died at the early age of 24 years. About a year before his death, he was united, both in the bonds of affection and wedlock, to a young woman, for whom he had the strongest love—and who was in every way worthy of his affection. At the close of a victorious golf match in September previous,—betwixt himself and his father,—known in the golfing professional world as Old Tom,"—and the brothers Park of Musselburgh,—he received on the green the sudden news of his wife's illness—and before be had time to leave for St. Andrews in a yacht, kindly put at his disposal by a gentleman, a second telegram announced her death in childbirth, and also that of the infant—just born. His sensitive nature never recovered this blow. His next public match was at the October meeting, when he and his father were pitted against Davie Strath and Martin, and after bringing the match almost to a successful issue—being 4 holes up and 5 to play—Young Tom so completely broke down, that he and his father lost the 5 holes and the match. After this, he was seriously ill, and nothing seemed to rouse him from the recollection of her who had passed away—life's interest having been snapped asunder by her early death. Shortly before his sudden death, a challenge was given by Mr. Molesworth of England, and Tommy's friends readily entered into it with the view of rousing him, and trying to infuse new life and vigour into his withered feelings; but he was very much out of condition, and he repeatedly remarked to his friends and backers that but for them he would not have continued it. He gained the match however.

Although born in St. Andrews, he was removed by his father at a very early age to Prestwick, where Old Tom went with his family and resided for many years—but on the death of Allan Robertson, Old Tom's noble colleague in many a tough match, he again returned to St. Andrews, where he yet plays an excellent game,—and it may not be out of place here to state that of all the great professional golfers, none have played so long and so well as Old Tom Morris— the father of the subject of this sketch. Young Tom's public career commenced at the early age of sixteen years, he was first brought into notice at a golf tournament held at Carnoustie in 1867, where he beat all comers,—professionals and amateurs,—the tournament being open to the world. On the back of this he played with and beat Willie Park of Musselburgh, a well-tried and excellent professional player. After this he was victorious on every green on which he played. His youth and success led to the most brilliant displays of golf probably ever known, and, in all cases, played so well that he was allowed to be—by all, the champion golfer of the world. In 1860 the Prestwick Club instituted a challenge belt to be played for annually there, to be held by the winner until won from him—but in the event of it being won in three consecutive years by the same player—(a feat considered almost impossible)—it was then to become his absolute property. It may not be uninteresting to give the history of the playing for this belt.

1860.	Won by	W. Park, Musselburgh	.	174
1861.	„	T. Morris, sen., Prestwick	.	163
1862.	„	T. Morris, sen., Prestwick	.	163
1863.	„	W. Park, Musselburgh	.	168
1864.	„	T. Morris, sen., Prestwick	.	167
1865.	„	A. Strath, Prestwick	.	162
1866.	„	W. Park, Musselburgh	.	169
1867.	„	T. Morris, sen., St. Andrews	.	170
1868.	„	T. Morris, jun., St. Andrews	.	154
1869.	„	T. Morris, jun., St. Andrews	.	157
1870.	„	T. Morris, jun., St. Andrews	.	149

So the trophy, which is an exquisite piece of workmanship, richly ornamented with silver plates, bearing appropriate devices —produced at the cost of thirty guineas—became the property of Young Tom, and is now prized as an interesting heirloom by the family. A challenge cup was substituted for the belt, to be played on the three greens, Prestwick, St. Andrews, and Musselburgh, by turn, when Tom was again victorious at Prestwick at a score of 166,—thus winning *four* consecutive times. As an instance of the smallness of his scores, when playing for professional prizes in 1869, he won with the smallest score ever known to be made on St. Andrews Links, viz., 77.

Out, 4 4 4 5 6 4 4 3 3, 37
In, 3 3 4 6 5 4 5 5 5, 40
77

It were endless to state the many great professional matches he played and won. But I may state that from his amiable and agreeable temperament and obliging disposition, combined with that indomitable spirit and determination which marked his play, Young Tom Morris became a great favourite with every one he came in contact with, and it is needless to say that his very sudden death at such an early age made him universally regretted throughout the golfing world, which is likely to result in a very substantial monument to his memory on the links of the principal scene of his success—St. Andrews.

From George Bruce, *Destiny and Other Poems*, 1876 pp 489-492

Further Books in this Series

MURDER AT THE ROYAL & ANCIENT – 1876

Prince Leopold, youngest son of Queen Victoria, is inaugurated Captain of the Royal & Ancient Golf Club. But is this the real reason for his visit? And why is there a series of bizarre deaths around this time? McArdle is called to investigate.

But there are more mysteries than mere murder. What is the true secret of German hotelier Johann Rusack? What links does he have to Chancellor Bismarck and Wilhelm I, the German Emperor? What is the true reason Queen Victoria likes to keep Captain McArdle on hand? How did McArdle get his Victoria Cross? And why is Dr. William McIntosh corresponding with Charles Darwin about worms?

Not to mention, will the 'Fifeshire Tight Horse' be a help or a hindrance?

McArdle, together with Constable Murdoch, McIntosh, Archie the caddie and a Prince of the Blood get to the bottom of a terrifying secret and a mystery kept hidden from historians for over 100 years. Bremner tells all!

MURDER ON THE OLD COURSE – 1877

Why are so many Committee Members of the Royal and Ancient dying while out on the golf course? Their deaths appear to be from natural causes (heart failure mostly) but McArdle is suspicious when called to investigate.

Not linked at first, there are other deaths in St. Andrews, mainly of professional people. At the same time, the University is in turmoil and may have to close. McArdle discovers the thread which connects these disparate facts when he foils the near-murder of one of the Cheape family of Strathtyrum.

Further Books in this Series

McARDLE MEETS CONAN DOYLE – 1881

Dr. Arthur Doyle (1859-1930) was a recently-graduated doctor in 1881, just returned from service as a ship's doctor on a voyage to the West African coast. Before taking up the offer of partnership with the enigmatic Dr. George Turnavine Budd in a medical practice, Doyle visits St. Andrews for a short golfing holiday and to study the scientific instruments of Brewster and Swan at the University.

There then follows a series of baffling thefts. A valuable astrolabe, one of Brewster's optical pieces (a kaleidoscope, which Brewster invented) and some irreplaceable early calotypes go missing, all at times when Doyle had had access to the collections. He becomes the prime suspect.

Rather than just accept his fate passively, the young Dr. Doyle launches his own investigation and comes up with clues and ideas which McArdle has missed, much to the Detective's annoyance.

In the end, they cooperate to track down the real thief, and it is Doyle's knowledge of the shady underbelly of Edinburgh which leads them to the culprit.

McARDLE and the GLASGOW BOYS – 1883

McArdle is called in to help Superintendent William Mackintosh of Glasgow solve a baffling series of art-related crimes. McArdle meets the young son of Superintendent Mackintosh, designer and artist Charles Rennie Mackintosh who helps him with his artistic knowledge.

McArdle and Mackintosh meet and investigate the group of young artists who became known as "The Glasgow Boys" (W. Y. MacGregor, Joseph Crawhall, E. A. Walton, George Henry, John Lavery, James Paterson and others). It is this experience which persuades the young Charles to follow his artistic and architectural leanings rather than join the Glasgow Police

Further Books in this Series

McARDLE and PINKERTON'S LAST CASE – 1884

McArdle, Inspector of the Fife Police in St. Andrews, is called upon to help the renowned detective (and fellow Scot) Allan Pinkerton solve a case that has baffled him for years and has oscillated between America and Scotland.

In the process, McArdle foils an assassination attempt on the American President Chester A. Arthur (over Civil Service reform, anti-corruption and immigration policies) and persuades wealthy businessman Joseph M. Fox, to introduces golf to the United States.

McARDLE & THE GREATREX CASE – 1888

This book concerns the revenge murder of Glasgow's famous Chief Constable Alexander McCall by John Greatrex, whom he had apprehended after a chase from Glasgow to New York some 20 years before when a Superintendent.

When McCall dies in office, in suspicious circumstances, McArdle's old friend, Superintendent William Mackintosh, invites him to investigate.

The hunt for the killer takes Mackintosh, McArdle and PC Murdoch to the Glasgow International Exhibition of 1888, where Mackintosh is Captain of the Glasgow Police Athletic and Rowing Club Tug-of-War Team The trail leads them to John Greatrex, recently released from a 20 year prison sentence and working under an assumed name as photographic assistant to Thomas Annan, the great Glasgow photographer.

e-mail: mcardle@brucedurie.co.uk
http://www.brucedurie.co.uk/McArdle

BRUCE DURIE